The Asset
By
A P Bateman

Text © A P Bateman

2020

All rights reserved

No part of this book may be reproduced, or stored in a retrieval system, or transmitted in any form or by any means, electronic, mechanical, photocopying, printing or otherwise, without written permission of the author.

This book is a work of fiction and any character resemblance to persons living or dead is purely coincidental. Some locations may have been changed; others are fictitious.

Facebook: @authorapbateman

www.apbateman.com

Rockhopper Publishing

2020

The Alex King Series
The Contract Man
Lies and Retribution
Shadows of Good Friday
The Five
Reaper
Stormbound
Breakout
From the Shadows
Rogue

The Rob Stone Series
The Ares Virus
The Town
The Island

Standalone Novels
Hell's Mouth
Unforgotten

Short Stories
A Single Nail
The Perfect Murder?
Atonement

Further details of these titles can be found at www.apbateman.com

For Clair and her unwavering support, as always

1

There was no more than three metres between her and the man directly in front of her, and ten more between her and the man directly beyond the first. The third man was twenty-five metres away, but he had an AK2000 assault rifle in his hands and that more than changed the game. She had fallen onto her side, the grenade knocking her clean off her feet. Again, she thought how crazy it was for her to be here. No back-up and an ill-conceived plan at best, but she was fully committed and so tantalisingly close to her objective, to get to the man she loved, that she couldn't afford to weaken at the thought of being injured or outnumbered. Because outnumbered she may well be, but outclassed, she was not. The concussive shock of the explosion had reverberated inside her, feeling as if her insides had been shaken loose. She had lost her baseball cap, her mousey-blonde hair spilling out and cascading around her shoulders. Slowly, she got back to her feet, turning to see the man now standing in front of her. His 9mm Sig Sauer pistol aimed at her, his eyes blinking disbelievingly and the expression upon his face telling it all. A woman.

Unexpected and at odds with the Albanians and the grisly scene he had just witnessed.

She held up both her hands, but as she straightened, she feinted a stumble. The man momentarily forgot himself, leaned forwards to assist her. Maybe he'd been brought up right. A long time ago. Before his chosen career path. Before the Russian mafia had eaten at his soul. Showing respect to women, instilled into him by his sisters, his mother, his grandmother. It was all Caroline needed and she faked another stumble, looking up and making sure that he now stood directly in front of the man with the AK2000. He was, so she drew the small but heavy Makarov pistol from her back pocket and shot him in the throat. He hadn't even begun his slump to the ground when she took another step forward and steadied her aim. When the man fell, she already had the vee and pin sight aimed at the man with the assault rifle twenty metres distant. She fired a single well-aimed shot at the man's forehead, then double tapped centre mass as he went down. Dropping to one knee she twisted to her right and fired three rounds in quick succession at the man in between, and adjacent to, the two bodies. He had been pulled in by the sight of her being a woman and putting up such resistance to their pursuit, and hadn't known it was she who had fired until he had seen the second man drop to the forest floor, and by the time he managed to fire back at her, he had already been hit by two of the punchy 9.2mm bullets, but his own bullet went desperately wide of his target and the next three went high and wide as he fell to the ground and the pistol flailed wildly in the air.

Caroline stood back a few paces and shuffled to her left. She did not want to be where the men had last seen her when his comrades had fallen. She had not yet confirmed that he was dead, and she did not want to be there if he managed to steel his resolve and fire wildly. She dropped the magazine, slotted another in place, but did not work the weapon's slide. She could count, after all. Now she was nine up. She aimed between the three bodies, rubbing her stomach gently, comfortingly with her left hand. She had grazed herself on the ground and could feel splinters and pine needles and wood bark on her skin. She was shaking, the adrenalin subsiding after such a peak of endorphins and the exertion of running up the slope and sprinting down the other side.

One of the men was still moving. Her compassion told her to walk over to him, kick his weapon aside and walk away. Let him die in peace or give him time to be recovered by the rest of his team. But she'd seen what he had done. He was a ruthless killer and would offer her no quarter if their situations had been reversed. Besides, she had been with King too long now, and her instincts had been honed through training, if not osmosis from working - and living - with such a man. There were too many variables involved in such an act. Too many things to consider and counter. She was outnumbered, after all. She aimed and fired, and the man's head rocked, then he rested still. The brutal action could well have saved her life and the lives of her friends and acknowledging the fact made her feel nothing for what she had just done. They would have done worse to her, once they had gotten over the fact that she was a woman. Undoubtedly, they would have soon taken advantage of that fact, considering who these men were and who they worked for.

They deserved no mercy, and least of all from her. And, as she picked her way through the forest floor, she just prayed she was still in time. Prayed that the man she loved was still alive.

2

Six Months Earlier, Thames House, London

"I want a man who will take this on and run with it…"

Amherst put his coffee down on the blotter on his mahogany desk and leaned back in his chair. He looked at the police commander and smiled wryly. "What you want is a man who will do this to the letter of the law. Someone who will work with the local police, perhaps with Interpol, build a case and along with the cooperation of the relevant country, have their day in court. But what you *need*, is a man who will get this done at any cost. Because getting these people into court in these countries will be nigh-on impossible and an exercise in futility." He paused. "You're firefighting. You have no chance of stopping these shipments, perhaps you will intercept a few, but on the whole, you're King Canute trying to hold back the tide. Your budget is down, domestic issues and the fallout from a collective worldwide health pandemic has left you pared to the bone. You simply cannot cope with the influx of organised crime from foreign shores." He shrugged and looked at Simon Mereweather. His number two, second in command of MI5. "Can we do this? Can we hustle in on a job traditionally more suited to those shits across the river?"

Mereweather nodded. "MI6 have their hands full with Russian problems. And this, although with a Russian angle, is crime and domestic, not governmental and political. The SVR and FSB are playing enough games to keep MI6 busy overseas. We'd be doing the SIS a favour by taking this on." He paused, inspecting a fingernail before looking at the SO15 commander. "We can help stem the flow, hold back the tide, so to speak. We can't have crates of automatic weapons on British streets, so I think it's in everybody's interest to cut it off at the source."

Commander Robinson nodded. "How will this work?" he asked cautiously.

Mereweather looked across at Neil Ramsay. He was operations manager, sometimes referred to as a liaison officer during missions. "What is your operational readiness for something like this?"

Ramsay was a quiet, somewhat terse man. His previous team had often joked that he was on the autistic spectrum. Certainly not *Rain Man*, but he needed all his ducks to line up in a row. There were distinct advantages to Neil Ramsay's 'condition', although not a man of action, he could see flaws in any plan and could often negotiate a solution several moves before others could see it. He tended to see the bigger picture, and the one beyond that also. "Rashid is good to go. Dave Lomu still won't come over fulltime and officially on the books, but maybe that's what we need for a task like this. The mercenary option doesn't look to be a bad option from where I see it."

"No mercenaries," said the commander. "We need the right kind of people. What has this Dave Lomu chap done, anyway?"

"That's better you don't know," Mereweather replied, giving the man a knowing smile. "He's a heavy hitter. If you want Russian mafia and an Albanian gang taken down, then he's definitely a man you want doing your bidding."

The commander nodded. "And this Rashid fellow?"

"Pakistani immigrant. Came here as a baby. He's a Muslim, not devout as far as I can make out. He was the youngest officer of Pakistani descent in the British army, went on to become a captain in the SAS. Did his officer training at Sandhurst, but as he was already a member of the Special Air Service, he was in the regiment for life, and not just the four years officers from other regiments can mandatorily serve. His speciality, if you call it that, is with a sniper rifle. He made one of the top ten distance kills on record. Two thousand, four hundred metres in Afghanistan. He took out a Taliban commander that the yanks and the frogs couldn't get to." Amherst paused. "He's the right man for this job."

The SO15 commander frowned. "He sounds like an assassin."

Simon Mereweather shrugged. "You're losing the fight against illegal weapons coming in. And you're certainly behind the crystal meth wave. It's a bloody tsunami, to be frank. And it only relies on meth cooks and chemicals. There's no chain to be broken like bringing in cocaine, opium, or heroin. It's a straight up chemical concoction, and Russia produces all the chemicals needed with an unlimited reservoir of resources. The only thing you can fight is the suppliers. And if you strike hard enough, you'll cut the source entirely. People aren't in a hurry to die, no matter how much money is involved."

The police commander shook his head, perplexed. "If we can stop the flood of weapons and drugs, just for a few months, then we can get a foot hold and start pushing back."

Amherst nodded. "You need breathing space. We all do. That's why it was a godsend having all those ISIS fighters in one place in Iraq, and later in Syria. When the military war on terrorism was at its height, we could get back to hunting down the terror cells at home. The soldiers and drones and tank shells thinned out the numbers for us and the ideologists all went out to the desert to spill their own blood."

The commander took a sip of coffee and placed it back down on the table between himself and Simon Mereweather. "I feel this snowballing, somewhat," he commented nervously. "I came to ask if our budgets and joint interests could align in some way to cut these threats at the source, and now I feel that your answer would be simply be to eliminate the threat, rather than help police it."

"Well, there's nothing simple about it," Mereweather interjected. "In fact, be under no illusion that to venture onto their turf, to Albania and to Russia, and destroy what mafia families and brotherhoods have taken generations to build, or what former KGB spies have done to get to the top of the pile and the body count in doing so, will be a damned sight more difficult to take down than to attempt to police it." He paused. "And you wouldn't get far policing it, either. Interpol have tried. One of our operatives did two secondments with Interpol to fight female trafficking for the sex industry. All she got for her trouble was heartache and misery and a handful of saved souls, when hundreds got through and were never seen nor heard of again."

Ramsay leaned forwards, his hand held up in much the same manner as one would summon a waiter's attention. "If I may just say…"

Amherst nodded. "Go on, Neil."

Ramsay looked at the commander and said, "What I think needs making clear, is that we are not thinking about sending Rashid off with a sniper rifle and other agents kitted up for a level of *Call of Duty*." He smiled and looked around, but nobody seemed to share his humour, nor knowledge of gaming.

Unperturbed, he said, "It's more of a game. A long game. But a game, nonetheless. It would take months to set in motion. But the long and the short of it would be intelligence gathering, classroom-based scenario building, field training in clandestine techniques and surveillance and then on the ground surveillance in the enemy's territory. From there, we'd work on getting close to the enemy. Infiltrating the organisations or setting those organisations up."

"Putting people in with them!" the commander exclaimed. "That would be a suicide mission!"

"We didn't say it would be easy," Amherst commented sardonically.

"You didn't say it would be impossible either," the commander retorted.

"It's not impossible; it's just difficult. But we can do it," Ramsay said. "Or at least, we can orchestrate something that gains trust. And then when we have trust, we make our move. It will take time for me to plan, but I already have the bare bones inside my head. Gabriel Manigault first committed it to writing, back in the early nineteenth century, but you will no doubt be familiar with the saying… *the enemy of my enemy, is my friend…* that's what we do. We take two beasts, and we set them against each other."

"But that's ludicrous," the commander said incredulously.

Neil Ramsay shook his head. "One of our agents did it before. I know he can do it again."

3

Cornwall

King had run along the beach from the rocky crag to the point where the tide was now too high and had created the small bay, that turned into a five-mile stretch of beach at anything below half-tide. He estimated that six circuits of this smaller bay equated to two miles, but he had lost count long ago and moved onto the seven boulders he had arranged in size order before he had started running his circuits. He picked up the smallest and started with twenty-five arm curls, then dropped it onto the shingle beach and bent down for the second and started twenty-five overhead presses. He had the whole workout planned from benchless presses, squats and clean and jerks. Five repetitions of these would then culminate in what he called the Sisyphus challenge. Rolling a huge boulder around his workout area until he could do it no more. Like the story in Greek mythology where Sisyphus, the King of Corinth is eternally damned to roll a boulder up a hill in the depths of Hades. Exhausted, drenched in perspiration, he would always finish up his workout with an icy dip in the sea. But now, as he watched the two suited gentlemen trudge along in the thick shingle towards him, he could see that it was over. He bent down and picked up the small backpack, retrieved the snub nosed .38 revolver and tucked it into his tracksuit pocket. To his right, nearer the cliff, a large boulder the size of a large van was embedded in the shingle and served as a perfect barricade. King edged nearer and watched both men hesitate. Tactically, King was all over them. No bullets could penetrate the rock, and the men were exposed in the open. King had a barricade, an escape route towards more boulders at the cliff base, and because of the shape of the boulder, he could also climb higher, lay over the top and have the high ground. Now it was over to them to make the first move. A part of him missed this. A part of him needed to feel under threat, so he could rise above it, channel it and take the offensive. Because being on the offensive made him feel alive.

The two men trudged on, but nervously so. King watched, then the familiarity hit him. Their outlines, their movements, their build. He was incredulous, had made his feelings clear last year. By the time he could make out their features, he could see the difference in the quality and cut of their suits. Ramsay's came from *Marks & Spencer* and Simon Mereweather's from Savile Row. King knew of the outfitters in question and was aware that would not only cost most people two month's salary, but the man had several of them for all seasons and occasions.

King did not fear either of the men, but he backed up to the boulder and studied the ground behind him. Thankfully, he did not see anybody flanking him and felt relieved. Not because of the lack of hostile threat, but for the fact he once considered these men to be his friends. With the passing of both time and political agenda, he hoped he still could.

The two men stopped walking when King stepped back out from behind the boulder. Mereweather nodded to him and said, "Hello, Alex."

"Simon," King acknowledged him and turned to Ramsay. "Hi, Neil. Not exactly dressed for a stroll on the beach. You just need a *Cornetto* and a knotted handkerchief on your head…"

"Caroline told us you'd be down here," he replied somewhat tacitly.

King nodded. That much was obvious, or they would not have known where to look. Maybe it was the change of lifestyle, the building project they had undertaken, or the simple fact that after so long operating in the shadows, doing the government's dirty work, he struggled with the 'normality' of his current situation. It all seemed so final.

"We've got a job for you," said Simon Mereweather.

"I'm not interested."

"It's right up your street."

"Things have changed," said King. "I'm out. We both are."

"It's a job for one person," Neil Ramsay said. "If you're worried about Caroline…"

"I retired," King replied. "We both have."

"I was under the illusion that Caroline was on sabbatical."

King shrugged. "You'll need to speak with her."

"Win the lottery, did we?" Mereweather quipped.

"Something will come up."

"Caroline's inheritance will help, I imagine. But it's not a sizable legacy, it won't last for ever."

"Nice to know nothing is off limits. I don't know why I thought they ever would be." King paused. "But what you consider to be sizeable, and what we consider to be sizeable are two different things entirely, Simon. I heard mummy and daddy own half of Hampshire."

Mereweather shook his head. "No, not quite half of it," he said wryly. "That would be Berkshire. I'm sure the family own half of that."

"Building projects escalate. A few more quid won't hurt," Ramsay added.

"Amherst made it quite clear he was going to clip my wings."

"He's had a change of heart."

"Then you can tell him to fuck off," King replied. "You can both fuck off, for that matter…"

"You're never really out of the game altogether, Alex." Mereweather paused. "You of all people should know that."

"After the last job, your office made it quite clear I should lay low." King paused. "In fact, I think after two months of laying low, you then used the term disavowed."

"Well, it wasn't exactly a *job*, was it? Officially, at least. You righted some wrongs, some *T*s and dotted the odd *i*. But you went rogue on us..." Mereweather trailed off, glancing uncomfortably at Ramsay. The whole team had followed King, Ramsey included. Retribution for fallen comrades and MI5's reluctance to act because of the political fallout. It had conveniently worked out for MI5 in the long term, but only by luck. And even then, by proxy. King had taken responsibility and Caroline had taken a sabbatical. King had been told to wait for a call, but none ever came. Later, he had been sent a letter telling him he had been disavowed, his files redacted. He was looking ahead now and had managed to get his head around his career with MI5 being over. Caroline was taking stock of her life, but a timely legacy from an aunt had bought her the luxury of time. For a few more months, at least.

"Things have changed," said King. He pictured Caroline sitting on the side of the bath wearing just her satin nightie, her legs crossed, and the pregnancy test she clutched resting in her lap. Too scared, and yet, too excited to look at it. He remembered how vulnerable, how beautiful she looked. Her skin glowing, her hair shining and her eyes beaming. He remembered how he felt inside. An emotion he'd never felt previously. A tangible element. He could only describe it as *complete*. And then the test had been negative, the moment evaporated and the reality cold and stark and real, the daydreams turned to smoke in the air. A false alarm, but something that they both felt more compelled to experience in the future. A new direction for them, and one they both knew to be impossible, or at least reckless and foolhardy living the life they once had. King looked at the two men resolutely and said, "I'm out of the game now."

Mereweather nodded and Ramsay said, "What about training?"

"That's what I was doing when you interrupted."

"Looks like you're training for a fight."

"I'm always training for a fight," King replied. "You never know when it's coming, but I won't be caught napping when it does."

Ramsay smiled. "I meant, what about training some agents for a specific task?"

"Like what?"

"Something you've done before, but this time on a much larger scale."

Mereweather nodded. "The idea is the same in principle, but where you improvised, or perhaps put just a few day's planning into it and rolled the dice, we have the luxury of time and resources." He paused. "We can make detailed plans, give the team the equipment they need, the back-up and support. Access to satellite imagery, that sort of thing."

"You've got good people, I'm sure a training program can be designed using the instructors you already have."

"Three months' work," Mereweather said. "Tier-Two salary, travel expenses and accommodation when not on site."

"I'm out."

"Full pension provisions, naturally."

"You'll start all that up again, anyway. I'm not happy that you pulled that. I was going to have a word with you. It was petty."

"You carried out an unsanctioned assassination. On a world leader, no less."

"So, you say. I rightfully decline to comment."

"The Secret Service investigation have a suspect. That man's name is a perfect anagram of your own."

"Coincidence."

"He worked on the victim's house."

"I'm not a tradesman."

"True," Ramsay interrupted. "We've just

seen his plastering."

King smiled. "And there you have it."

"So, you're still denying it," Mereweather nodded.

"I caught up with the man behind the death of one of our own. He committed terrorist activities, and an attack on British soil. If the Yanks want to answer to that, then bring them to account. Otherwise, both sides can shut up. Call it quid-pro-quo. I know nothing about the death of the world leader in question."

"I know you did it," Mereweather persisted. He looked as if he was about to add something but noticed the coldness of King's stare and did not continue.

King frowned. "And you thought it would be wise to pull the pension on a man who you thought could do that? It's a good job I considered you a friend, Simon. No, you'll start that up when you get back to the office, and you'll back date it as well. I don't want to be the one to tell you that I know where you live," King paused, staring at him coldly. "But I *do* know where you live, Simon."

Simon Mereweather did not reply, but King was left in no doubt that the man would see it done. First thing on Monday morning, his pension plan would be back in place.

"It's just training, Alex," Ramsay added, breaking the tension. "We know that you no longer want to work in the field."

"Rashid is in." Mereweather paused. "I'm making him team leader. Or at least, I am now that you're so adamant you don't want the job."

"Good for him," King replied. "If he's the one on the ground, perhaps he'd better help train the other agents."

"Are things okay between you?"

"It doesn't matter anymore."

King looked towards the sea. The shore break was pounding directly onto the shingle beach like it so often did on this stretch of coastline. It was deep just offshore, so no swells formed and built further out. The western reaches of the Atlantic simply swelled close to shore and unleashed pounding waves which often caught out the unwary paddler. Other stretches of the southern coastline had surf and golden sand beaches, but here it simply crashed upon the rocky shore. King lost himself in the sight. He and Rashid had reconciled, but it had not been the same. He hadn't seen the man he would call his best friend since they had shaken hands at the airport in Toronto, and King still carried the weight of an innocent's death with him and knew he always would. The last operation had seen the team disperse, unlikely to come back together. Once Caroline's sabbatical had been approved, they had settled in Cornwall and started to renovate the old coastguard cottages they had bought at a property auction, with the idea of living in one and renting the other out to supplement their funds. King had been slow to complete the maintenance tasks, but now he had a good reason to put roots down. After a lifetime of never knowing family, or what it was to be a part of one, he liked the idea of starting one with Caroline.

"Alex?" Ramsay ventured.

King snapped to. He shrugged benignly. "I'm not interested. Come back to the cottage and I'll get the kettle on, raid the biscuit barrel. Let's leave it at that."

4

Four months later
Albania

"The man you can see on screen is Besmir Muka, an Albanian national. Five feet nine or one-point seven-five metres and approximately twelve-stone, which I'm sure those of you under thirty-five will know as seventy-six kilos." Rashid paused the footage and said, "Note the titanium case. It's rumoured to hold close to two million euros, one point five million pounds sterling or two million US dollars. He takes the cash to one of twelve possible cover businesses in Tirana, six times a week."

"Twelve-million a week!" exclaimed Mac. He was a short Scotsman with red close-cropped hair and a face only a mother could love. He whistled a long high to low and shook his head.

"And they say crime doesn't pay," Goldie commented. He was a Londoner and could have bantered on a fruit and veg stall in Borough Market all day long. Except that he had been a sergeant in the SBS, the Royal Navy's equivalent of the SAS based in Poole. He was an extreme athlete, running fifty-mile endurance races in his spare time. He also gave up on a place on the British triathlon team in the London Olympic Games when he was deployed to Afghanistan. The nickname came from his constant whining that he could have taken gold. Colleagues in the special forces rarely missed an opportunity for banter or a nickname.

Rashid held up his hand. "Besmir Muka is one of at least a dozen bag men. This Albanian gang show more profits than some of the FTSE 100 Index companies." He paused. "And tomorrow, we're going to hit two of them. One at eleven hundred hours and the other at twelve hundred hours. Four miles between."

A tall man in his late thirties leaned forward in his chair. His name was Tom Hendy, but they called him Philosopher because he had a two-two degree in leisure studies. Back when people had enough loans and grants for pointless degrees. The economic banking crisis had put an end to degrees in canoeing and abseiling, and by the time Tom Hendy needed to put his studies to employment, he had decided to join the Army, but the degree got him into officer training and he had reached the rank of captain before doing a four year stint in the SAS. He had later joined the Gurkhas because of his interest in climbing and the chance to trek and train with the Gurkha regiment in the Himalayas. "That sounds tight," he said. "Hitting a bag man and getting to the next drop before word gets out, with only an hour in between." He shrugged. "It's not a lot of time to get on site, but it might as well be hours in terms of keeping it quiet."

"He's right," Mac agreed, thumbing towards him. "He's not called Philosopher for nothing..."

"What's the chain around his wrist?" said the fourth and last of the agents. He was black, stocky and in his early thirties. He was a former army helicopter pilot and wasn't a typical MI5 recruit, but he had flown several missions for 14 Intelligence Company and had got on well with one of the intelligence officers and when the officer had later joined MI5, he had recommended him. Leroy Wilkinson was known as Flymo, after the hover lawnmower brand, because he flew and hovered so low.

"Titanium," Rashid replied.

"Not coming off with a set of bolt croppers from B and Q, then," Flymo commented.

"Can we pick the lock?" asked Mac.

"Not enough time," Rashid answered.

"I can blow it," said Goldie. "A small ball of PE4, slip some Kevlar around the bloke's wrist. The detonator will be bigger than the charge, but it might just allow him to hold onto the wrist."

"An axe is a lot less bother," Philosopher commented. "We haven't got time to piss about. Nobody said we weren't just wasting this guy, either."

"Is he a hostile?" asked Flymo. "Do we just go in shooting?"

Rashid stood up and pointed at the screen. "Here, here and here…" He pointed at three points on the image and pressed play on the remote. "Three support vehicles. One or two men per vehicle. It's sketchy, because the amount of men changes. But there are always three sets of back-up wheels. So, if it all goes tits up, there are potentially four getaway vehicles for them. And at least five bodyguards to stop it going down."

"Armed?" asked Flymo.

"You can bet your arse on that. All of them carry a short and there will be longs in all the vehicles. AK's most likely."

"Then we go in hard," said Mac. "Silenced pistols. Walk up behind them simultaneously and give them a bullet behind the ear. Take the bag man out, use an axe and get the hell out of there."

"I'll be the wheelman," said Flymo. He stood up and walked over to the table with the flask of coffee and poured himself a cup. Black and strong. He spooned in half a dozen sugars. He had often joked that he liked the spoon to stand up in it. To attention, not stand easy. "I'll do what I have to do, but wet work isn't in my skillset."

"I can't say that I enjoy doing it," said Rashid. "But like we trained for and studied for back home, we can't make this particular omelette without breaking eggs. A lot of eggs."

"Aye, just think of the guns and drugs coming into the UK with this bunch," said Mac. "*Dunny* think about it." He held up his fingers like a child acting out a gun. "Tap, tap, tap and move on."

"They're a means to an end," said Rashid. "MI5 being what they are, have only allocated a budget that gets us here. To go all the way, we need to raise funds. But doing it like this means we also sow the seeds of doubt in both organisations. The Albanians hold the ground. This is Tirana. It's ground zero, so no rival ethnic gangs are going to try a takeover here. Nobody is either brave or stupid enough."

"Apart from the Russians," said Philosopher. "Or us, so it would seem."

"Exactly. Now, the Albanians get hit and ask, 'who was stupid enough to do that?'" Rashid paused. "But it will take them all of five seconds to blame the Russians. According to our source in the Met's International Crime Taskforce, Romanovitch was unhappy at the Albanians when T'Briki negotiated a new percentage. He took Romanovitch's guns, and his chemicals to make the crystal meth, but simply sent less money back. Percentage changed, and that was that. Romanovitch begrudgingly accepted the terms. What else was he going to do? The weapons were ex-Soviet stock and had a huge mark up, and the chemicals are all produced in Romanovitch's backyard, so he's making hundreds of percent profit. However, to save face he wasted six of T'Briki's men. And their entire families. He went along with the percentage, but he had sent a message back to the Albanians. And it's only a matter of time before the simmer becomes a boil and Romanovitch renegotiates, or possibly cuts out the Albanians altogether."

"They don't fuck about, do they…" said Goldie quietly.

"No, they don't," replied Rashid. "So, we need to do this thing right. Capture isn't an option I'd want to be left with. So, to avoid that, we go in as hard as the Russians would, and we don't leave a trace." He allowed the film to play on and stopped as the subject entered the post office. The image blurred and for a moment, a coat covered the lens of the camera. The person filming stood at a grim selection of postcards, the subject just in view and unlocking the case from his wrist. The camera captured the key being handed to a serious-faced man behind the counter. The man turned and walked through an unmarked door.

"Inside man," Philosopher said. "One of Romanovitch's?"

"Yes."

"So, the case is locked, the key is left wherever they make the transfer and another key unlocks it at the post office. Why not just have the man take the case?"

"Because someone on the payroll at the post office packages it into bundles and sends it through the mail. Inside poster tubes, coffee cans, small packages and large. Some of it even gets repackaged into well-known delivery service and internet shopping boxes. Counterfeit boxes if you could believe people get such things printed."

"What about doing it when the man gets his key out?" asked Mac.

"We could try it at that moment," Rashid replied patiently. "But this post office isn't just a front for laundering money, it's operating as a genuine business and service. So, there is a chance of collateral damage if it all goes to shit." He paused, looking at each man in turn. "Which we all know it does the moment a shot is fired. But also, that counter is solid. If the case goes over the top, a shutter can be raised by a state-of-the-art gas piston release. You won't even see it rise. It will simply be down one moment and up the next. We could shoot at it until it's a bloody colander, but it will just flex and remain in place."

"I suppose it's not out of the question for Romanovitch to have guys the other side of the counter?" Philosopher asked. "Armed men, not just a man with a key."

"Undoubtedly," Rashid replied. "So, we need to get this done before they join in the fight or are witnesses to what is going down outside. Most likely, they'll assume police involvement and stay put."

"So, what about our other friend?" Flymo asked. "It seems rather cold blooded."

Rashid nodded and froze the screen. He switched channels on the remote to an AV channel and a man appeared on the screen. He was sitting on the plain concrete floor of an empty room. It was the cellar beneath them. He was hooded, his hands taped behind his back and his legs taped together at the knees and ankles. There were bloodstains on his shirt. The CCTV camera recorded constantly. "I know," he replied. "When the time comes, I'll do it."

5

The weapons were all Russian ex-military stock. Perhaps over egging the pudding, now that even the Russian mafia had realised the best quality weapons and most effective calibres were manufactured in the West, but it told a story and the story they wanted to tell was that Romanovitch's organisation was behind this.

Each man carried a Makarov pistol in 9x18mm. Flymo was driving, so he carried his without a suppressor in a shoulder holster under his lightweight jacket. The other men all had a bulbous suppressor attached to the muzzle of their weapons. Not as quiet as the fantastical, near-silent Hollywood 'silencers', but a hell of a lot quieter than without, nonetheless. Mac carried the hatchet, and he'd worked on the blade with a whetstone to give it a razor's edge. Both Goldie and Philosopher carried AKS-74U machine carbines. Short, powerful, and capable of a fearsome rate of fire. They could also be concealed under their jackets.

The car they had chosen was an Audi S8. Near supercar performance, four-wheel drive, a powerful V8 engine and plenty of room inside. To the south of their location, approximately one mile distant, they had parked a BMW 3 series estate with the keys stored on the driver's side front suspension spring. A mile to the east, a Ford C-Max was parked in a side street with the keys stored similarly. Neither vehicle was involved in Plan A, but it gave them options if it all went south. Inside both gloveboxes was a loaded pistol and a burner phone with the numbers of each of the men stored on it. Each man had this phone's number in their own personal burner, so contact could be made with whomever got to the vehicle first, and pickups could be arranged. There was also an envelope containing two-thousand Euros emergency funds, and an extensive gunshot-trauma first aid kit, bottled water and a change of clothes for each of them was stored in a sports bag in the boot. They hoped they would never need either vehicle, but if they did it would mean they would certainly be glad of the precaution.

Rashid had taken up position outside the post office. He was browsing a city map with a 'you are here' arrow. He had a comms unit attached to his belt and a wrist mic and earpiece threaded through the sleeve of his jacket.

"Target on route, three minutes..." Mac said, his harsh Glaswegian accent grating in

Rashid's ear.

"Have that," Rashid replied quietly.

"Two CP's in a grey Skoda Superb," Goldie announced. *"Should be with you in thirty seconds…"*

Rashid waited, counting down in his head. Sure enough, the two close protection operatives drove into view and parked the Skoda under the shade of a cypress tree near the square. Rashid did not look at them, but he could already see Philosopher ambling towards them. He was pretending to talk on the phone, but he checked in on the comms.

"On them in thirty…"

"Second CP unit heading in from the south. Three men. Two up front and one in the back seat," said Flymo. *"With you in thirty…"*

"Third team passing me now. Two men," Goldie said. *"Behind the target."*

Rashid watched the black Mercedes E Class sweep in and park on the opposite side of the road to the first close protection team. The third team drove on past and parked at the western edge of the square.

"If the next bodyguards to the party park on the eastern edge, we can keep our arcs of fire pointing outwards, no chance of blue on blue."

"You wish," Flymo scoffed, then added, *"Fuck me, we're on. They're holding back right beside me."*

"You'll have to go live," Rashid told him.

"I'm the driver!"

"It's too good an opportunity to miss."

"My weapon isn't silenced, and I'll never engage three hostiles without getting shot! I'm a fucking pilot!"

"On route to Flymo!" Mac shouted breathily. *"ETA two minutes!"*

"Not enough time!" Rashid snapped. "The target has debussed and is on foot. I'm moving now…"

Rashid reached across and gripped the butt of the Makarov under his jacket. He turned slowly and started across the cobbled square. He could see Goldie and Philosopher doing the same. Mac ran past the second close protection team and Rashid could see the two men stiffen in their seats, then visibly relax as the red-headed Scotsman shot past as if late for a bus. It worked to Philosopher's advantage, because the two men were momentarily off guard. Rashid turned his attention to the target, it was up to the others to control their vectors.

"And three... two... one... Go! Go! Go!" Rashid said into his mic and drew his weapon. He aimed the Makarov at the target and fired three shots. Two in the heart and one in the head. With the target down and the others engaging, he scanned to see where he was needed most. He was positioned centrally and could see that each of his men had swerved into the road or the square and had engaged from the inside out, keeping their arcs of fire away from each other, and of the other's targets. Textbook. Except he could see that Philosopher had taken a knee and was frantically clearing his weapon of a stoppage. Rashid took a knee, too. Making himself a smaller target and enabling a steadier aim. He aimed at the vehicle in front of Philosopher and fired five rounds in quick succession. It was enough to keep the Albanian's heads down and Philosopher was already springing to his feet and darting behind the car, where he emptied the new magazine through the rear window. The men in the front seats didn't stand a chance and Rashid saw the windscreen splash red from the inside. Rashid changed over to a new magazine, remained low and surveyed the scene around him.

Behind Rashid, Flymo had taken on the third team with his pistol, but he was taking fire from an automatic weapon and sprinting for a rubbish bin for cover. Mac had arrived and ignored his silenced pistol and gone straight to the Kalashnikov concealed under his jacket. He fired short bursts through the rear windows, and it was over in less than a few seconds. Goldie was already heading in Flymo's direction, having taken out both of his targets in two double taps with no return fire. He'd be bragging about that one for the duration of the mission.

Rashid turned back to the primary target and looked at the titanium handcuff and chain attaching his arm to the case. Mac had volunteered, and he wasn't going to argue. He passed Mac as he headed for the car. "Hurry up, we need to get out of here," he said. Mac said nothing and ran past him, already taking the hatchet out from his belt. He didn't envy the task, but then again, nobody envied what Rashid had agreed to do next.

Flymo was back inside the Audi and both Philosopher and Goldie had arrived and were taking up positions nearby. Reloaded and watching for more Albanian gang members, 'have a go heroes' or the police. Flymo looked up as Rashid neared and popped the boot open. Rashid nodded as he jogged past. He rounded the vehicle and grabbed hold of the man inside, heaving him out.

Igor Yahontov was one of Romanovitch's most recognised enforcers. He had acted as a go between with the Albanians many times and had gone missing one week previously. He had a predilection for underage girls and satiated his appetite for them in Bulgaria on the Black Sea coast where a casino and hotel used as a front by Romanovitch's wing of the Russian mafia facilitated such perversions. It was the one factor that had enabled Rashid to cope with the thought of killing an unarmed man. When they had snatched him in the dead of night, Igor Yahontov and two other Russian gang members had been with a twelve-year-old girl and had raped her repeatedly, tying her to the bed and forcing her to do unspeakable things. Bleeding and traumatised, Philosopher had taken her to a nearby hospital and Rashid had made a call to the Georgian embassy, where they would send someone to take care of one of their nationals. Igor Yahontov was vital to their plan and so were the other two, but only by the conspicuousness of their absence. Igor Yahontov had spent a week in the cellar, but the other two men had met their fate soon afterwards, and a shallow grave. Whether it was the heat of the moment, or the fact that Mac had teenage daughters, he had seen to both men and spoken no more about it.

Goldie slashed the tape around the man's knees and ankles and handed Rashid a captured Glock 19 from one of the Albanian bodyguards, while he set about slicing at the tape around Igor Yahontov's wrists.

Igor Yahontov was unsteady on his feet. He swayed, blinking as Rashid removed the hood. Rashid said nothing but pushed the man towards the square and raised the pistol. He looked the man in the eye, the image of the young girl coming to him as he fired two shots into the centre of his chest. No head shots. They wanted an easy identification later. Igor Yahontov dropped to the ground and twitched wildly. Rashid could see there was no coming back from the injuries and a merciful shot now would only screw with the forensics. He picked up the two ejected shell casings and walked over to the shot-up Skoda, pressed the pistol into one of the body's hands and dropped the empty brass cases on the ground. He stood back to see Mac sprinting back with the titanium case in one hand and the axe in the other.

"Right, let's get out of here," Rashid said, eyes everywhere, as the rest of the team got into the Audi. He looked back at the body on the ground. It had stopped moving and the first of the brave public were appearing from doorways and sidings, peering out tentatively.

Rashid leaned back in the seat as Flymo accelerated the Audi S8 wildly. He breathed a deep sigh. It was done. They had kicked down the gates of hell and taunted the devil.

Now they needed the devil to reply.

6

The Ural Mountains, Russia

The house was a former palace to the Tsar. It had escaped the uprising of the Bolsheviks and the years of communist rule, chiefly because the communist leaders all enjoyed a little luxury of their own, and partly because of its location and strategic advantages. It had been requisitioned and used as a party meeting place, and then the KGB had used it as a training facility and place to debrief its spies and execute the spies of their enemy. There was rumoured to be over a hundred unmarked graves in the grounds, but Ivan Romanovitch could testify to a great many more. Now that he had made the property his own, part of the hostile takeover the former KGB turned mafia had instigated after the first decade of capitalism to follow the break-up of the Soviet Union, he now used the property as his headquarters, and the security arrangements in place would shame many governments and world leaders.

They had taken lunch on the terrace. Below them, three bikini-clad women swam and frolicked in the pool. They were happy and playful. Cocaine did that to young women. That and the promise of money, a lifestyle otherwise beyond both their peasant means and dreams, and of more cocaine to come. Romanovitch watched them as a pretty service girl brought the silver tray of caviar and blinis to go with the chilled vodka and champagne. They had already eaten slices of homecooked bread, which Romanovitch had sliced off with a serrated bread knife and served with slithers of salted pork fat and grated garlic. He looked up and caught Vasyli leering at her. As the girl left, the man who ran his drugs operation and acted as his chief enforcer watched her walk away, her hips swaying gently.

"What have I told you about the staff?"

"Don't fuck them," Vasyli replied.

"A good housemaid or cook is hard to find," he said, sweeping a hand towards the girls in the pool. "Fuck one of them, if you have to."

Vasyli grinned. "Any of them?"

Romanovitch shrugged. "The blondes are enjoyable enough, but the brunette doesn't quite make you believe in her." He paused. "Try her. If she does not please you, then she can go to one of the whorehouses and I'll have her replaced. If she does please you, well then, she's yours." He smiled. "To do with as you please."

"But Ivan, it is not my birthday!" the man smiled. He looked past Romanovitch, his smile fading. "They are here…"

"Ah, good." The gang boss turned and watched two men walking towards them. They were hemmed in by six of Romanovitch's security. Each of them ex-Spetsnaz – Russia's toughest soldiers and the world's largest special forces unit. "I want you to watch this," he said. "I want you to understand the situation."

"Boss," Vasyli nodded, but the frown told Romanovitch the man was none the wiser.

The two men stopped short of the terrace and five of the security men filed off, and the one remaining led the two men to the table. Romanovitch greeted them warmly and asked them to join them. He poured four glasses of vodka and passed the glasses around.

"Na Zdorovie!" he said and downed the shot of vodka in one. The other men did the same and Romanovitch poured four more glasses. "Na Zdorovie!" he said again and downed his measure. The other men did so more slowly, and he laughed.

Romanovitch watched the housemaid walk across the well-manicured lawn and asked her to pour the champagne. He watched her, as did the other men. She was a beautiful young woman of twenty-five and from the Ukraine. He had instructed every one of his men that she was out of bounds. He had enough women around the place. So many that his wife did not bother to visit anymore, preferring their Majorcan retreat in the summer months, and splitting her time between London, Switzerland and their St. Petersburg mansion in the winter.

"Ivan, we are here, we have toasted each other's health, and now we have business to discuss," said the larger of the two men.

He was tall and bald and heavily tattooed. He was number two in the *Albanian Brotherhood of Kontroll*, which did exactly what it promised. It controlled Albanian organised crime. Or as much of it that could be without Russian interference. By contrast, his brother was shorter and more rounded and had a good head of hair. Perhaps their mother had been indiscreet. But whether or not one of them was a bastard, the two men were as close as brothers could get, and he was number three in the brotherhood, and seated beside him, with his eyes on the bottle of chilled vodka.

"Do you care for more of my vodka, Yosef?"

The shorter, more rounded man nodded. "Please…"

Romanovitch waved the girl away as she reached for the bottle to pour. "No, my dear, I have no further use for you today." He smiled as she nodded and walked away. His gaze lingered for a moment, certainly long enough for the other men around the table to notice. He seemed to realise and shrugged at them, then poured the bottle for Yosef and smiled. "Potato vodka from Kyiv. Double distilled. You like?"

"Very much, thank you."

"Then you shall have a case when you leave."

"Thank you, I will toast your health each time I drink it."

The taller man leaned forward. "As I said, we have much to discuss," he prompted irritably.

"You dare to interrupt me at my home?" Romanovitch asked, staring at him.

"No, I…"

"You ripped me off!" Romanovitch cut him off. "You failed to deliver on two instalments."

"Your men stole from us!"

"Four million, five-hundred thousand Euros," Romanovitch said quietly.

"Exactly!"

Romanovitch smiled at him, but his expression mocked both his surprise and indignation. "You have brought this to me today, with interest? I expect no less than five million."

"I have come to tell you we will not tolerate…"

"Enough!" Romanovitch slammed his fist on the table. He looked up at both men and said quietly, calmly, "You have not delivered two payments. You take my chemicals, my aluminium filings, so you can make your crystal meth, but you have not delivered what was agreed."

"Ivan, with respect, your man Igor Yahontov was found dead at the scene of the first attack on our men. Less than an hour later, we were hit again." He paused. "Igor Yahontov stole your money, not us!"

"And how was Igor able to hit you again, when he was found dead at the scene of the first hit?"

"Because he was a part of it! Because more of your men have turned against you!"

"Igor Yahontov went missing last week, along with two more of my men."

"Exactly! And the filthy pigs took your money!"

Romanovitch shrugged and nodded, but was quiet for a moment before asking, "Igor Yahontov, do you have my money?" He cupped his ear and frowned mockingly when there was no answer. "You have no reply." He shrugged, then pointed at the pair of them in turn. "But *you* are here, and Igor Yahontov is not."

"Then we are at a stalemate."

Romanovitch leaned back in his chair and nodded. "Indeed." He rubbed his chin thoughtfully and smiled.

Each of the security guards moved simultaneously. Yosef found two pistols jammed into him, one each side of his neck, while three men subdued his brother and dragged him out of his chair. He struggled at first but stopped struggling when a fourth man pressed the muzzle of his pistol into the nape of his neck.

"I think we are in need of a visual aid here," said Romanovitch, getting out of his chair. He poured himself a measure of vodka and downed it in one gulp, before picking up the bread knife. The tall, thin man was pressed down onto the lawn and Romanovitch cut the man's throat, both wrists, then with the help of the three men, turned him over and sliced across the meat of the backs of his thighs until both femoral arteries were severed. The fountain of blood that had spouted from the carotid artery slowed as the other arteries were cut, like turning off a hose.

Romanovitch stepped away from the man and casually took a linen napkin off the table and wiped his hands. Yosef was struggling, but as he watched his brother dying on the grass, he struggled less until the fight drained from him altogether. He got the message. If Romanovitch was going to kill him, then he would have done it by now. And Romanovitch wouldn't have bothered making a show of cutting across six of the man's arteries. The Russian had wanted to make a statement. There was no going back, no chance of survival and no negotiating for his brother's life. From the first cut, his fate had been sealed. The rest of the cuts drove the point home to the surviving brother.

Romanovitch sneered at the Albanian as he stared vacantly at his brother's body. He threw the soiled napkin on the ground and poured two glasses of vodka. He slid one across the table towards Yosef, then picked up his own glass, cradling it as he spoke, "T'Briki has insulted me greatly by sending his number two and three in command. The limp-dicked inbred peasant should have been here to tell me what happened. He should have compensated me without question." Romanovitch paused. "Two cases. Small change. But it is the principle. You taunt me with such behaviour. The little dog has yapped harmlessly all this time, it has even humped my leg..." He smiled. "But now it has bitten the hand that feeds. And for that, it has been taught a valuable lesson..." He raised his glass and stared coldly at the Albanian. "Toast with me, Yosef. Here ends the lesson. Na Zdorovie!"

Vasyli's eyes were on the body, and he ignored the fact that no vodka had been poured for him, and that no toast was being made with him. What was Romanovitch saying to him? He was sweating, his heart racing. Could Romanovitch know he had helped himself to funds? He vowed right then and there to replace it as soon as he got back to St. Petersburg. To his right, the girls still frolicked in the pool, oblivious to the killing of a man a mere twenty metres from them. Vasyli no longer thought about the brunette. The fact that as the chief enforcer for Romanovitch he had been oblivious of the man's plans, and that the six bodyguards had known all along what would go down, filled the man with dread, and he realised that the killing of the Albanian number two had been as much for his benefit as the poor man's brother.

Yosef raised his glass and knocked back the vodka. He was shaking and had turned pale as he placed the glass back down on the table.

Romanovitch smiled. "Good! Business as usual," he said. He clicked his fingers at the nearest bodyguard and said, "Dimitri, please escort Yosef out." He paused, looking at the Albanian as he stood unsteadily. "I will make arrangements for your brother's return."

Yosef tentatively followed the bodyguard, flanked by two more. Vasyli stiffened in his chair as the three bodyguards remained, acting on their earlier instructions. He was unarmed, as all Ivan Romanovitch's guests were, and had a foreboding feeling in his gut as he glanced down at the body on the ground.

Romanovitch stood up suddenly, and Vasyli flinched. "Dimitri!" he shouted, waiting for the head guard to turn around. "See that Yosef receives a crate of the vodka. It's the least we can do!" He chuckled to himself and turned to Vasyli, looking at him seriously. "Now, that is how to show the little dogs who's boss. I don't expect to have to give visual aids to my enforcer, as well as my underlings."

"No, boss. You will not have to again."

Romanovitch nodded. "The Albanians did this," he said. "They snatched my men and made Igor Yahontov the scapegoat. Let me ask you, would Igor do such a thing to me?"

"Never," he said. "Nobody would betray you," he added, as much for his own benefit as to emphasise Yahontov's loyalty.

"Then the Albanians are playing a dangerous game. Maybe they made a move and have seen the error of their ways. Or perhaps they plan more like this. They would be fools if they did." He paused. "How much of my chemicals and aluminium filings do they have in reserve?"

"About enough for one hundred million euros production."

"That nets us sixty million euros." He shook his head. "So, they get forty million, and then what, we shut down their supply? No, it's too short sighted."

"Perhaps they have another supplier?" Vasyli ventured. "Or perhaps they will try to renegotiate the split."

"They would be fools to try that again."

"Then they must have another supplier."

Romanovitch leaned closer to him and said coldly, "Then I suggest you find out, before I have somebody remove your eyes, your balls, your hands and your feet and leave you on a Bulgarian street to beg for stale bread." He paused, poured himself another vodka, then topped it up with the chilled champagne. He did not pour a drink for Vasyli, and he looked at him as he sipped it slowly. "It should not have come to this today. See that we are not left playing catch up again."

7

**One week later
Kosovo**

The building was an old schoolhouse and it had stood deserted and dilapidated since it had been the scene of ethnic cleansing slaughter in 1998. On that terrible day, three teachers and forty seven children under the age of eleven had been executed by forces of the Federal Republic of Yugoslavia – consisting of soldiers of Serbia and Montenegro – because of the area's affiliation to the Kosovo Liberation Army, and alliance of Albanian and Kosovan forces. T'Briki had purchased the building from the Kosovan government and renovated extensively. There was talk in the area of it being made into a shrine, but T'Briki had turned it into a private residence and eight years after its purchase he had sold it to a business with a company registration in Liechtenstein. The company in question was one of his own, but the trail ended at a shell company with its home banking facilities in Switzerland.

T'Briki and the *Albanian Brotherhood of Kontroll* used it as a secondary headquarters and its existence was a closely guarded secret known by only a key few. His inner core. Set in the hills, and now enclosed by forest after the area had been lain to waste and deserted after the ransacking and pillaging by Kosovan forces, the old schoolhouse was isolated and private. Overlooked only by a wooded peak some two kilometres distant.

    T'Briki poured red wine into five glasses and they drank in silence. It was a fine wine, and one of the bottles which had been in the cellar of an old chateau he owned on the Albania-Greece border. When they had finished their glasses, the gang boss said, "To fallen comrades…" The four men in front of him murmured their agreement. T'Briki poured more wine, finishing the bottle, then said, "And to settling scores…" The men drank down the wine, as was tradition, in one go. "My condolences, Yosef…"

    Yosef nodded solemnly. His brother's body had been sent back for burial, but in typical behaviour befitting this wing of the Russian mafia, Romanovitch had sent the body back in six separate wooden vodka crates. Along with another crate of the vodka he had briefly enjoyed on the terrace near the pool. There had been a card attached bearing Ivan Romanovitch's compliments.

"I want him dead," Yosef said quietly.

T'Briki nodded. "And you shall have your vengeance, my friend." He paused, looking at the other men in turn. "But we need to keep the status-quo, need Romanovitch to think we have toed the line, and that we dare not over-step our boundaries again."

"And what will we be doing meanwhile, to avenge my brother's death?" Yosef asked. "We went there under your orders," he stated flatly. "My brother is dead because Romanovitch was insulted by your absence. Disrespected that you would send us, and not go yourself. He killed my brother because he outranked me, and I was spared my life to return and give you his message. How glad you must be, that you did not dare to go…"

T'Briki stood up, staring coldly at the man who showed so much insubordination and so little respect. The wooded peak was visible through the bay windows behind him, as was the setting sun, and he was framed momentarily in a golden hue, which made him look eerily powerful. Andreas Galanis, a large Kosovan of Greek descendance stood up, his hand reaching for the skinning knife he always wore on his belt. He was known as The Shepherd, because that is what he did for most of his life before joining the brotherhood. He would often kill, skin and butcher goats for feasts when the brotherhood met at his farm on the Albania-Kosovo border. T'Briki glanced at The Shepherd and shook his head. The big man sheathed the blade and sat back down. Loyalty affirmed.

Yosef rose steadily to his feet and looked at his boss. He dipped his head and said, "I am sorry. I did not mean to disrespect you. I am still grieving…"

The Albanian never got to finish his sentence. The bullet punched a neat hole in the glass behind T'Briki's head, struck his cranium through the occipital and exited through the man's throat. Yosef was struck in his left shoulder by the same bullet and spun like a top, the misshapen bullet slowing in velocity and hitting him like a brick at two-hundred miles per hour. As he fell, he caught sight of the brotherhood boss slumped on the floor, eyes open but still and bleeding out of the entry and exit wounds at an alarming rate on the hard, wooden parquet. Above the chaos that ensued, he heard a distant rumble across the valley as the sound of the gunshot caught up with the bullet.

The Shepherd was crouched beneath the table and had bizarrely drawn his knife for protection. Yosef belly crawled to him and groaned as he rolled onto his back to assess the damage. Galanis sheathed his blade a second time and looked to the man who had been so rapidly promoted. Galanis was several rungs down the ladder and had only been present at today's meeting because he was the brotherhood's number one killer.

"We need to get to the rear of the building," said Galanis. "To the vehicles…"

"It may be an ambush," Yosef replied breathlessly. "There could be others waiting!"

Galanis took out his two-way radio. "Security! Shot fired! Report!"

There was a short pause, then a bemused reply came back, *"Nothing to report here, we thought it was somebody hunting on the hill."*

"Well, he's just successfully hunted the boss! Get the hell out there and find him! The shot came from the peak!"

Galanis reached for a napkin on top of the table and folded it, handing it to Yosef to press against his shoulder. "He'll never get there in time, you can hear it in his voice." He knew it would take the guard an hour to trek the two-thousand metres of forest and incline to the peak. Whoever had made the shot would be heading the other way for sure. He ducked further under the table and said, "Let's get out of here." He caught hold of Yosef's arm and dragged him closer. Mere seconds ago, he had drawn his knife to show his support to his boss, and now he was helping that same threat across the floor and out of the line of fire. He was a cog in a machine. He had survived by being loyal, and that had not changed. A week previously, Yosef had been number three. Now he was the boss of the *Albanian Brotherhood of Kontroll.*

Yosef looked at the man, then smiled and took hold of his hand. As he struggled and crawled, his shoulder on fire from the bullet wound, he vowed vengeance on Romanovitch and the Russian scum working for him. He would avenge his brother. And he would need the killing skills of The Shepherd. The man who killed and skinned and butchered the goats for their feasts.

8

Rashid had watched the scene unfold in his scope. It had been a highly testing yet satisfying shot. Two thousand, two hundred metres with a .338 Lapua magnum, in this case the Russian-made Kalashnikov VSV-338 sniper rifle.

The evening sun had created taxing thermals across the ravine, but watching the nesting ravens soar, and using a laser thermometer to read the temperatures throughout the valley, Rashid had been able to make the necessary adjustments. Even so, he had over compensated, planning to hit T'Briki between the shoulder blades and sever the man's spine, and in doing so, miss the man standing in front of him. After compensating for the recoil, Rashid had seen the man with the wounded shoulder make it under the table and disappear from view. According to their contact, the man was known as Yosef and would now be made number one in the brotherhood. Rashid only hoped that Yosef would recover from his injuries and assume the title.

Rashid continued to scan the room through the window, then sighted the crosshairs of the scope over the other windows checking for a counter-sniper. He scanned the sides of the building and could see the flash of motor vehicles through the foliage. He assumed they were retreating, but in the event that they were heading for the peak, he had no more than twenty-minutes to get clear. He rolled over onto his back and made the weapon safe, then slipped it into the gun slip and wiped the Russian stamped bullet case and left it on the flattened ground where he had lain. He rolled onto his front and belly crawled into the cover until he was twenty feet deep in the brush and out of sight of any potential sniper.

They had netted just over four and a half million euros from their two heists and that gave them some serious operating capital. Rashid could hear the whump of the rotors and roar of the jet engine of the helicopter. He was now running through the last of the brush and soon reached the path that took him around the peak and onto the grassy and stony plateau beyond. Flymo had responded to his text and taken off from the field where he had been waiting five miles away.

Rashid's heart was pounding with the adrenalin and effort of the run in the warm evening air. He could see the Bell Jet Ranger banking hard half a mile ahead of him. Flymo was seriously dropping in altitude, too. When he righted the aircraft, he brought the nose up sharply, the tail rotor slicing at the grass below him, and the helicopter stopped dead in a hover two hundred metres away. As the nose balanced, the craft hung in the air with its skids less than a metre off the ground. Rashid slowed to a jog, ducked his head, and leapt through the open door. Goldie took the rifle from him and shifted over leaving Rashid to close the door behind him.

Flymo took off in a reverse lift, dipped the nose and banked to the right. Both Rashid and Goldie in the rear and Mac, who occupied the front seat, made a noise between a cheer and a grunt, having been treated to the most sensational, adrenalin-fuelled display of expertise that felt like the most extreme theme park ride imaginable. Within a minute, they were behind the next peak and out of view from any of the brotherhood, with the third job, and second phase of the operation under their belts.

9

**Three weeks later
St. Petersburg, Russia**

The warehouse was situated on the west quay of The Big Port of St. Petersburg, which meant that Romanovitch could both import and export through the Baltic Sea, or by train north, east and south. On occasion, he would run freight via ship up the Gulf of Bothnia and overland it through Sweden and Norway to various seaports – anything to prevent forming a pattern or routine – but once the freight left by the Baltic Sea and entered the vast shipping routes of the North Sea, the world was his oyster.

    They were making a waterborne assault, so Goldie was leading this one. As a former sergeant in the SBS he was in his element, and although the SAS train using the same craft and techniques – often alongside the SBS – Goldie had a wealth of experience and had been at the helm of various boats for hundreds of hours and in all sea conditions. As a former Army Air Corps pilot, Flymo brought nothing more to the party than goodwill, and was given the role of eyes and ears. From a van they had purchased and then kitted out with monitors, receivers and recording devices, Flymo monitored the many wireless cameras that the team had covertly planted over the past three nights from a few miles to the south. Using a rubber inflatable boat with a silent electrically powered outboard, the three men had swept through the moored boats under the cover of darkness and into the port from the southern side. The cameras and audio equipment had given them the chance to draw-up an in-depth plan from the safety of their rented farmhouse, while knowing exactly how many hostile forces, not to mention innocent personnel were in the vicinity when they carried out the raid.

Goldie, Philosopher and Mac eased the rubber boat into the slick, black water on the shingle beach. The water was cold, their wetsuits letting water in between their boots and the ankles of the wetsuit legs, which would soon warm between their skin and the neoprene of the wetsuit. Each man had a diving knife strapped to their ankles, with tactical belt rigs and holsters made from hard plastic and webbing around their waists. They each carried a well-greased Sig P225 9mm pistol in their holsters with two spare magazines. 9mm

Heckler & Koch MP-5 carbines were strapped to their chests along with spare magazines and pouches containing the tools they would require. They also wore wetsuit hoods and PNVG's or night vision goggles on their heads, which they would snap down in place when they needed them. Philosopher carried the homemade charges, while Mac carried an extensive first aid kit upon his back and Goldie carried a waterproofed tablet with a 3D diagram of the warehouse using data collated from plans, photographs and digital imaging they had taken during the week. The tablet could also bring up single image footage of the cameras they had installed. From his position across the bay, Flymo had communications to them all and could survey every camera on the bank of monitors in front of him.

    Rashid watched the warehouse through the thermal imaging optics attached to the top of his scope. Below, the scope was infrared and x 8 magnification. The weapon below that was a Steyr HS .50 calibre rifle. The weapon was loaded and made ready and five brass shells were lined up in a neat row on their sides on the insulated groundsheet Rashid was resting on, two hundred and sixty-five feet above the ground on the platform of a crane, a full one-thousand metres from the working side of the warehouse. In front of him, the lights of the port created some flaring in the lens, but the black waters of the Baltic corrected it quickly. Behind him, the city lights of St. Petersburg burned fiercely, a hub of restaurants, nightclubs, and hotels.

"Control to God. Penguins are on route."

"God to Control. Have that." Rashid smiled as he replied to Flymo, surveying the scene like God from the heavens with a lightning bolt at his fingertips.

Rashid watched the small inflatable reappear from behind some boats and pull close to the quay. He traversed the scope across the quay. There was movement in the shadows, and he dialled back the magnification, which in turn dialled up the intensity of the passive infrared. A single guard relieving himself beside some wheelie bins.

"God to Penguins. X-ray fifty metres in, eighty metres east of your position. Armed with a long." Rashid lifted his eye from the scope and moved the rifle's muzzle a full metre to his right. He sighted on the main gates where port authority security manned the gates with AK-74 assault rifles slung over their shoulders, talked and smoked with Russian soldiers on the other side of the barriers. Despite being early summer, the night air was cold, and the guards walked small circles, stamping their feet, and patting their own arms. Only a month before the port would have been frozen with icebreakers piloting the ships to their moorings and docks through the ice.

"*Received…*" Mac paused. *"Port authority or acceptable loss?"*

"Acceptable for sure." Rashid replied, consigning the man taking a piss to his fate. They had a job to do and they were doing it. He moved the rifle again and re-sighted on the man. He'd finished what he was doing and was working his way around the warehouse in a clockwise rotation. "God to Penguins, wait one. X-ray is in front of you… now rounding the edge of the building… you're good to go…"

"Penguins, this is control. Seaward side is clear. Four x-rays on north side, one on each end. The four x-rays are static and pouring something hot from a flask. They're shooting the shit and chewing the fat. Mobile x-ray is still moving clockwise. Seaward side is all clear."

Rashid could confirm Flymo's report, but he kept quiet and watched the three men climb the steps, having tethered the small rubber boat to the bottom of the steps. Now that his team were exposed, he settled in behind the rifle and took plenty of tension up in his shoulder, and a little on the trigger. He tracked the crosshairs along the windows and towards the far eastern corner of the building. When he tracked back, he could see Goldie and Mac ferrying the gallon petrol cans across the open ground from the quayside to the building. One in each hand, both returning for another trip. A gallon of petrol holds the same detonation yield as a pound of plastic explosive, just as long as detonation is achieved, rather than ignition. The secret was in the amount of charge used, and they had constructed charge packs from a potent mix of gently heated petroleum jelly, pre-condensed bleach, chemical fertiliser and sugar, which was then poured into moulds with standard RDX detonators at their core. Each charge was about the size of a jam jar and while Mac and Goldie made another trip, Philosopher attached the charges to the petrol cans using cable ties. When the other two men returned, making twelve cans in all, Mac started attaching the detonation cord to the finished cans, while Philosopher applied the last four explosive charges.

"Control to Penguins. Movement. Coffee break is over. One x-ray heading clockwise on east side, one x-ray heading anti-clockwise on west side. Contact imminent…"

Rashid watched the east side, his finger tightening on the trigger as the guard came into view. He followed the man round, waiting to see what happened next. He would have to assume the men could take care of matters up close, but the warehouse was over two-hundred metres long and a push for the team's 9mm weapons in the darkness. The guard hesitated near the wheelie bins and Rashid saw the man take the rifle from his shoulder, where it had been hanging lazily on its sling. That was enough, and he zeroed in on the man's centre mass. Normally he would take a head shot, but he was a kilometre away and had a .50 at his disposal. He was about to leave a hole the size of a large apple. He took up the final resistance of tension on the trigger and the weapon hammered back into his shoulder and sounded like a cannon in his ear. He worked the bolt and the .50 shell case ejected and clattered on the ironwork of the crane and he picked up another bullet, then dropped it into the chamber and worked the bolt forward. When he re-sighted, the target was down and lying still. Rashid tracked to his left and could see Goldie crouched low, putting the final adjustments to the charge. He tracked further along the building and he could see the tall frame of Philosopher dragging the body of a man towards the wheelie bins and Mac sheathing his diving knife. They had managed a silent kill, but he wondered whether the .50 had been audible from their position, given the distance and sounds of the city behind him and the port in front. He tracked back to the east and focused on the port authority guards and Russian soldiers. They were all looking his way and the cigarettes had been dropped on the ground.

"God to Penguins. X-ray down, but I've screwed the pooch. The port authority guards and soldiers know what they've just heard, so they'll be getting busy any minute. Out." He took a breath and said into the mic. "Control. Give us a heads up."

"Have that. Two x-rays down on seaward side. Two more heading both ways. Soldiers are coming through the barrier and the port authority

guards are talking on comms. There are vehicles on the way, searchlights on top. The soldiers are getting ready to get on the vehicles."

"Have that," Mac said in his broad Scottish accent. *"We're going noisy any minute…"*

With that Rashid saw muzzle flashes and heard the pop-pop sound of small arms fire a full second later. Right now, it was four against three, but he still liked their odds. But the unexpected always happened in firefights, so he turned the rifle towards the port entrance and sighted on the lead vehicle. He gave a little lead, then fired and by the time he had gotten over the massive recoil of the rifle, he could see the lead four by four swerving, then veering towards the guard's security hut. It crashed through and sent wood and bricks scattering across the concrete. He worked the bolt and loaded another bullet. The second four by four had slammed on its brakes and Rashid wasted no time in putting his next bullet clean through the bonnet and engine block, where steam and smoke started to vent and the driver got out and fled for cover. The soldiers were scattering also, taking cover, and setting up firing positions. Rashid reloaded and looked for a material target. He had earlier made note of potential targets and he found the fuel pumps some two hundred metres north of the soldiers. He adjusted his aim, but from an elevated position and a thousand metres distant with a .50 he was just getting into his stride and sent an incendiary round into the base of the pump, where it ignited instantly and sent flames a hundred feet into the air. The sight flared and he snatched his head away, blinking and cursing his loss of night vision. He turned the rifle back to the warehouse, but the team was now out of view.

"God to Control, sit-rep!"

"Two x-rays down on west side. Penguins setting charges. Two x-rays on east side. They've taken cover and are watching the port authority guards five-hundred metres away. Vehicles burning, fuel pumps on fire. One x-ray has now fled. The other is heading for the seaward side of the building."

"Have that," Rashid replied and moved the weapon back to the far end of the building.

"He's edging along. Now three metres from the corner. Two metres… one metre…"

Rashid fired at a spot six inches out from the corner of the building and one and a half metres off the ground. He recovered from the recoil in time to watch the man step around the building and walk into a .50 calibre bullet travelling at nine-hundred feet per second with a closing energy of 9000 ft/lbs at a thousand metres. The man was practically broken in two.

"Control to Penguins. East side is now clear."

Rashid moved the weapon along the building but could no longer see the team. Instead, he focused on the threat of the mounting guards and soldiers half a kilometre away from the warehouse. There were a few brave soldiers edging out from cover and he put a bullet onto the ground fifty feet in front of them, where it sparked intensely and he watched the men scatter, this time returning fire vaguely in his direction, but falling way short of his position. One thousand metres and over two hundred feet of elevation was way off the capabilities of a Kalashnikov and the bullets were dropping harmlessly into the sea.

"Penguins to Control. Devices set. Working exfil."

"Control to Penguins, have that."

Rashid watched the three men bolt out of the shadows of the warehouse, weapons raised and covering the open ground to their left. He saw a man dart out from behind some shipping containers, his rifle raised. "Penguins! X-ray two-hundred metres to the east, armed with a long!" He sighted on the man, but he was moving quickly, and he struggled to track his movement smoothly enough for a shot. He cursed. He hadn't seen the man and Flymo hadn't, either. He could see muzzle flashes sparking in the night, highlighted in the green hue of his night vision. The team were still too far off for an accurate shot with the MP-5 carbines, but they were raining rounds down around him, and it was enough for the man to stop running, drop to one knee and take a well-aimed shot. Rashid took up the tension on the trigger and fired. A full second later, the figure sprawled forwards and his rifle spun off to the side.

"We're clear and on route," Goldie said through the comms. *"Light her up!"*

Rashid smiled as he packed the rifle away and strapped the slip to his back. He picked up the control unit and switched it on. There was an illuminated panel which showed a signal in the same way a mobile phone did. It indicated four bars, but he had checked it earlier and knew it would be. He flicked the arming switch, then pressed the button, not looking at the warehouse until the blistering, simultaneous explosions had flashed, and the noise rumbled towards him. When he did finally look, the warehouse roof had sunk, and all four walls had fallen inwards. The building was ablaze, flames licking the sky some hundred metres high and smoke was billowing into a mushroom cloud three times higher than the flames. The fire roared but continued to grow in intensity as the contents of the warehouse started to combust and ignite.

"Job done," he said quietly, then clipped onto the rope and stepped over the railing, before abseiling the two-hundred and sixty-feet to the ground below. He disconnected and climbed over the great bundles of caged boulders that had formed the man-made island on which the crane stood. Behind him the flames grew in intensity, and the darkness had become light. The cages of boulders, some eight feet cubed had snagged weed and debris and driftwood at the sea edge and seagrass had grown to form a shoreline. Rashid had moored his boat directly to the cages, hidden by the seagrass. He took the rifle off his back and dropped it into the boat along with the harness and backpack. The rubber boat flexed as he got in and untied, then cast off with the tiny oar. He started the electric motor and it silently kicked into life, propelling him across the bay towards the moored ships and smaller boats. As he left the burning sight of the quay behind him, and the night grew darker with every metre he travelled, he slipped his night vision goggles down and snapped them into place. Ahead of him, he could make out the second rubber boat heading silently out of the port and down the coast.

Rashid grinned. It was going well, and they had made their fourth successful strike, but this time at a larger, and altogether more dangerous enemy.

10

One week later
St. Petersburg, Russia

"English?"

"British."

"What's the fucking difference?"

"One of the voices was Scottish," Major Diminov replied. He was an officer with the SVR, Russia's foreign espionage service. He was in his late forties but looked to be in his late fifties. A life starting with poverty and culminating in excess had not been kind to his system. Hard service, deception and stress had not been kind to his face, in particular his eyes, which were cold, lifeless and devoid of emotion. "We can do better than that, though. The man with the call sign *God* has traces of a Birmingham accent, most likely from a place called Oldham, and almost certainly of Asian descent."

"Asia is a big place, Major Diminov," said Romanovitch pointedly. "We are in Asia ourselves, after all."

"Northern India or Pakistan."

Romanovitch nodded. "So, a Scotsman and an Indian-English immigrant."

"Or Pakistani."

"And the others?"

"Our linguists are certain the man known as *Control* is British, but of Afro-Caribbean descent. The other two voices are white-British one from South London, the other most likely from the Southampton area."

"A mixed bag," he said. "A team, all individuals, but collectively British." Romanovitch paused. "A wanton act of vandalism, nothing more. Nothing stolen. And certainly, nobody of any importance killed."

"There's more," said Diminov, leaning across the table and handing the Russian mafia boss his phone. "Those are pictures of Commander Robinson entering Thames House, the headquarters of MI5. Not exactly my opposite agency in the United Kingdom, but the one that hunts down people like me operating on their soil. Commander is head of SO15, the police counter terrorism unit."

"So?" Romanovitch shrugged, swiping over four photographs of a man in his fifties with grey hair and an unremarkable appearance.

"Those images were emailed to me when I started my enquiries. A small team of SVR agents have the police chief under surveillance. He has been quite vocal in his condemnation of Russian intelligence services interference." He paused. "As has the British Home Secretary. She has cited Russian crime and state-sanctioned interference as one of their biggest threats."

"But she would be right," Romanovitch smiled wryly. "Your agents in Salisbury? A most audacious assassination attempt of a double agent and defector."

Major Diminov reached back across the desk and took his phone out of Romanovitch's hand. "I am helping you, not requiring your judgement."

"And I am paying you a fortune!" Romanovitch snapped. "Don't *ever* forget that!"

Diminov nodded, reminded somewhat of both the man's lack of fear for members of his country's intelligence services or armed forces, but also of his considerable reach. It was rumoured that Romanovitch had moles in multiple government departments, and as one of them, Major Diminov could certainly testify to that. "Your contribution to my son's, your godson's, education fund will never be forgotten, nor overlooked, my friend…"

Romanovitch scoffed. Diminov was a slippery one, always covering his back. That was how he had risen to such heights in military intelligence. The rank of major was nothing out of the ordinary, but the unit he commanded within the SVR was legendary. It would not be out of the question for this meeting to be recorded, and the intelligence officer would never assume he could talk openly about the subject of his monthly bribe. He leaned forward, elbows on the desk, his hands steepled. "Bribe, sweetener or *fund* for my *godson*, whatever we call it, you had better deliver." He paused. "If this police chief, Robinson, is looking into my affairs, then I want him gone. No mistakes and no delays. No agents caught on CCTV, no Novichok or bullshit with poisonous umbrellas. Just a bullet in the head. Nice and public."

Diminov nodded. "And this team of saboteurs?"

Romanovitch opened the drawer next to him and took out an A4 padded envelope. He tossed it across the desk at the SVR agent. "Find out who they are, then find out *where* they are," he said. "Then call me."

Major Diminov nodded. He peered inside

the envelope, which was stuffed full of neatly stacked bundles of fifty and one-hundred-euro bills. He tucked down the flap, but the bundle was too large to fit into his pocket. "Just call you?"

Romanovitch nodded. "Just call me."

"And the Albanian problem?"

"That is in hand," he said. "As we speak. But I am sure that the two problems are one and the same."

"What will you do?"

Romanovitch stood up and walked to the window. The city of St. Petersburg sprawled before him, the Moyka River glistening in the bright, early summer light. For three days after the raid on his warehouse, some four miles distant, he had seen the smoke from the smouldering remains of his property. Tens of millions of dollars' worth of petrochemicals and equipment had been destroyed. His operation had been set back years. And now there would be questions. He wasn't too worried about the government – he had enough people on the take, all the way to the top. But the opposition parties and the bedroom journalists operating on social media, websites and YouTube were tenacious and proving incorruptible. He had lost count of how many he had 'disappeared' but another would always take their place. For the first time in his career of crime, and certainly since he had taken over from his deceased brother's mantel, he had questioned whether it was the right time to liquidate his assets and lie low. He could still live a luxurious life in the South of France. But he couldn't take the defeat. The sense of being pushed into such decisions. He turned and looked coldly at the Russian intelligence officer. "What will *I* do?" He paused. "Rest assured, Major. I will have these people's heads. I will cut them, personally, from their shoulders and I will do it in front of them, so they know they have been defeated. And I will do it slowly, and with great care, and I will laugh as I do it…"

11

**One month later
Cornwall, England**

King had discovered that what he had initially thought of as relatively unskilled work had in fact been far more skilled than he had originally perceived. Like when the world first experienced lock down and key workers were found to be those stacking the shelves of supermarkets or driving a delivery van. Solicitors and financial advisers and estate agents were suddenly barely thought of, and the importance of what was to be deemed essential worker had far outweighed the higher earning professions with true value and worth being placed above salary.

He had previously learned to plaster and paint, and the skill had proved invaluable as cover for his last, and unofficial mission. However, laying blocks and bricks had required a steeper learning curve, and that had taken him into the realms of tiling and roofing and guttering, and whenever he thought he was getting ahead of the game, another factor came into force and he had yet another DIY hurdle to master.

There had been no repeat of the pregnancy test. No false hopes or spikes in euphoria at the thought of becoming a family. It wasn't an issue, but each month Caroline had spent a sullen few days lamenting what wasn't to be before getting on with things, and life was settling into the same routine. King hadn't thought about it much at all. The building project was ongoing, although they had completed the rental cottage to net them an income and had been left starting over and living within a building site once more. He supposed it wouldn't be the right time to start a family, although they hadn't exactly been careful in that department. They would simply allow things to happen, but he knew that Caroline was starting to worry that it hadn't.

King was making the most of the late-summer sun and adding to the pile of split logs that should keep them going over the winter. He was shirtless and using the chore as exercise, wielding the ten-pound axe through the whole logs, then when he had a decent pile, he would throw them like a rugby ball to the mounting pile under the lean-to some twenty feet from the depleting pile of unsplit wood. Caroline had gone for a run, but King knew it was more about sorting out her head than simply keeping fit. She would pound the clifftops for an hour or two every day. If he was honest, he welcomed the solitude. He needed time to think, too, but not just about starting families and chalked-up failures each month. He missed the action. He missed the intrigue and subterfuge. But more than that, his constant thoughts about the life he had lived, the acts for which he felt the need to atone, were evermore present in this softened civilian life. As busy as he was developing their property, his mind simply wasn't busy enough for him to live with himself.

King looked up as the bell sounded at the bottom of the lane. He had laid a simple old-fashioned garage forecourt style contact wire across the entrance. Nobody calling on the house noticed it, but it rang a bell just once inside the porch. He bent down and picked up his shirt, then realised he had not picked up one of the two pistols he had secreted from previous missions. To his dismay, he could not remember the last time he had carried a weapon. He always carried a folding lock knife, and during his time renovating the property he used it for certain tasks every day, but he realised he had been carrying it as a tool instead of an actual weapon. King cursed himself, wondering what his old mentor Peter Stewart would have made of it. As he walked around the side of the house and into the porch, he could hear the cantankerous Scottish drunk lambasting him for his complacency.

King opened the drawer and picked up the Walther PPK. He did not bother working the slide and checking the breech because the tiny pin above the hammer was poking out indicating a round was already chambered. A brilliant feature he had often wondered why other manufacturers had not copied. He tucked the tiny pistol into his back pocket and put on his shirt as he walked back outside.

The car was a black Jaguar saloon, and he recognised the London number plate configuration. It was a new registration, so he assumed MI5's budget was still strong after so much government investment and bailout to businesses, workers and the NHS. The country was now in recession, but government departments would always do OK. He watched it manoeuvre between Caroline's Mini Cooper S and his own battered Land Rover Defender. Neil Ramsay got out of the passenger seat and Simon

Mereweather opened the rear door and stepped out, blinking in the sunlight. Someone King did not recognise opened the driver's door, stepped out and did a quick assessment of the area. He looked like a bodyguard, but he'd missed King standing in the shadows of the late afternoon sun. Ramsay nodded when he finally saw King, and the bodyguard did his best not to look too bored as he waited beside the car.

"The house has come on since we saw it last," Simon Mereweather said. "How is Caroline fairing with the boredom?"

"Who said she was bored?"

"Sorry, I just assumed. You two didn't exactly have the quietest of lives before all this rural idyll."

King shrugged. "Well, we're making up for it at last."

"I bet," said Mereweather.

"I don't see her watching *Cash in the Attic* with a cup of tea and wearing a pair of slippers," Ramsay quipped. "Not quite the picture I'd paint of you, either."

"She's gone out for a run," said King. "So, you can both be gone before she returns." Mereweather smiled, looked around him. The sea was glistening in the distance, with the fields an array of colour with yellow rapeseed, tall grass for silage or hay and wheat creating a patchwork quilt of hues. King said, "Get on with it, Simon…"

"Rashid's team has disappeared."

"Disappeared?"

"Vanished," Ramsay reiterated.

"What was the job?"

Mereweather looked around him. The bodyguard-come-driver was staring at the sea with his back to them. The deputy director of MI5 looked back at King. "Can we discuss this inside?"

King shrugged. "Fair enough." He led them inside and into the kitchen. The cabinets and fixings were all new, but the walls were still to be tiled and painted. There were test colours on the wall, some with ticks beside them, others crossed out altogether. King put the kettle on and took four cups out of the cupboard. "So, what was it?" he asked again.

"You once crossed paths with a man called Romanovitch," said Mereweather. "A Russian mafia leader."

King looked at him, but he was picturing the man before him, Caroline being held captive by an adversary out for vengeance and the killing of Romanovitch being the price of her freedom. He could see the man lying still on the hard floor after their struggle, his head split open, his eyes staring wide. That day on the coast of the Black Sea in Georgia seemed so long ago, and the deception which had followed had cost lives. Rashid had been there that day, at the exchange. Ready with his rifle, protecting King at a distance.

"What about him?" King asked tersely. "He's dead?"

"But his brother is not. Ivan Romanovitch picked up where his brother left off, and over these past years he has built up a large network of drug manufacturers, weapon smugglers and people traffickers. We have been working on intelligence from SO15 to shut the organisation down. Together with an Albanian outfit called the *Albanian Brotherhood of Kontroll*…"

"That's organised crime, not terrorism. SO15 are terrorist hunters."

Mereweather nodded. "Romanovitch has his fingers in a lot of pies. It is suspected he has people inside the FSB and SVR. Romanovitch's weapons have ended up in Islamic extremist hands, so he has found himself firmly within

SO15's remit." He paused. "The great policers of Islam don't seem to mind raising funds by selling drugs either and Romanovitch sells the chemicals to the Albanians, who then sell the crystal meth on to Islamic extremist groups over here."

King shook his head as he poured hot water onto the four teabags, splashed in milk and before he could stop himself, he had shovelled a spoon of sugar into all four mugs. He hesitated, then shrugged. That's how he took his tea, and anybody wanting it differently was simply wrong. He stirred them well, then hooked out the teabags and slid one of the cups towards Ramsay. "Give that to the driver, Neil," he said and picked up his own cup. Ramsay looked affronted, but walked out with the cup, nonetheless. "What was the brief?" King asked, then sipped some of his tea.

"Rashid was to lead a team of four more men in subterfuge and assassination, to pitch both gangs against each other. And then, like a wise fighting-cock, watch the other two fighting-cocks rip each other to shreds, then attack the winner when they are both wounded and exhausted."

"Great analogy," King replied. "But it seldom works out that way. The winning fighting cock has the edge because it has lost the fear. It doesn't feel pain, because its blood is pumping with endorphins and besides, it has the taste for blood…"

"It worked when you pitted that Russian gang against the Italian mafia." Mereweather looked up as Ramsay walked back inside and picked up his mug of tea. "It worked for you," he added.

King nodded. "But I was in a pinch and running out of time. I did what I did and rolled the dice. They did not have the time to figure things out." He paused. "I was in and out. This sounds like a long-term, protracted affair. It sounds as if somebody wised-up."

"Indeed," mused Mereweather.

"Or there's another possibility," said King.

"Which is?"

"Do I know this team?"

"No."

"How well do you know them?" King asked. "Can you trust them?"

"Implicitly," replied Mereweather. "Especially Rashid."

King shrugged. "I know Rashid, and I would vouch for him all day long. But I don't know these other four men." King paused. "I take it they have hit the gangs financially?"

"And then some," Ramsay interjected. "Six laundering hits, and then when the gangs used different methods, they went after the money men. They hit them up for millions. Both in Russia and Albania. More than twenty million euros in all."

King shrugged. "Enough to disappear on…"

"But I still don't think Rashid would…"

"Of course, he wouldn't!" King snapped. "But that doesn't mean the others wouldn't have killed him and taken off with the money." He sighed, shook his head. "Shit…"

"We have a contact. An asset," said Mereweather. He took out an envelope, placed it on the kitchen counter and slid it across to King. "All the details are in there, along with a cash card, a bank account and a credit card, all in your name. Unlimited funds."

"Within reason," Ramsay added. "And it needs accounting for, so you can't finish your renovation off with it."

"Piss off, Neil." King shook his head. "I'm out, and I meant it at the beginning of the summer. I no longer work for you."

Mereweather nodded and stood up. He finished his tea and placed the cup down on top of the envelope. "I understand."

"So, you'll need to take that back with you," King told him, looking at the envelope.

Ramsay sipped some tea, grimaced at its sweetness, and placed the cup and its barely touched contents back down. "It was nice seeing you again, Alex."

King nodded. He removed Mereweather's cup and slid the envelope back towards him. "I meant it, I'm out."

"I thought Rashid meant something to you."

"He does. Or did." King shrugged. "In this game, it catches up with you eventually. If you want to dance, you've got to pay the band…"

"But it didn't catch up with you," said Ramsay.

King took the pistol from his pocket and rested it on the counter, still in his hand with his finger near the trigger. "And that's a miracle. But because I stay prepared and I've stopped taking chances." He paused, thinking about how off guard he had been earlier. He needed to sharpen up. "I've dodged bullets and people who would do me harm my entire adult life. And with my childhood, I was lucky to make it, full stop. And now, that's it for me. I'm out and hopefully I'll live long enough to start a family with the woman I love."

Mereweather smiled. "Then, I wish you well and we'll be on our way." He paused. "But I'll leave you the envelope. I understand your reasonings. And fatherhood, if you're lucky enough to experience it, tends to focus one's eye. Until they're teenagers and then you'll do everything within your power *not* to be home," he smiled, managing a chuckle.

King smiled and slid the envelope towards him but frowned when Mereweather ignored it. "What's going on?" he asked.

"We're done with this," he replied. "If there's any chance of finding out what happened, then it lies with you. If Rashid and his team have buggered off with the money and are in hiding, then I guess we'll find out at some stage. If they are being held captive… or indeed have been killed… then it begins and ends with you finding out. We can't be any more involved than we have been. The team were effective, too effective perhaps, and there are people who want to find out what was going on and who was behind it. Crossing swords with those people is not on our department's agenda."

King shook his head. "So, that's it? You dangle Rashid's life in front of me like a carrot, and if I don't bite, he's done for?" He paused. "You bastards…"

"Well, like you said, you no longer work for us, Alex. We can't very well use a stick, so the carrot is all we've got."

12

Tirana, Albania

King looked at the copy of the police report. It had been requisitioned by Interpol and bore the agency's stamp all over the photocopied sheets. Then the Met had gotten hold of it and it bore several stamps requisitioning the report. MI5 had received the report clandestinely, so there was nothing to link the Security Service with the documents. He studied the post office in the tree-lined square. He would have called it a piazza but wasn't sure if it translated in Albanian. The chalk lines indicating the resting places of the bodies had long-since been rubbed away by pedestrians, as he doubted the area had any rain in the past few months. It was a dry climate, similar to that of Greece, and would rain more during the autumn months as the air and sea cooled against the heat of the sun-baked land, but summer rain would be rare indeed. He looked up for CCTV cameras, but there was nothing more than he already knew about from the report and the images he held on file.

He folded the report and tucked it back into the back of his trousers, leaving just under half of it poking out. Not ideal, but he had hired a motorbike and it had come without panniers. King swung his leg over the frame and sat down heavily on the hot seat. He pulled the bike upright and kicked up the stand. The bike was a Suzuki SV650 which he had chosen for its convenience in city traffic, ease of parking and a terrific turn of speed which could embarrass most supercars to one-hundred miles per hour.

The traffic was light, and King weaved in and out of the slower-moving vehicles to maintain a good pace. He always found he rode more recklessly than he drove. The speed and manoeuvrability became addictive. Part of the reason he did not own a motorcycle – because he would get a taste of it and unwittingly embrace the infallibility without recognising the vulnerability.

He left the main road and started riding loops of the square, widening the route in concentric circles, and watching both sides of the streets. He spotted the BMW merely by the amount of tree debris and dust covering it. There were dried seed pods, sap and fallen leaves all over the windscreen and bodywork. The dust was thick and covered the glass all around and it was evident that nobody had driven the vehicle in months. Only the fact it was parked in a quiet residential neighbourhood accounted for the fact that it had not been stolen or attracted attention from vandals. King parked the motorcycle on the opposite side of the road beneath the shade of a tree and spent a few minutes studying the street. He then got off the machine, took off the open-face helmet and hung it on the handlebar as he watched the road behind him. There was no CCTV and the houses were a few metres set back from the road with overgrown gardens and hedges giving the residents privacy. King approached the vehicle and dropped into a press up, holding himself just a few inches from the hot tarmac to survey the underside. He saw the key resting on top of the rubber bush above the shock absorber spring, but he ignored it until he had checked the other wheel arches and the rest of the underside of the vehicle. IEDs or tracking devices could be easily planted and left for the unwitting driver to return, with lithium batteries lasting for years. King also knew enough about vehicle searches that you did not see just one thing and make a move. He checked all the wheel arches and the underside on the opposite side of the vehicle, then satisfied it was clear, he picked up the key fob and walked back thirty metres or so and used a parked vehicle for cover as he unlocked the BMW using the fob. It unlocked without drama, its lights flashing twice as the locks lifted and the alarm was immobilised. King walked back to the car, glancing about him to see if he was being watched. It was a quiet, tree-lined street and by the way the hedges and fences bordered the edge of the pavement, he could already tell that it would require a great deal of effort by someone who wanted to spy on the street. Anybody watching from the top windows of the houses would have their view obscured by the trees lining the pavement.

King opened the door slowly, checking for wires, but he had already decided that the vehicle had been left for a quick getaway. That is, if it indeed had been used by Rashid and his team. Plenty of people dropped off a car and left the keys within easy reach for someone, but this car had been here for weeks, if not months. The dust and grime, seed pods and dried leaves had left a layer of debris so thick that King could barely guess at the colour underneath. He pressed the fob again, saw there was battery charge enough to bring the display to life, so he sat down in the driver's seat and started the engine to save the battery and brought up the telephone options. Next, he took out his iPhone and connected to the vehicle via Bluetooth. When he had the device paired with the vehicle, he scrolled through the screen of his phone and selected an app. There was a brief pause while the two devices paired through the app and then he followed the prompts and rested the phone next to the satnav and scrolled through the BMW's iDrive to the satnav and waited for the data to stream. King opened the glovebox while he waited and found the envelope of money and the loaded Makarov pistol. He took the money out of the envelope and folded it before tucking it into his pocket. As he got out of the seat, he slipped the pistol into his back pocket as he walked around the vehicle and opened the boot. King could see all he needed to. A comprehensive first aid kit and small carry-on bags with changes of clothes. He had operated in the same way, left an escape option ready more times than he cared to remember. Someone generally came behind him and moved the evidence. Usually a junior agent out of harm's way but still in the field getting some miles on the clock.

King got back into the car and checked his phone. The app had opened a program on a backdoor MI5 server and had downloaded the last 250 megabytes of data from the satnav's history. It included GPS journey start and end data as well as average speed and the time of each journey. King opened the email which the program had sent back to his email provider and checked the folder. He entered the GPS coordinates of the start location and studied the map. He doubted Rashid and his team would be there, but at least he had another lead to go on.

13

The road on the map was a gently meandering ribbon of red which cut a swathe of colour across a page of white and beige and green. In reality, it was a potholed and uneven track which had been hewn from the rock using dynamite and lives which had not been valued under communist rule, and had fallen away into the abyss in parts that made it strictly one lane at the most dangerous of points, and barely two lane for the remainder.

King was glad he had taken the car. The particular motorcycle he had hired was more suited to smooth tarmac and would have proven to be a treacherous ride on this surface. A trail bike would have fared well, but either way, the potholes were easily the worst King had seen, and had already removed a section of spoiler at the front of the car when he had misjudged the severity of the first major pothole. He was now approaching a thousand feet above sea level and the pine forest reminded him of mountain passes in Mallorca, with jagged rocks jutting out and trees defying nature and setting roots down in the tiniest of crevices. However, it was wilder country than that Spanish tourist island, and he had already seen small deer and some large wild boar not far from the road, as well as the remains of several snakes on the road surface. He knew from past experiences that snakes soaked up the night-time heat on roads, and the fact he had seen remains told him that the road was used more often than its appearances would suggest. He had seen a few battered hatchbacks and some recklessly driven supply trucks heading towards him, but he had neither caught up on a vehicle, nor had one in his mirror for almost an hour.

With approximately four hundred metres to go until he reached the GPS coordinates indicated on the satnav, he pulled off the road and left the car in what appeared to be a hunter's or farmer's track. The map showed a plateau of land beyond the trees, and he assumed it could be accessed from different directions for subsistence farmers to exploit for grazing. There were thick mounds of pine needles covering the track, indicating nobody had driven on or herded cattle or goats along the track for a considerable time and he figured the car would go unnoticed parked here, out of sight of the road.

It was late summer, but the Albanian sun bore down on him, dry and relentless. The pine forest made for some shade but smelled like a hot sauna. He could taste the heady pine air in his mouth, feel it robbing him of his senses as he attempted to tune into his surroundings. He checked the Makarov pistol. It had been made ready, but the hammer was set forwards. Being a double action pistol, it would only require a stronger initial pull on the trigger for the first shot. After which, subsequent shots would cycle and leave the hammer held back, requiring a less frenetic pull. The Russian weapon was both rugged and crude, but generally kept working when its modern, expensive, and cutting-edge western counterparts had jammed and cracked and failed to cycle.

King quickly found the property. He was approximately sixty feet above it and one hundred and fifty metres away when the forest cleared enough for him to take the full layout into view. It did not look like a working farm, and nor did it look to have been used as a storage facility or haulage business. The road and location would not have made a great deal of sense for a venture like that. But it had been something. Once. It was now dilapidated, and the forest had started to claim ground, with younger pines and saplings and brush sprouting up between buildings. The house was basic. Four walls, a flat roof and two storeys. It would have been painted, but only once and a long time ago. King could not tell in which colour, but houses out here were generally white, and then cream, and then flaked, and then bare concrete. Touching up was something he doubted people had heard of, and neither was buying paint a second time. There was an array of out buildings, but King did not need to watch for too long to see that it was deserted and had not functioned as a farm in a long time. There was no loose hay or straw blown or scattered across the yard, no sign of manure. He studied the eaves of the buildings, the facias for CCTV, security lights or alarms. Nothing.

Working his way back into the woods, he walked down the incline adjacent to the property. By the time it levelled out, he was only fifty metres away and level with the yard. Midday with the sun directly overhead, clear skies and little shade. Not the ideal conditions for a tactical advance. King took a tentative step out of the shade of the fringe of trees and into the light. He checked his shadow. It was behind and to the left. So, he knew which way was north to keep his bearings. And the fact the shadow was behind him, even slightly, meant it would not reach his destination before him and give someone a tell.

The open ground was hot, despite the altitude, and he could feel the warm air rising from the smooth concrete surface. By the time he reached the first outbuilding, he was perspiring. He drew the pistol and wiped his brow. The door was a double-fronted wooden structure which had seen many seasons. Ice cold and searing heat. The planks had bowed so much that he could peer between the twisted timbers and see that the building was empty. Regardless, he opened the door outwards and blinked through the dusty beams of sunlight, like cinema projections interspersing the darkness within.

King could see tyre tracks on the hard earth floor. He bent down and took a picture of them, figuring he would compare the photograph with the tyres of the BMW. At least it would give him the definitive answer as to whether the vehicle had simply visited this place, or whether it had been stored here, meaning that Rashid and his team had used this property as a base. King closed the door behind him and skirted the perimeter of the property. The larger barn intrigued him. The doors were huge, and the doorway was high, indicating that perhaps a large vehicle could be stored inside. Maybe a lorry of some description. But it lay beyond the house, and there was no point bypassing the building and to do so would put him at risk. He glanced through the nearest window but could see little. Dust and grime, and what he thought to be a layer of pine sap, from dispersed seed pods had coated the glass and rendered it impervious. He tested the door, but it did not yield. Around the back, the glass was the same. The windows probably hadn't been washed in decades. Again, the same as the paint. Once, and that was enough.

King looked around him, found a decent sized rock, then smashed the window and got ready with the pistol. He crouched, using the wall and the frame as cover, but nobody came. The place was deserted. King cleared the glass from the frame using the rock, then climbed through. The floor was tiled, the walls whitewashed and still clean, bright, and intact. He headed for the kitchen because that is where signs of habitation were most easily confirmed.

The colour of the water in the taps when they are first switched on – especially from bore holes where a property such as this would most likely source its water - whether the fridge was running and the condition of the food inside, how hard crumbs were on surfaces – kitchens told an easily read story.

The water ran clear and there were tinned items in the cupboard. The fridge had been left running but was empty and the freezer box had a few pizzas and some packets of frozen minced beef. Basic fare. But the pasta and sauce and tinned beans and meats in the cupboard made King think it catered towards a more Western diet than the average Albanian. No olives, pickled vegetables, or cured meats. These items were certainly more like the sort of food a team of British ex-soldiers would get through as they planned and organised for their mission. He looked around for debris, and there were the odd crumbs of bread on the floor. They were dried and popped underfoot. He went through the rest of the cupboards and found nothing, then turned his attention to the other rooms. Basic, square bedrooms with roll mats on the floor, sheets half-made on top. No possessions. No tells. King surveyed the rooms. There was nothing to tell just how long the property had been empty, but he could see that the plan had been to return. Rashid knew enough not to leave evidence behind, and the bedding would be prime material for DNA sampling. King was surprised the farmhouse had been left as it was, which told him that the last thing on the men's minds would be not returning.

Satisfied the building was at least free from threat, King went back outside and headed along the perimeter using the shadows of the forest for cover. When he reached the larger outbuilding, he could see that it was constructed much like the first, with timbers warped from the cold and heat and time. The doors were concertina style, with four folding doors, two on each side. King studied the padlock and the shackle it was locked through. The doors had been reinforced with plywood and metal sheeting around the locks. King bypassed it, knowing the Makarov and its shortened- case 9mm cartridge would do nothing to the hardened steel lock, so he worked his way through some briars and ran a hand along the timber planks that looked more bowed than the rest of the facade. He pocketed the pistol and took out his folding lock knife. It was a stubby model Buck knife with a three inch blade and he jimmied it between the planks and levered it enough to dig his fingers inside, where he clutched the plank and heaved, using his foot to press against the barn and get all of his weight into it. The plank started to crack, then split altogether and he put the knife away and got both hands onto the next piece of timber. The seasoned pine timber pulled out easily, and he soon had enough removed to slip inside. But first, he took a moment to squat on his haunches and study the inside of the building. He chuckled to himself as he took in the sight. Rashid wasn't messing about. He had certainly gathered resources. The Bell Jet Ranger helicopter sat in the centre of the building, its skids tethered to a purpose-made trailer that worked like a manually operated load-bearing fork-lift trolley. The main rotor had been anchored forward and aft by webbing straps. Along the far wall, a selection of tools, fuel cans and manually operated fuel pumps kept the show on the road.

 King slinked inside and allowed his eyes to adjust to the gloom. It was stifling hot and the air was thick and it was an effort to breathe. The floor was made from earth, which had compressed and hardened over time. King studied the flooring, frowning as he walked towards an area of newly laid concrete. The rest of the floor was like so many he had seen in poorer, sun-baked regions like Iraq and Afghanistan where he had operated clandestinely for close to a decade. The earth could harden so much that he had seen mud huts deflect .50 calibre bullets. So why would an area of the floor be turned over to concrete?

King got his answer when he pulled a piece of tarp away and half coiled, half folded it. In the end, he simply walked backwards and tugged the sheet away, leaving it where it fell. He looked at the safe, submerged in the concrete. It had been a good effort and would not have been easy to secure. A digger could have extracted it, but the whole barn would have to come down first. Hand tools wouldn't cut it, either. A pneumatic pick would take somebody days to extract the safe, which had been laid on its back flush with the floor. Which meant they would have had to have dug out a hole six feet deep, part filled it with concrete, laid the safe in on its back and filled the void with concrete. An arduous and time-consuming task for five men, but it meant that whatever they were storing would be safe from a random attack. King could see that planting charges would take days. Getting to the sweet spots of the safe would take heavy excavation. A gang without the specialist knowledge required would have to plan it right and allow at least two days and have a range of equipment to do it. King had cracked a few safes in his time, but he could already see that it would take more equipment than he had in his pockets. Certainly, more than he would find in the house. Making a homemade charge would not be enough for this beast, not unless he could drill to specific points. And even still, he would stand little chance to view the contents if they were blown to pieces and on fire from the super-heated residue of the IED. He took out his phone and photographed the make and model of the safe, then dragged the tarp back over it and headed for the gap in the wall he had created.

Outside, the brightness of the early afternoon sun in the cloudless sky was debilitating after the gloom of the barn. King blinked away the white light, but both heard and felt the gunshot as the bullet slammed into the corner of the building just inches from his shoulder. He dodged back and drew the chunky

Makarov from his pocket. He cocked the hammer back, the safety disengaging. Another gunshot. A dull thud. Small arms fire. Most likely a weapon in the same ballpark as the Russian pistol. King darted around the rear of the building, the briars snagging and tearing at his jeans and skin, ripping his T-shirt. He spun around, aware he had had his back exposed for too long. Once he had backed through the thorns, he reached the fringe of the forest and headed right, back towards the farmhouse. He figured anyone taking shots at him would not expect him to return, even by a roundabout route. If the person behind the gun was tactically trained, they would be following up their shots by advancing. Piling the pressure on. King had been there. But he wasn't your average prey.

King had simply rounded the barn and was edging his way around the other side between the building and the farmhouse when he saw the flash of movement. He raised the pistol, edging forwards the entire time. When he reached the corner of the building, he squatted low, edged out weapon first, stealing a glance at the man who was now advancing on the far corner of the building, his back to him and his own pistol aimed out in front. The man had adopted the classic Weaver Stance and was shuffling forwards his left foot always in front and shoulder width apart, his left hand cupping the underside of the weapon's butt. King opted for the strong-arm retention stance, carrying the weapon close to his chest to avoid snagging and ready to punch the weapon out straight when he wanted to bring the weapon on target. He had found that by using this technique, he could also use his left hand and both feet in unarmed combat techniques, only falling back on the pistol when he needed to. It gave him more options than the man who would be viewing everything through his weapon's sights. King stood up and hustled forwards. The man was already easing around the corner of the building and as King caught up, and the man realised his prey was in fact behind him, he struggled to bring the weapon back around onto his target. King launched a front kick into the man's right kidney, and as he dropped his foot forwards onto the ground, he punched out the weapon and struck the man under his ear with the muzzle of the pistol. The man cried out, still trying to get his pistol up to aim, but King clamped his hand over the weapon and the man's entire right hand, then pulled and pressed his own elbow into the man's own and spun his weight back onto his right foot. The man's arm was locked tightly, and he had to go with King's momentum to avoid his arm being broken. The brain is extremely good at this – sending messages to the limbs to do anything to avoid being broken - which is why you can see small people spin bigger people in the air in any dojo. At a shade under six-foot tall and fourteen stone, King was not small by any means and the man was thrown over savagely, landing on his backside, but this time his arm was locked tightly with King standing above him, pressing down on the straightened limb and bending his wrist.

King tucked his own pistol into his waistband and relieved the man of his own, which allowed King to get better resistance on the wrist. The man tried to get up, but King merely took half a step backwards and the hold doubled in resistance and the man howled.

"Okay! Okay!" he shouted. King did not really know for what, because he was beaten, and King held all the cards. "I give in!"

"Leroy Wilkinson?" King paused. "AKA, Flymo..."

"Who the hell are you?" He snapped, but relaxed and let out a breath as King released his grip and stood back two paces, the pistol now in his right hand and held close to his chest. "You're Box?"

King watched the man rub his arm and wrist. He figured the man would feel it in his shoulder tomorrow. He had taken in the man's features during the scuffle, but the moment he had spoken, he knew he was on track. "Recognised you," he said. "From your file."

"You're the clean-up party?"

"Is that what the operation needs?"

Flymo shrugged. "Fucked if I know. They've gone off radar, and any contact for Box has gone unanswered."

During the Second World War MI5 had used the address PO BOX 500. Even today, 'Box' was how many people in the know referred to the Security Service.

"You're on your own, son." King paused. "Five have tested the water, it was bloody freezing, so you're done."

Flymo got up unsteadily and held out his hand for his weapon. King ignored him. He wasn't about to give a man who had just been cut loose a weapon. He would have to earn

King's trust first.

"Then what capacity are you here in?" he asked. "Not tidying the loose ends, are you?" His eyes were wide and did not leave the gun in King's hand. "Oh, for Christ's sake…"

King had learned to read people over the years. White people typically drained of colour in the face when they were scared; they also reddened when they were angry. But black people were more difficult to read. It all came down to their eyes. And King could tell fear from anger in the man's wide, pleading eyes. He could tell agitation, too. Their eyes were a flashpoint, a beacon of emotion. Right now, Leroy Wilkinson was terrified.

"I'm here for Rashid."

"To tidy loose ends…"

King shook his head. "I'm here of my own accord."

"*You're* King…"

"I don't know you."

"Rashid mentioned you." Flymo paused. "Christ, your eyes… You're looking at me like you want to tear out my throat… He said you had cold eyes." He shook his head despondently. "You *are* going to kill me, aren't you? You just want to know where Rashid is, first."

"Have you got a key to the barn?"

"Yes."

"Open it."

Flymo shrugged. He put his hand in his pocket and froze when he saw the muzzle of the pistol in King's hand rise slightly. King nodded for him to continue and he slowly retrieved a shiny key.

"Please…"

"I'm not going to kill you." King paused. "Not unless you give me good reason to. Can you get that safe open?"

Flymo shook his head. "I don't have a key for that."

"What's inside?"

"Money."

"A lot?"

"And then some."

"From the Albanians?"

He nodded. "And the Russians, too. We've hit them all over. Albania, Kosovo, Bulgaria and in Russia."

"You've been busy."

"Too busy," said Flymo quietly, as he opened the lock and unfolded one of the doors. "They must have been ready for them. Either that, or their luck simply ran out."

"Where?"

"The Greece border with Albania. They were doing a recon. It was too far for the chopper to drop them in. I had tasks to do, get more fuel for the chopper and do some maintenance on it. I haven't heard from them since."

"Shit."

"Exactly." He paused. "I took the chopper up, stopped at a couple of airfields along the way to refuel, then flew a few circuits of the area. Damned if somebody didn't take a few shots at me. When I got back, I noticed three bullet holes in the canopy near the base of the rotor. I think they must have been aiming for the Jesus nut."

"The Jesus nut?"

Flymo nodded. "Only one damned nut holds the rotor in place with the rotor mast. We have to put our faith in Jesus for keeping the thing together."

King smiled at the thought. "So, what was your contingency plan?"

"You know? I don't think it ever came up. We'd been hitting the Albanians all summer, making it look like Russian involvement. We'd done the same in Russia a couple of times, too. We've cost them hundreds of millions of dollars in lost revenue, closer to a billion if you factor in the structural and resource and logistical damage we've done." Flymo paused. "I took the bird up again, but this time the first airfield wouldn't allow me to refuel. I know when somebody's been gotten to, and the airfield manager definitely had a lot of pressure piled on him. He came up with some bullshit story to stop me taking off, I soon realised he'd made a call to the same people who had put the pressure on him. I got the hell out of there before anybody came to meet me. Got back here on fumes alone."

"Where were they when they went dark?"

"They were scoping out a place the Albanians use as a rear echelon base. Any problems and they bolt into Greece or Macedonia. It's an old chateau style building. Used to be a vineyard before the Commies drank all the wine and forgot to look after the grape vines."

"Sounds like we need to get in there and take a look."

"Well, we can't take the bird because it's too far. And besides, we're just two men," Flymo shook his head. "I'm not sure if it was campfire bollocks or whether Rashid just liked a good yarn, but he mentioned you a lot. Not classified shit, or anything like that. No operational history. But just how many times you've beaten the odds, got the job done. When we all voiced how some of the tasks that we were up against were simply too stacked in the enemy's favour, he would drag out another anecdote about you."

King shifted awkwardly. "Did he say he'd saved my arse more times than I care to remember?" He paused. "Certainly, more times than I've saved his."

"No."

King thought about how things had become strained between them. How his actions had cost Rashid personal loss. But the man had been there for him again when it mattered. He thought about Caroline and the fact he'd most likely still be in rural Cornwall had it been anybody else but Rashid who had gone missing. He owed the man, and that was that. They had argued and Caroline had given King an ultimatum. And yet, King was here. If he succeeded, he did not yet know what would happen between them. He had tried not to think about failure.

"How much money is in that safe?"

"No idea. MI5 funded us the travel expenses and a few grand to get us started but that was it. Nothing like the budget we needed for payoffs, bribes and expenditure."

"Sounds about right," King agreed. Operations like this made criminals out of patriots.

"We took enough out of the money we liberated for the vehicles, working capital and the helicopter, of course." Flymo paused, still looking at the gun in King's hand. "The chopper has kept the Albanians behind us. We can strike and retract before they know what has happened."

"Shoot 'n skoot."

"Exactly."

"How much fuel do you have? In airtime, that is."

Flymo shrugged. "Three hundred miles to a tank with a thirty-minute reserve, I guess we've got enough fuel now for seven refuels."

"So, you're pretty much tied to operating in about a one-hundred-and-fifty-mile radius from here. Say, one-forty allowing for take-off, landing and some low-level evasive action."

"I reckon."

"You must have exhausted what can be done here."

"We had. Hence the recon on the mountain property." He paused. "It was part of Rashid's onslaught. Never give them time to regroup. If we hit them there, they would know that they could be got at anywhere."

"And he thought it was their main hub?"

"It made sense."

King nodded. "And it's high in the mountains near the Greece border?"

"Yes."

"So, too far."

"That's what my maintenance task was. To rig something to give us extra range. Like camel packs of fuel, or something. I haven't figured it out yet." Flymo paused. "But I couldn't continue if I wanted to."

"Why?"

"Funds. Rashid never came back, and I can't open the safe."

King nodded. "We need some eyes and ears on that place."

"We?"

"What else do you suggest?" King answered tersely. "A thorough reconnaissance before we go in."

Flymo frowned. "I'm still not convinced you're not going to kill me."

King tucked the pistol into his pocket and showed the man the palms of his hands. "Relax. I'm not going to kill you. I want you to work on those fuel tanks."

"But, like I said, I'm out of funds."

"You have transport?"

"Yes."

"Okay. You follow me back to town and I'll get you the funds you need. While you're there, I'll give you a shopping list. You can bring the things I want back here, then get on with the task of making that bird capable of flying twice as far."

"Twice as far?"

"At least."

"But we can't put surveillance on their base."

"Let me worry about that." He paused. "Do you have the coordinates?"

"Yes."

"Write them down for me before we leave."

Flymo nodded. "Okay, but we certainly can't hit it with just the two of us."

"All I ask is that if or when the time comes, you get me in and you get me out," said King. "If you don't show up for extraction, then I'll hunt you down and I'll kill you."

Flymo looked at him, took in King's eyes and expression, then said, "I believe you."

14

Novyalaski, Russia

Novyalaski was a one-horse town. Except the horse had wandered off and left the residents to it years ago. And King could see why. He had arrived three days before and started to build a legend that he was a fly-fisherman looking for an adventure. It wasn't a bad plan as there were a myriad of lakes with hundreds of streams feeding them and several businesses had sprung up selling tackle and bait and offering quadbike hire and even guides to the seasoned fisherman turned adventurer. The only problem was King realised he knew nothing about fly fishing. He had Googled what he could and had purchased some equipment before he had left the country, but now that he was faced with building on his legend, he wished he had taken a different approach. Still, it wasn't like there would be that many people out there to see he barely knew one end of the rod from another.

King had checked into a hotel, or more accurately, a bar with a few rooms out back. Breakfast had been included and consisted of some hard cheese, bread rolls, cured pork or bacon fat, pickled cabbage, and a shot of vodka. Like most Russians in the area, if he so wished he could be drunk by nine, depressed by eleven, comatose by two. But he wasn't staying around the town to succumb to its limited delights, and had hired a beaten up quadbike with two spare fuel cans strapped to the back, and the guy had thrown in an old Mosin Nagant 7.62x54mm bolt action rifle and four rounds of ammunition for the bears. Or wolves. He had offered to take King out back for a lesson but shrugged when King checked the action and looked over the weapon. It was clear he knew his way around a rifle. The man then explained in poor English not to try and outrun a bear on the quadbike, because it could only do fifty kilometres an hour, but the bears could reach fifty-five kilometres an hour in short bursts. King looked at the four brass cartridges in his hand and hoped bear encounters would be rare but reflected that at least he would be better prepared than when he had last crossed paths with one.

 The terrain was Arctic tundra meets Great American Plains, and once he had gotten out of the rounded, grassy foothills, the wooded mountains reminded him of the Black Hills in South Dakota, and he figured that Russia and the continental USA had been joined once and that, geographically at least, the two nations were extremely similar.

King checked his phone's GPS. The signal was low, although he was surprised that he had any signal at all. But he had a compass and a map and had reset the odometer on the quadbike. He already knew the lay of the land and after an hour, he skirted a small town and continued parallel to the road, around a mile away from it until it crossed with his course and he carried on heading North East. He knew the town was significant to the area, as it served as a junction for the Trans-Siberian Railway and a vital supply route. King's ride would now steepen significantly as he left the road, the town, and the railway line behind him and headed into the mountains. The only roads within an area of eight thousand square miles were now narrow undressed tracks, and of course the main road behind him. The area was vast, and there were parts where you could drive three hundred miles in any direction without meeting any form of human habitation.

After another hour, King stopped and got off to stretch his legs. He unstrapped the rifle and slung it over his shoulder and walked up the steep slope to the peak. He could see for miles in every direction. Horizon to horizon. The town was visible, but only barely, a faded sprawl on the cusp of what he could see. He estimated twenty miles, but the elevation meant he could pick it out against the grassy plains surrounding it. To the North East, he could see a network of narrow roads, but it then dawned on him it was in fact one road – a twisting ribbon weaving through the peaks, with possibly twenty hairpin turns as it gained in elevation towards the summit, then reappeared on the peak behind, then the one behind that. He was near. He was in the same time zone, at least. The vast country had eleven of them, after all.

He walked back down to the quadbike and checked the fuel. It needed a tankful, which took half the first can. Seeing as he'd started off with a full tank, that meant he could only go on for half the tank, and that did not leave room for the gradients he would now be faced with, nor the fact that he could become lost. Just half an hour of looking for a landmark or an alternative route would eat into his fuel supply. He reflected, as he took out the Primus stove and poured water into his mess tin, that the country was beyond comprehensible scale. On a previous mission, he had once encountered a forested area larger than France, and he knew that the Boreal Forest was six times larger than the entire Amazon rainforest.

"Took your time."

King smiled, as he tossed two teabags into the mess tin, along with some powdered milk. He looked up and frowned. "I thought getting a brew on would bring you out."

Dave Lomu nodded, as he headed down the slope from a clump of alder brush. "Got any scran?"

"Salted pork fat?"

"Crackling?"

"No," King smiled. "Raw pork fat soaked in salt and then dried for a bit. But not too much, because it feels pretty soft. Like lard."

"You're kidding…"

King dug into his day sack and took out a packet of biscuits. He tossed them at the man mountain in front of him and stirred the brew. Dave Lomu was six-foot four and eighteen stone, his skin as black as coal and he had left his native Fiji at sixteen when a British Army recruitment ship had sailed into port and whisked himself and other young men away with stories of a better life. King did not know if the better life had materialised, but Lomu had excelled in the army, made it into the SAS and after a stint as a security contractor and mercenary, was eventually recruited by MI5 on a contracting basis. Known affectionately as 'Big Dave', Lomu was famed for both his appetite and his strength.

"So, what have you seen?"

"Romanovitch isn't there anymore. He's taken off to St. Petersburg. Apparently, the place is normally like a Russian version of the Playboy Mansion. Romanovitch comes up here on the pretence of hunting and fishing, and while he does a bit of both, he also has hot and cold running women on tap."

"Standard," said King. "Russian oligarchs and crime kingpins alike. Russian men in powerful positions see having sex with women outside of marriage as a confirmation of their status. They'll often seal a business deal with an orgy."

"I'm in the wrong job."

King laughed and poured the soupy brew of tea into two metal cups, handing one to Lomu who had finished half the biscuits. "Think of Rome and the Roman Empire. That's what half these Russian tycoons think they are building."

"Still, I'm in the wrong job."

"And the asset?"

He shrugged. "I followed them to town, some of the staff, I mean. No idea who the asset could be. The cook and the maid went into town twice."

"Accompanied?"

"Not until recently," he replied. "Apparently one of Romanovitch's men follows loosely now. I was told he should probably have been more high-profile. He keeps tabs on the staff, then stops off for a drink in a bar, then gets back to following them around for a bit. Something's changed in the dynamic. Since Romanovitch has been in St. Petersburg the place is run on a skeleton staff, where before there were plenty of his men there." Big Dave paused. "It's not been an easy assignment. They're bloody racist here. I don't think many have seen somebody my colour before. Comments, stupid questions. I haven't exactly blended in. I don't think Black Lives Matter would get much of a foothold here."

"Sorry but needs must."

"Great, scraping the barrel, then?"

King laughed, drank some tea, grimacing at the taste. "Sorry, forgot the sugar."

Lomu dropped a couple of biscuits in his and swilled the cup around so they dissolved in the brown liquid. "They'll sweeten it up."

"Christ…"

"So, got your head around retirement, then?"

"Doesn't look like it, does it?"

"Then, what the hell are you doing here?"

King shrugged. "Rashid."

"He's tough. And he's a big boy. He knows the score."

"I haven't got many friends."

"You've got a beautiful woman and the chance to start a new chapter. Given your history, you're lucky to have made it this far." He shrugged. "I don't get it."

"Like I said, Rashid."

"Bullshit, man! You miss the action!"

King shrugged, sipped some of his tea.

"We've all been there for each other. The team, the guys back in the regiment. It goes with the territory. You watch your buddy's back. But you also know that things happen and sometimes you will lose. You need to be ready for that, and Rashid will have been. He knows that, and *you* know that. I think this is more about what happened to Marnie, than going to the aid of a former soldier who knows that shit happens, and that it may be time for him to stand easy, service done."

"I thought you wanted to change careers and be a Russian oligarch? Not a psychotherapist…" King snapped, annoyed with the intrusion into his business.

"Just say'in."

King drank down the terrible brew. But he reflected that it wasn't so bad. He'd had worse. He'd once made a mess tin of tea with his own piss in a wadi in Iraq, so he wasn't near leaving it just yet.

"Where's your transport?"

"Down the other side of the hill," said Big Dave. "You're going to love it. I don't think Discoveries or Range Rover Vogues have made it out this far yet. Not to the average Russian, at least."

15

Dave Lomu had secured a truck. A four by four with military history, roughly modelled on early Jeep design. It was called a UAZ 469 and had four seats, two bench seats and a canvas roof which may have once been waterproof, but King held out no hope in the event of rainfall, judging by the eight-inch gash in the fabric above his head. But its four cylinder, seventy-horsepower engine started, ran and didn't sound as rough as King had expected, although a great many horses had bolted from its engine over the years and the vehicle struggled up some of the steeper inclines.

King had stashed the quadbike in the treeline, but he needn't have worried, the odds of somebody stumbling across it was higher than winning the lottery. Twice. He had taken the rifle with him, and his day sack and Big Dave had picked up a battered and worn AK-47 supposedly for the bears, but more likely for whatever Russian threat stood in their way. King quietly reflected on the country and its people as he bounced away over the rough ground. The United States was full of hunters who used rifles costing many thousands of dollars with optics costing even more, argued in internet forums about the muzzle energy, velocity and ballistic properties needed for hunting brown bears and how it differed for caribou or moose, or that smaller projectiles with a higher velocity were needed for mountain lions. Just as debated was what kind of back-up pistol was needed and shot placement required for certain animals. The Russians just slung what in hunting terms was a relatively low powered assault rifle over their shoulder, sunk a couple of shots of vodka and headed off into the wilderness. If they were to shoot a bear and the bullet did not prove enough for the creature's size and mass or motion, then they just mowed it down on fully automatic. The same went for the vehicles. The UAZ was rough and basic and thirty-five years old, but it still worked and somebody somewhere had put their faith in it when winter temperatures dropped to minus thirty degrees Celsius and there was nobody to come and help them. He had always believed the Russians simply made use of what they had – borne from years of poverty and repression - and when something worked, they just stuck with it. They were not a nation of progress, but they were stoical and practical and resolute. And in his experience, that had always made them a formidable race.

"How much further?" King asked.

Big Dave was using a Garmin GPS and had stuck it to the dashboard with rubber suckers that kept bouncing out every mile or so. He now had it tucked between his legs, close to his groin. He fished it out and handed it to King. "Here, it's nice and warm…"

"Piss off!"

Big Dave laughed and said, "Seven miles." He tucked the satnav back between his legs, still amused at himself. "I reckon we should go the last mile on foot."

King nodded. He had told the babushka back at the bar that he may be camping under the stars tonight. She had looked suitably unimpressed and told him that he would still have to pay for the room. She had then sold him sausage, cured pork fat, stale bread, and a quarter bottle of vodka at a premium. King had picked up the biscuits and some indescribable cake as well as the powdered milk from a convenience store that seemed to sell mainly vodka and cabbages. King always travelled with his own teabags. Monkey brand. Nothing fancy.

When they had travelled the remaining six miles, Big Dave parked the truck beside some trees near a small lake fed by a fast-flowing stream from the base of a waterfall. He could see trout jumping, late summer mosquitoes swarming the surface, providing the fish with a buffet. King mused that it probably wouldn't have been all that difficult to catch a fish in a place like this as the water looked to be teaming with trout.

Big Dave hoisted a large bergen upon his back and cradled the AK-47, which looked like a toy in his giant hands. King shouldered the rifle. It was loaded, but he had not worked the bolt chambering a bullet. He wasn't familiar with the rifle's trigger and nor the condition of the weapon for that matter. Bolt action rifles can fire if a jolt shifts the bolt from its lug, sending it forward on its spring. The weapon looked well used, which meant it would have worn considerably over the years, its tolerances changed from when it had left the factory. If he needed it, he could make it ready almost as quickly as he could release a safety catch.

"Let's get out of here before those mozzies realise there's fresh meat out here," Dave commented. He led the way, taking great strides up the hill towards the waterfall. "We'll veer off from the stream at the top, get away from those biting bastards."

"Okay," replied King. Lomu had done the recon. He'd been out here shortly after King had arrived in Albania. King trusted the man's judgement. The fact he had taken leave from an assignment to help King spoke volumes. The man was close to Rashid, too, so he had taken little convincing when King explained that there was no official rescue and the team would be written off. Despite the man's attempts to delve into King's reasoning for coming out of his short retirement, there was an unwritten agreement among men like King and Rashid and Lomu, that they would always go the extra mile for a colleague because one day, it might well be them.

The grass plain, which had many sporadic spinneys of trees and tiny lakes soon gave way to thick pine and birch forest. It was one of a dozen thousand-acre forests which had been left to grow after huge deforestation in the region. King knew that a hundred miles further to the west logging concerns were tackling a forest larger than the entire United Kingdom, so they would probably never be back this way again and nature would soon reclaim the region.

"There are a lot of bears here," said Big Dave. "They're what they call grizzly bears in the states. Or similar, at least. Maybe not quite so big, but way bigger than black bears. They're filling up on trout, feral cattle and sheep, as well as reindeer for the winter. Also, blueberries and chives, too. There are thousands of acres of wild blueberries out here. And mile upon mile of chives. But nobody can be bothered to pick them."

King nodded. In Alaska he'd been close enough to a hungry grizzly to smell its breath. He hoped he would never see one again. "The people have reindeer, trout, chives, and fresh blueberries on their doorstep, and they eat salted pork fat, raw cabbage and stale bread. Go figure."

"They're all too drunk out here to be bothered with anything. I've never seen people drink vodka with breakfast. I don't like to generalise, but they're all alcoholics! And there's a distinct lack of get up and go. It's a depressing bloody place."

King nodded. "I had a shot of vodka this morning. When in Rome. I had to have something to keep the bloody pork fat down."

"Yeah, the food is off. I could eat a fry-up

right around now, that's for sure."

"What's the lay of the land once we're through the trees?"

"Romanovitch has cut a perimeter of one-hundred metres. Between his fence and the forest. Then it's like something in Beverly Hills."

"I checked on Google Earth. It was an old overview, but the grounds looked like a scene from the Somme, like no-man's-land," said King.

"He's had extensive landscaping done. A full-sized eighteen-hole golf course designed by a top greenskeeper, as well as garden terraces. The property was once owned by a tsar and then the communist party and the KGB." Lomu paused. "I don't think the Commies went in for country club chic, so Romanovitch has been busy," he quipped. "Then he had a specialist swimming pool designer from Spain design and construct the pool."

"And I bet inside is filled with antiques and art from around the world. Stolen, no doubt."

"Well, you'll find out soon enough."

King nodded. He would. If he was lucky.

16

St. Petersburg, Russia

"You have balls being here, Galanis. I'll give you that."

The Shepherd shrugged. "I bring with me a message. I hope that because I am alone, the messenger will not be shot." He paused, nodding knowingly. "Or butchered and sent back in many vodka crates."

Romanovitch smiled. "I do not imagine further visual aids will be required. Or at least, not yet."

"I have a message, and I hope to live long enough to take your answer back with me to the brotherhood."

"To Yosef," Romanovitch stated flatly.

"Yes."

"He should thank me for his promotion."

"He is grieving." Galanis paused. "He hopes his message will be accepted in the manner it was delivered. In good grace."

"One can only live in hope," Romanovitch said with a mirthless smile. "I suppose it would depend upon the message."

Andreas Galanis nodded. Yosef had said that the Russian would not make a repeat of their last visit if he alone went to meet with him. What would be the point? That was all very well, but Yosef would not be there to find out. However, Galanis had agreed, although since he had landed in Russia yesterday and arranged the meeting, he had had his doubts. He had not been able to travel with his trusty knife, and right now, he wanted to slice out the Russian's throat and bleed him out like a goat he was about to butcher. He had contemplated procuring a weapon and secreting it upon him, but he knew he would be searched, and the Russian mafia boss' men had done exactly that. And then some. The humiliation of a rough body cavity search showing a degree of nervousness from the Russian that had not been there before the troubles. Yosef and Galanis had gambled – admittedly with all the risk on Andreas Galanis' part – that the Russian will have seen the escalation. Felt it, even. He would not do anything to lose face, but he would be both intrigued enough to listen, and keen to see a return to stability and the status quo.

Romanovitch regarded him, then nodded to the guard behind him. He tried to suppress a smile as the Kosovan flinched. "Vodka and caviar," he said.

Galanis visibly relaxed, but his heart would continue to hammer against his chest until he was back in the air and bound for Albania. Even then, given the Russian's reach, it would be a nervous flight. "Thank you," he said.

Romanovitch clapped his hands together. "So, what is this proposition your new boss has for me?" He paused. "Incidentally, we did not assassinate T'Briki. But I suppose you know that by now?"

"We know a great many things."

"Having said that, Yosef should be grateful to me. His brother would have been next in line of succession, but now he has the top job. Now he is the Albanian equivalent of me!" He laughed raucously, clapping his hands together twice. "Which is like saying a rat is the same as a pedigree dog! You will agree with me, no? With you being a Kosovan-Greek and all. The Greeks are a noble people. The Greek gods, the mythology, and the history, that is. Not the bankrupt nation of café owners and waiters they are today, who sell their own children so they can eat! No, they were once a nation of great adventurers and scholars. The Kosovans, not so much. But still, better than Albanians, no?" He looked up as a member of the house staff brought in a silver salver of blinis, sour cream, and caviar as well as chilled vodka in a carafe, with a few slices of shaved garlic dropping gently from the surface. "Put it on the table," he said sharply, then looked back at Andreas Galanis. "So, let me hear your news."

The man known as The Shepherd took a deep breath and leaned back in his chair. He had refrained from doing so up until now, uneasy at the bodyguard standing directly behind him. He watched the maid leave and the bodyguard take up position beside the closed door. Yosef had recounted how six of Romanovitch's bodyguards had encircled them on that fateful day, and at least the Russian had not put on a similar display. All he had to do was sell this. Sell like never before, because his life depended on whether Romanovitch took the bait and sent him back to Albania with a yes.

17

The Ural Mountains, Russia

King looked at Big Dave incredulously as the man pulled out a foil-wrapped sandwich and took a giant bite. "Did you bring enough for everyone?"

The big man shrugged. "I thought you'd be prepared."

"I shared my biscuits."

"Dave doesn't share food…"

"Duly noted," King replied and took out the bag of food the babushka had put together for him. The sausage was greasy and hard. King took a bite and had to saw his teeth through the gristle and fat.

"Rather you than me, mate."

King watched the man eating his sandwich. "That looks like a bloody Subway," he commented. "Where on earth did you get that?"

"I picked a few up in Yekaterinburg," he replied. "Well, ten of them. Just meats and cheese with some mayo. The salad wouldn't have lasted long."

"It looks stale. I do hope it's stale," said King.

"Don't worry about me. Good luck with yours though, mate. That looks like a pony's dick."

King tossed the sausage back into the bag. "Thanks for that image." He reached into his pack and took out the cake, wrapped in paper. He looked up as Big Dave stared at it. It was like a light-coloured fruitcake but with layers of pastry in between that looked soft and buttery. King broke off a piece and chewed. "That's really, really good," he lied. It tasted stale and dry. "Wow. So sweet and moist…" He grinned as he wrapped it back up, watching the big man salivate before him. "Too bad, King no longer shares food, either."

"Bastard."

"Born and bred."

Big Dave chuckled, raised the binoculars, and surveyed the ground ahead of them. They were halfway up a gradual slope which rose approximately sixty feet above the property, with enough trees to shield them from view, but with enough sparsity to give them a relatively clear field of view as well. At the bottom of the slope, the ground had been cleared to create around a hundred metres of flat grassland before the fence.

"You're in the shit, sunshine," Big Dave announced. "Looks like trembler devices on the fence. And CCTV on the corners of the main house."

King nodded. "Standard. The intel said as much."

"Intel?"

King smiled. "You don't bring a knife to a gunfight, and you don't go after an enemy without learning about them first."

"Yes, Sun Tzu." Big Dave grinned. "Have you read the Art of War?"

"Flicked through it."

"Learn much?"

"A bit."

"I thought it was a bit shit, really. Should be called the *Art of Stating the Obvious*." Big Dave continued to study the property through the binoculars. "So, the asset has been feeding intel? I thought they were a sleeper."

"This is where we find out if Ramsay is on the ball or not."

"And if he isn't?"

"Then it will get really shooty, pretty bloody quickly." King handed him the rifle. "I'll take the AK."

"Dave doesn't share."

"Yeah well, he bloody does today." King picked up the AK-47 and ejected a round. He slung the rifle over his shoulder and took out a roll of duct tape. Lomu watched incredulously as King wrapped some around the bottom of the shell case and then handed it to him. "Technically the seven-point-six-two by thirty-nine-millimetre cartridge from the Kalashnikov is seven-point-six-two short. It will work in the Mosin Nagant rifle, but probably only the once before the case expands short of the breech and blocks the chamber. The rim of the round for the Mosin Nagant is lipped instead of recessed, so the tape will hold it in the breech. It's not ideal, and you may only get one shot, but at least it will give you five rounds instead of a paltry four. After that, it doesn't matter because you'll be out of bullets anyway. At a range of two hundred metres you will have an additional two inches of drop over the longer cartridges."

"Is it safe?"

"In that thing, then yes. They're as solid as a rock, which is why they are still standard peasant issue since World War Two. It may flash some hot, unburned powder out of the bolt vent but should be okay."

"Should?" Lomu nodded, frowning. "How do you know about the wrong ammunition working in a weapon?"

King shrugged. "I've been out there on my own. I've had to improvise. There wasn't always a Chinook and a fire support group there for me on my missions." He paused. "Right, exfil. If it all goes tits-up, I don't expect you to come in for me. Provide covering fire if you can, if I'm in the open, that is. Then pull back to where we parked the truck. Wait for thirty-minutes if you can get away with it, then pull back a further two miles south-east and give me ninety minutes."

"Then what?"

"Hit the road."

"Just like that?"

"Just like that."

"It isn't much of a plan."

"It's the only one I've got," said King. "But Ramsay's intel is usually spot on. Better than his chances of hitting a bullseye on the range, or of him buying a round at the pub."

Lomu nodded, considering the options. "I can shadow you in the treeline. The gradient will give me the tactical advantage. But you've still got to cross a hundred metres of open ground." He paused. "You'd better make that call."

King studied the display of his smartphone, pulled a face. "No signal. Great."

"Better get higher."

King nodded, but he delved into his day sack before leaving and retrieved a folded canvas roll. "What sort of phone have you got?"

"A Samsung."

"Great, give it to me."

Big Dave shrugged and tossed King his phone, told him the passcode number as King caught it, then trudged up the slope. The trees were birch and pine and there was the heady scent of pine in the air. From the top of the slope, he could in fact see that it was a false summit, and there was a steep slope to a valley with a stream, and a climb he estimated to be a thousand feet which peaked half a mile ahead of him. King could see that the stream would feed the small lake where they had parked the truck. He checked the compass and saw that the heading was dead-on. Good to know, in case he lost the compass or became disorientated. But he was hoping it would be a simpler task that lay ahead of him.

King checked his phone, and then looked at Big Dave's. Nothing. He opened the canvas roll and selected the coil of copper wire. He fashioned two large rabbit ears, twisting the wire tightly to join it together, then laid it on the ground while he searched the forest floor for a suitable branch. He soon found an eight-foot bough and started to trim the branches from it with his knife. Then he hooked the rabbit ears over the tip and raised it as high as he could, hooking one of the ends left from cutting the branches over a branch high in a pine tree where he carefully released it and let it dangle. The rabbit ears were now fifteen feet above the ridge, with the wire trailing to the ground. King used a pair of snips to cut the wire, then turned his attention to taking the back off Big Dave's phone. It would not have worked with the sealed unit of the iPhone, but King knew the aerial output of the Samsung could be tapped into to provide a boost. In a pinch. He pressed the end of the copper wire against the screw fixing the internal antenna of the phone in place, and in contact. He carefully turned the device over and saw that he had a two-bar signal. King knew there was little accuracy in such things. You generally had a signal, or you didn't, and the five-bar holy grail was usually no different after three bars, and a true signal was more like eight, although displays only went as high as five for simplicity. King dialled Ramsay's number from memory. The MI5 planner answered on the fifth ring.

"Neil, King. I'm on Dave Lomu's phone."

"I can see that."

"I've got no signal. Alert the asset. Give them this number."

"Text only, that was the deal. Go carefully. Intel is showing that Romanovitch is in St. Petersburg, but he'll have some heavies there for sure."

King thanked him and hung up. He kept the copper wire pressed against the screw, keeping the circuit connected. He thought about Ramsay and the *heavies*, sometimes he thought the man would have been better suited to another decade. The nineteen-twenties or thirties, perhaps. Back when MI5 was in its infancy and men in tweed suits and homburg hats spoke in hushed tones and code words under dim streetlamps in the London fog.

The text came through. *"I have it..."*

King typed, "I need you to get me in," then sent the text.

"East side. Get to the pool house. Security switched off for fifteen minutes, no longer…"

"Confirmed. East side."

King let go of the copper wire and clipped the back onto Lomu's phone. He deleted the messages and the call history and slipped the phone back into his pocket. He ran down the slope, slowing and approaching Lomu's position cautiously. Big Dave was ex-SAS and it wouldn't be a wise move to rush up on him. He kept the muzzle of the AK-47 down and crouched low as he neared the treeline.

"On you…"

"On me…" Lomu replied, stepping out from behind a tree twenty metres from where King had left him. "Any joy?"

He tossed the phone back to Big Dave and nodded. "I've only got around ten minutes," he said.

"And the security?"

"Down. But not for long."

"Don't like it."

"Not loving it, myself."

"The word trap springs to mind," he said. "What were they like? To talk to, I mean."

"Text only," replied King. "That was the deal."

"Right…"

King headed for the east side, Big Dave picking up the pack and rifle and following him. They kept back from the treeline, stepping over fallen branches and small granite boulders. King stopped when he could see the pool and the pool house. It was an impressive sight, shaped like a palm tree with alcoves to relax in in the shapes of the fronds and a decent area to swim lengths in the shape of the trunk. The pool had been designed to get the best out of the rising sun and faced south to have the sun for most of the day. With the house set back, King suspected the pool would be cast in the suns setting rays as well. There were no guards in the grounds, and King could see why the pool house would make a good meet – there were few windows on the east side of the house, and the pool house obscured the view of the fence from the property.

"Keep me covered."

"Don't go further than the pool house, I won't have a decent shot." Big Dave paused. "I don't even know if this thing will shoot true. The sights are set for what, two-hundred metres?"

"In that calibre those open sights will be good from point of aim at one-fifty to three-fifty allowing for a foot of drop."

"Check."

King stepped out of the treeline and crossed the ground to the fence. Romanovitch was secluded this far out in the mountains, so King had assumed the fence would be a deterrent for bears and wolves more than turning the property into a fortress. Romanovitch only travelled with his bodyguards and as the place was being used primarily as a hunting lodge, it would be fair to assume there were more than a few guns inside. He figured the tremblers would alert someone if a brown bear was giving himself a backrub, or perhaps trying to get to one of the bevvy of beauties Romanovitch often kept out here in his personal harem and take them to lunch in the forest.

King crouched at the perimeter fence. It was eight feet high with a strand of razor wire on top. Perhaps the Russian did fear more than bears all the way out here. King took out the canvas roll and took out a pair of wire cutters. He then plucked a blade of grass, licked the tip, and held the stem between his thumb and forefinger, touching the wet end to the fence. He did not feel any tingle. Either it had not been electrified, or the asset had switched off the security devices as promised. He could not test the trembler devices, so had to hope for the best and set about cutting a straight line down the wire from just under a metre high. The fence was taut, and he had to cut a horizontal flap. He replaced the tool and pushed the assault rifle through before tentatively crawling after it. King picked up the rifle and walked confidently to the pool house. No fast movements, no tactical drills. Simply covering the ground with as little drama as possible. He couldn't see anybody in the grounds, but as he drew nearer the pool house, he saw a curtain twitch within and his grip tightened on the pistol-grip of the AK-47 and his finger edged closer to the trigger in readiness. Still not touching the trigger, but tantalisingly close.

The glass door opened a crack, the person inside distorted by a Venetian blind. King kept the weapon casually aimed at the ground, but loose enough to bring to bear.

"We haven't much time…" the woman said, pulling the sliding door open. She was slim, distinctly Eurasian with attractive, chiselled features. Her hair was black and shaped in a page boy bob, and she wore little makeup. "I am Alaina. I have been in contact with Neil Ramsay, and Interpol before that." She paused. "We have an agreement. An arrangement."

King nodded. He did not introduce himself. He did not know the details of her agreement with MI5, either. "Do you have it?"

She nodded. "I do." But she did not move. "But there's been a change of plan."

King raised the rifle a touch. Just enough to cut her clean in half at the waist if he kept his finger on the trigger. He wasn't in the habit of letting a double cross change his chances of survival. "I don't like the sound of that," he replied.

"I have what you need. But I want to go with you." She paused, her bottom lip trembling slightly. "Ramsay said he would get me out. But I do not want to wait."

"Then that isn't the deal," he said. "The borders are open. If you want to leave the country, you can."

"But I have been promised a visa. In the UK. To live and to work, but only if I do what I was asked to do, and if I do not, then I will be blacklisted."

"If Ramsay gave you his word, he meant it. He will not let you down."

She shook her head. "I am Romanovitch's maid. But I have seen the way he looks at me, the way he has warned his men off me. He is attracted to me. I fear he will not resist the rule he has for good house staff. He will soon come on to me, and I will not be able to turn him down." She waved a hand towards the forest. "There are people buried out there. People who have displeased him. The cook talks of a personal assistant, a former Miss Ukraine, and Miss World runner up who turned down his advances. She says the woman is buried out there somewhere." She shrugged. "Nobody knows for sure, but..."

King frowned. "For my mission to work, I need Romanovitch to believe he is untouchable. If you leave now, he may become suspicious."

"I can't take the chance."

"Hold on," he said. "Hang on in there. It will be alright." He could understand the woman's concerns, but he had enough of his own to contend with. Although he realised the insincerity of his remark. "Now, where is the USB?"

Alaina reached for her pocket, but hesitated. "Please..."

"I need it," he said sternly. "The deal still stands. You will have to speak to Ramsay, but he won't renege on your deal. He is trustworthy, believe me."

"He promised me money. Along with tickets and a visa."

"But *I* would never deliver those." King paused. "I'm simply here to collect what you promised you could supply."

She looked at him tearfully, then reached out slowly and touched the back of his hand. "Please…" She looked like she was about to sob but caught herself in time. "He will come back, and he will take it further this time. He touched me before he left, had a strange look in his eyes when I did not respond and busied myself. I know he will try something, and if I am to survive, I will have to let him do what he wants. I am not like the other girls he brings here. I am not *that* way. If they refuse, the cook says they are sent to his brothels. God forbid he sends me to one of those hell holes."

King thought about Caroline's work with Interpol. How she had worked as part of a trafficking taskforce in Georgia in response to her being held hostage a year before. The threat of ending up in a place like that had been real. It was a horror she still lived with and it would never go away. Alaina looked terrified, and he believed in her desperation.

"Do you have the soap?"

She nodded. "Please, Sir, just take me with you."

"Show me."

Alaina took out a new bar of soap which had been soaked in warm water before a key had been pressed halfway into it, on both sides. On the other side, she had inserted the key a few centimetres to gage the key head. The soap had then been dried. It was crude, but the process had made a good template of the key he would need.

"And you're sure this is the right key?"

"Absolutely," she nodded. "He wears it around his neck, and I took it from his dresser when he was busy with one of his women." She shuddered, then said, "I'm sorry, the memory even scares me. It was a tense moment, where I prayed the whole time that I would not be caught."

"And the USB?" King asked, unperturbed.

She took the device out of her pocket,

wavering as she held it out in front of her. "Please, don't be heartless. I can come with you, now. I won't get in your way."

"It will look suspicious."

"I copied the key, and I copied his hard drive!" She shook her head. "He will never know!"

King looked at her, trying to read her eyes. She was upset, that much was obvious. But could he trust her? He kept thinking about Caroline and her incarceration in Georgia. What if things had gone differently?

"Who is here?" he relented.

"The cook, her husband who cuts the golf course, tends the gardens and does maintenance jobs. Anoushka, one of Romanovitch's harlots. And Draco, a bodyguard. The rest of his bodyguards are with him in St. Petersburg while he meets with the brotherhood."

"The brotherhood?"

"The Albanians."

"You know about them?"

She nodded. "I know all about them," she replied.

King sensed a hail Mary. She probably knew nothing more than what she had overheard about meeting them. Or perhaps she knew a hell of a lot more. Maybe a snippet that would help him. "This bodyguard, Draco, worries me. Where is he?"

"On site," she said quietly. "I have no idea where, but he made advances on me earlier today," she added. "I rebuffed him, and he wasn't happy. I told him I would tell Romanovitch. Draco knows that his boss wants me, he will assume I ran away from him, and I imagine he'll play it down. The last thing he'd want was for Romanovitch to know he made moves on me. He will know that I'm not coming back and will probably come up with a story."

"It's a big reach."

"Please, don't leave me here. Take me back to London with you."

"But I'm not going back. Not yet."

"Then I can help you." She paused. "Whatever you are planning to do to Romanovitch, I can assist you. I know all the members of his organisation. I know the people who can help you, those who will have the information that you may need to bring success to your mission."

King glanced at his watch. "It's not as simple as that." He knew Alaina had been recruited by Interpol, then handed over to MI5 at Ramsay's request. The woman would not have signed up for that, but there had to be a reason why she had agreed to pass information onto Interpol. A catalyst. And as he watched the woman in front of him, he wasn't so sure it would have been for pocket change, a ticket, and a visa. There had to be more. But time was ticking by and he had to make a decision. As his mentor Peter Stewart would have said, time to shit or get off the pot. "Okay," he said, almost regretting it at once as she flung herself at him, wrapping her legs and arms around him tightly.

"Thank you! Thank you! Thank you!" she nestled her face into his shoulder and King struggled awkwardly to free himself of her tangle of limbs. "You won't regret it, I will help you."

King managed to break free. He was flustered. The smell of her body – clean and mildly scented of jasmine - the tingle of her warm breath against his neck, the feel of her firm breasts rubbing on his chest, and the hardness of her pubic bone against him had stirred something inside, and he felt not only embarrassed, but ashamed that he had felt a rush of blood and a shallowness of breath. His thoughts turned to Caroline, their home, the life they had carved out for themselves. He had risked everything in being here. Risked it all for a friend who had known the risks of the ridiculous games they played and duties they performed from the outset. But it was more than that. King knew deep down that he was a wolf, not a sheep. He had missed the exhilaration of an assignment, the anticipation of action. He had missed his old life. Now it seemed a fool's errand. What mattered was a tiny cottage on the cliffs in Cornwall and the woman within.

"Do you have access to a vehicle?"

"No. I get a lift into town with the cook, but Draco always comes now. I go to a café and buy a book from a book shop while she shops for food, then she picks me up. Draco drinks in the bars, never wants to leave."

"So, how will your absence be explained? There's nothing but wilderness out there."

"Maybe that is good? Maybe Draco will think I fled because of him and got lost or walked into a bear. There are a great many bears out here. Packs of wolves, too." She paused. "If he thinks I left because of him, he will not dare tell Romanovitch."

King thought back to the man giving him the rifle and bullets when he had hired the quadbike. It seemed a plausible explanation, and at least it would have a ring of truth and that, in turn, may stop Romanovitch from searching for her once she got to London. From there, she could go anywhere and with the identity Ramsay would have arranged for her. In the system, a new name, and a new start. Untraceable.

Alaina looked at her watch. "The security system is performing an update," she said. "We only have three more minutes until it goes online again and then the fence will detect movement and the cameras will start recording again. It's now or never…"

"Okay," he said decisively. "Follow me and keep close."

King waited for Alaina to pick up her bag, then led them out of the pool house. He glanced back at her. She was still checking her watch. As they rounded the edge of the terrace, she screamed.

"Draco!" she exclaimed.

King turned to his right and saw a large man in a leather bomber jacket. He was surprised to see King and fumbled for the Uzi 9mm submachine gun he had slung on a strap over his shoulder. King started forwards, he judged he could reach him before he got the Uzi ready, but Alaina got in his way. The man looked up at them both, raising the weapon. He was shocked, and King could see the hesitation and bewilderment in the man's face. King was quicker but could not bring the weapon to bear. He shoved Alaina aside and fired from the hip. It was enough to shock the Russian, who flinched and fired wide with a volley of fully automatic gunfire. King dropped to one knee, brought the weapon to his shoulder and a four round burst sent the man sprawling backwards.

"Is he dead?" Alaina asked. She was close enough for King to smell over the hot residue of spent cases. "He will tell Romanovitch that I went with the intruder!"

King saw the man moving. His outstretched hand was close enough to the Uzi to make a difference and King fired a single round and the man went still. He dragged Alaina by her sleeve and snapped, "Get moving!"

They reached the fence and King shoved the Kalashnikov through and followed, picking it up and taking a defensive position as Alaina struggled to push her bag through the gap in the wire. King snatched the bag from her and kept his eyes on the house. He had planned to reattach the fence with copper wire, crudely covering up his entry and exit to the grounds, while maintaining the electrical contact which would power the trembler devices, but it seemed pointless now. One of Romanovitch's men was dead, and there was no covering that up. Alaina was in too deep, now. Romanovitch would be out to find her and punish her. King knew enough about the man to know he would stop at nothing. The nice and tidy lost in the wilderness and eaten by a bear scenario was no longer a reality now that his bodyguard was full of holes.

"For fuck's sake!" Big Dave lifted his head, breaking cover. He got to his feet and cradled the rifle as they approached. "This wasn't the plan!"

"The plan has changed."

"Clearly."

"This is Alaina."

"Hi," Alaina said quietly.

Big Dave ignored her. "Did you get the USB?"

King nodded. "And the mould of the key."

"So, why the baggage?"

"I'm not baggage!" Alaina exclaimed. "I will help. I know things."

Big Dave shook his head and snatched the AK-47 off King, thrusting the old rifle back at him. Then he turned around and powered up the slope, his telegraph pole legs pumping like pistons as he weaved through the trees.

King winked at Alaina, then regretted it when he saw her smile. His aim had been to defuse the tension, not signal intent. There was something in the way she looked at him that made him think she was grateful to him. More than he would have preferred her to be. He slung the Mosin Nagant rifle over his shoulder and picked up his day sack. He did not look back at the woman until he reached the top. She was struggling with the bag and he swiped it off her and slung it over his other shoulder, then set out after Big Dave, who was striding down the slope towards the waterfall.

When they reached the truck, Big Dave turned around and said, "This wasn't part of the mission."

King stopped and stood directly in front of him, his eyes hard and cold. "The mission is whatever the hell I say it is." He paused. "There's nothing else for Rashid. No second rescue attempt, or investigation. If I hadn't have taken it on, then MI5 would have washed their hands of him. Simon Mereweather and Neil Ramsay are operating this out of the back door. Amherst doesn't have a clue this is happening."

"We don't even know what happened to them, let alone if any of them are alive to rescue," Big Dave replied tersely. "Now you've got baggage to slow you down."

"Well, maybe you can take care of that?"

"No way," Big Dave replied. "It's all a bit *To Kill a Mockingbird* out this way. I'm not pairing up with a white Russian chick. I'll be called out in no time."

"Have you seen the size of *you*?"

"Doesn't matter out here. All the men are missing teeth and have calloused knuckles and look like they want a good scrap. Half of them are drunk and the other half are either getting drunk or hung over. They're all packing guns as well, it's like the bloody Wild West." He paused. "Besides, I should be somewhere else. And I'm heading there tomorrow."

"I will go with *you*, yes?" Alaina asked King nervously.

King nodded. "I'll get something sorted. Don't worry." He opened the door and gestured for her to get inside. He then turned back to Big Dave. "Look, I have my reasons."

"I can see. There's a couple of good reasons under that blouse. Thirty-two D cup, would be my guess."

King ignored the jibe. "Romanovitch is showing an interest in her, has also warned off his men from so much as looking at her. She knows that if he makes a move, she will have no choice but to submit to it. If she refuses, then she could be buried out in the wilderness. That or end up in one of the man's many brothels." He paused. "After Caroline's experience being abducted, and her latter work with the Interpol sex trafficking taskforce, I couldn't refuse." He got in the passenger seat and said, "Now, I'll deal with it. So, get in the bloody car and get us the hell out of here."

18

By the time they had reached the bar with the rooms out back, King was exhausted. The ride back across the wilderness had been more difficult with Alaina riding pillion, and the seat had been a snug place for two. Alaina had ridden behind, her arms wrapped tightly around King's waist with her own bag strapped to the rack and keeping her pressed into him. Every now and then he would feel her warm breath on his neck, catch the aroma of her and feel her firm breasts pressing against his back. He was only human, a red-blooded man, and he was both surprised and ashamed to have found the experience arousing. Once they had parked beside the porch, King had shown her into his room and headed to the bar to speak with the babushka. To his consternation, there were no more rooms available and the quick-witted woman had quickly added a surcharge for the double occupancy, for the man who was supposed to be sleeping out under the stars, but had returned from a fishing trip with a beautiful woman instead. King did not object, it was simpler to shrug it off than draw more attention than was necessary, and he had no choice but to stay the night with his house guest. He imagined going fishing for the day and returning with a woman to share his room would not be the most obvious turn of events. But this was the Urals on the edge of Siberia and weird was just part of everyday life. As if to confirm this, a naked man staggered past him wearing nothing but a fur *ushanka* on his head and a pair of well-worn military boots with a tangle of laces to trip on. He nodded at King and offered him a swig of vodka from a half-empty bottle and shrugged as King refused, then staggered on past. His buttocks looked to have been whipped, but he didn't seem to be suffering because of it. King shook his head and headed back for the room. As he reached the door, he heard a gunshot, then some whoops of laughter and the sound of breaking glass. King considered what this town would be like in the winter, isolated for three months and in a state of lockdown from the outside world. It didn't bear thinking about and he rapped twice on the door, then opened it and stepped inside.

Alaina was in the shower. King could see steam escaping from under the door. He fancied a shower himself but was now regretting the size of the room. He looked at his phone, got as far as typing out the first six digits of Caroline's number, then deleted and locked the screen. He never kept numbers and contacts on his phone when he was on a mission. He never made a personal call, either. He wanted to call Caroline and tell her that he missed her, ask her how she was doing. He wanted to tell her not to worry, that he was OK, but he knew he couldn't let his guard down. Couldn't let his two lives cross over. He was an agent now. His task was to find out what happened to Rashid. He could not afford to play happy couples. He looked up as Alaina came out of the bathroom. She had a towel wrapped around her and tucked in place under her armpits, and her hair was wet and slicked back. Her skin was flushed and radiant. The water had been too hot. She smelled of soap and shampoo and conditioner. The towel was short and barely covered her below.

"I needed that!" she exclaimed. "What a ride! I'm sore in places I shouldn't be!"

"I'll go out and get us some food," said King. "After I've cleaned up. Better for us to eat in here than let you be seen around town. There's only two bars, but people may talk."

"But we're miles from Romanovitch's property!" Alaina protested. "Besides, he is in St.

Petersburg, and Draco isn't going to tell anyone what happened." She paused. King had found the observation callous, and she seemed to pick up on the fact. "It's unfortunate that you had to kill him, but now that he's dead, it's a possibility that whoever broke in, for whatever purpose, took me hostage. Maybe it went wrong. Maybe they killed me somewhere out in the wilderness. That is a scenario they will assume, and one that will help us." She walked towards him, drips of water running down her neck and across her bare chest. She caught King's gaze and checked the tuck of her towel was still firmly in place. "It's worked out well for me. I got a clean break. And now I can reward you…"

"Reward me?" King bristled, taking a step backwards.

"Yes," she said. She was close to him now, and King could smell the freshness of her body, feel the heat emanating off her from the shower. "By helping you take down Romanovitch." She took a step backwards, as if suddenly aware of their proximity to one another. "What else did you think I meant?"

"Oh, exactly that," he said. "I wouldn't want anything else."

"Oh, really?"

"No."

"Then you are gay, yes?"

"No."

"Then you are not like the other men I have met. Every man wants something from a woman." She paused. "Every man will take favour or payment through sex. It is in their nature."

"Not all men. Not the majority either, I would hope." King shook his head. "It's sad that you haven't moved in better circles."

"I haven't been as lucky as some people."

"You make your own luck."

She scoffed. "What would you know? Western middle-classes. You know nothing of hardship!" She bent down and picked up her bag and dropped it onto the bed. She rummaged through the clothes inside and pulled out some underwear. "I have struggled! It took me until the age of twenty-four to get a job that paid more than a pittance, and then I discovered what the man did for a living. How my chances of remaining a house maid and avoiding being turned into a live-in whore dwindled with every visit the man made to the house. I have worked there for two years, and always it is a relief when the man returned to the city or travelled to the

Black Sea to be with his wife." She struggled into a pair of satin briefs, then allowed the towel to drop and made no effort to cover her breasts. King averted his eyes, but possibly not as quickly as he should have. She turned sideways on to him as she put on her bra, but it made little difference other than to show off her ample breasts from another angle. "You do not know of hardship or a lack of opportunities. And you are judgemental because of it."

    King could have told her about an absent mother, of never knowing a father and stealing food for his siblings. He could have told her about a tower block with urine-stained stairwells and faulty lifts the local prostitutes jammed closed and used for five-minute transactions. He could have told her about the day he discovered his mother's body lying in her own filth, a strap cinching tightly around her left arm, the empty syringe in her cold right hand. The bare-knuckle fighting for quick cash, of prison, of life-changing ultimatums and a chance to serve his country. But he denied her any of it. He left her words hanging in the air, as heady as her soapy aroma and the steam still wafting from the bathroom.

"What is wrong? Does the truth hurt?" she asked, pulling on a pair of jeans. She pulled a baggy sweater over her head and said, "I have seen what the man can do. I have seen how he gives the girls all the cocaine they can take and gets them dependant, then gets all the sex he wants before he grows tired of them. Then they end up in one of hundreds of brothels he owns throughout Russia and Europe. In London, even."

King looked at her, studied her young face, her vulnerable eyes. You could tell a lot about a person by their eyes. King's told you to keep walking. Alaina's were passionate, but not for carnal pleasures. They were passionate because of emotion. "You were passing information to Interpol, weren't you? Before Ramsay contacted you. You were helping them." He paused. "Not because of what you have seen and a sense of doing what is right, but because you have lost someone. How am I doing?" She looked back at him. Guarded, but her expression was starting to soften. "A sister, perhaps? Younger, most likely," he said with knowledge of what Caroline had told him about the Interpol trafficking taskforce and the girls she had managed to save. "Small town, no opportunities. A young girl goes for a job in the bright lights but is soon swallowed up by a different life. She becomes a commodity in a rich man's world."

"Please..."

"And the older sister stayed in the small town. Perhaps she was meant to go, too. Perhaps there was only enough money for one bus ticket."

"Please, stop."

King carried on unperturbed. He could see the change in her, the façade lowering. "So, did you get the job and then contact Interpol? Or was it the other way around?"

"Why does it matter?"

King shrugged. It mattered. But he didn't voice his concerns. "But you've bottled it," he said.

"Bottled it?" she asked, screwing up her face.

"Run out of nerve," he replied. "Hence the out. Interpol let Ramsay know about an asset they had in place in Romanovitch's organisation and he contacted you."

She shook her head. "No, my Interpol handler contacted me first, then I contacted Ramsay."

"Because you saw a way of doing what was asked of you, then negotiating your deal for the information MI5 asked for, and not continuing passing information on to Interpol." King paused. "Which tells me, you were having a crisis of confidence and losing your nerve, or…"

"Or what?"

"Or there was no point staying on to find your sister. Like, it was a pointless task and you needed a change of plan." King said quietly. "Where are you from?"

She wiped her eye, but not before King saw a tear. "The Ukraine."

"And your sister was a former Miss Ukraine, perhaps?"

She nodded. "She left Titiiv with hopes and dreams of furthering herself and soon became PA to a wealthy businessman and hoped she would learn enough to start her own company someday," she said. "She didn't know in what, but she would find an opening and save money and build contacts. I knew she had worked closely with Romanovitch and knew if I could get a domestic job with him, then I would be able to ask the right questions, listen to conversations." She started to sob. "But the cook told me about Dina and what they think happened to her when she refused to have sex with Romanovitch. Like them, I was in so deep by then, I couldn't just leave, and I feared things going the same way for me, or worse."

King nodded. "And now you've given up?"

"No! I have not given up!" she snapped. "But I am no longer searching for her, no longer holding onto the hope that she is alive. And while I am in the wolf's lair, I am in danger."

"And now you need to cut and run."

"No," she said, wiping the last of the tears away with a resolute swipe. "Now I want him dead."

19

London

If there was one benefit from rising to commander and head of SO15, the police Counter Terrorism Command, it was the opportunity to mix business with pleasure. Dining out was a legitimate expense for the purposes of networking and the expense account for this facility was not inconsiderable. Especially when Robinson made it his point to dine in places renowned for their value with certain colleagues and opposite numbers, which allowed him to carry over funds for the occasional luxurious experience with others, naturally people of more importance and benefit to his tenure. In this case, the Home Secretary and her husband accompanied both him and his wife to *The Ivy*.

"Russian and Balkan crime continues to rise," the Home Secretary commented, placing her cutlery down on her plate.

"How was your curry?" Robinson asked, having been somewhat miffed that she had gone for something so generic, even though it had been deconstructed. But it was sea bass and Thai spiced with swirls of coconut cream and served on a crispy noodle cake, so he had managed to let it go.

"Delicious," she replied.

He nodded and said, "Russian crime is the one thing we can count on to keep climbing. That and knife crime among the degenerate classes." He stabbed the last piece of calf's liver and wiped it around the jus and melted onions. "Black on black knife crime is the most worrying. For the statistics, that is. And with Black Lives Matter at the forefront, we are finding it difficult to stop and search. It's a political and social hot potato. All ethnicities in the under thirties bracket are a close second, but nobody praises us stopping and searching them, just vilifies us when we stop a person of colour."

"I hear you. But we need to do something about knife crime. It usually affects the same sort of people, and that starts with community policing. But many of these estates are police no go areas. If you go in, riots start and pretty soon the newspapers are full of race headlines." She paused. "The vast majority of those killed, would likely have pulled a knife on somebody else sooner or later. Yes, a death on the streets is tragic, truly so when the person is an innocent victim. But really, some of this is thinning the herd…"

"With respect, a death on the streets creates a spiral of vengeance."

"Exactly."

Robinson looked at her incredulously. "And that vengeance escalates. Innocent bystanders become victims. Families are destroyed. People die, merely because people have already died."

"Knives are too easily accessible. Nothing will change until we make them more difficult to purchase. Or make it impossible to buy such large knives."

Robinson shook his head. "No matter what you do, most of us have a bigger knife in our kitchen drawer than are used in ninety percent of the stabbings we see on our streets. In fact, many of the knives used are kitchen utility knives. Thin, sharp, and easily concealed. Any more legislation on knives is like peeing in the ocean." He paused, catching his wife's glance. "Forgive me, darling, but it's exactly the case." He put down his own cutlery and took a sip of his wine. The Home Secretary's husband had been quiet throughout the meal, as had his wife. Like a couple of bookends. Both had ordered the roast chicken. Another choice which had annoyed him, not least because it took a mandatory fifty minutes, but because roast chicken was a mid-week dinner in his opinion, and not something you ordered at a place like The Ivy, no matter how much foie gras the chefs put in the stuffing. He had let the matter go with his wife, because the dish relied upon two people sharing and the Home Secretary's husband had made a great deal about ordering something 'ordinary' from the exquisite menu. It was just like her to support her husband when she would have preferred the lobster. Robinson did not know whether the man had done it purposely to irk him, or whether he was simply fed up accompanying his high-profile wife to yet another meeting where he was nothing more than a plus one.

 The waiter came and cleared the plates, and another followed behind tidying the table for the next course, which was presented to them in menu form, while the sommelier topped up the wine from the ice bucket. It was a polished operation, and Robinson reflected that despite his guests ordering from the more questionable options, he had experienced yet another excellent meal. The Ivy was a safe pair of hands, with a well-deserved reputation built upon various talented chefs, as well as the many celebrities who helped create its façade. Many people spoke about how good the food was without having been there or known a single person who had.

"The Russian crime thing you mentioned is a reference to their mafia?" the Home Secretary's husband asked.

Robinson was caught off guard, the man had barely spoken for most of the evening. "Yes, Harold, that's right. Russian organised crime is a scourge on Western Europe. And the uncomfortable truth is, there are connections to Russian mafia and brotherhoods in virtually all *legitimate* Russian business. That is why the former Prime Minister announced seizures on undisclosed Russian money, but as your good lady will tell you, Britain PLC can't do without Russian investment. It's a double-edged sword."

"Indeed," the Home Secretary agreed. "But by them teaming up with the Balkan mafias, we are still getting drugs, prostitution and weapons smuggled across our borders, but left without the Russian's holding the smoking gun. We know what they're doing. They know that we know what they're doing. But we are left without the evidence needed to put pressure on the *legitimate…*" she scoffed. "Russian organisations."

"What about the Russian government?" Sally Robinson asked. "Can't the British government put pressure on them?"

The Home Secretary laughed, taking a mouthful of wine. "The Russian's neither care, nor fear any sanctions we may consider. We need their oil and gas and we have nothing in the same league as their military might. No, I'm afraid that Russia is the big boy in the playground and we're poking our head around the toilet door hoping to be left alone." She paused. "And the Russian president is the biggest gangster of them all…"

"Careful, honey," Harold laughed. "Don't get on the front pages with a quote like that!"

Robinson grinned. "I think present company can be trusted."

"I'm thinking about the waiting staff." He stopped speaking as one of the servers glided towards them and asked if they would like desserts. Robinson went for the cheese selection and the Home Secretary decided on an espresso. She said she had a speech to prepare for and would be up until the early hours. Harold kept coming back to the baked Alaska, and as it was a 'serve two' dessert, Sally dutifully accepted his request to share. Robinson decided he would not invite them again, but he ordered them a box of the homemade chocolates to go with his own to take home.

"This is wonderful, though," said the Home Secretary as the waitress bustled away. "I do enjoy this place." She raised a glass to him and said, "To the expense account!"

"To Wetherspoons and Harvesters!" he replied, chinking glasses. "Where much of my business has to be endured to balance the books for a meal like this!"

The Home Secretary smiled. "Oh dear, we may have to look at upping your expense account, after all."

They all laughed, but Robinson laughed harder than the others as he thought about how he had side-lined funding to cover the costs of the team from MI5. He hoped they were nearing a positive result. Hoped they could hold back the tide against the surge of Russian crime. He would not be able to claim credit for the MI5 team's 'sanctions', but at least the crime statistics would fall dramatically under his watch.

***

From his table - three removed from Commander Robinson, the Home Secretary and their respective partners - Major Diminov was seated at a booth beside the stained-glass window, where he sipped from his Courvoisier as he paid the bill. With a cover charge and tip included in the price, he refused the prompt on the card machine to leave a discretionary tip, shaking his head and thinking how Western capitalism had peaked, but under no illusion that it had. There would always be surprises when he travelled abroad but he could see the changes happening in his own country more and more. His homeland had changed so much since the fall of the wall. Barely out of his teens when it had happened, he had welcomed the progressive evolution of his country and its people, but like so many of his comrades, now wished for a middle ground between the two extremes his country had experienced in just a few decades.

Diminov had chosen only a main dish – to enable him to be ready when the group finished their meal - much to the consternation of his dinner date. But she was being paid over five hundred pounds for the evening, so she could get on with it without complaint. She was on the books of one of London's top escort agencies, and her presence in the CCTV footage that would later be scrutinised by the police and both MI5 and MI6 would undoubtedly throw up another avenue of investigation and keep them busy long after he was back behind his desk in Moscow tomorrow evening.

Diminov took out his phone and typed out a text. He sent it as he watched the foursome drain their glasses and look to make a move to leave. He kept his phone on the table, then smiled and felt relieved when he saw the reply. He nodded to his date as he slipped the phone back into his pocket. She finished her glass of champagne and picked up her clutch, dutifully following the man as he walked past the table. He hesitated for a moment in front of the Home

Secretary, and a stocky man in a dark grey suit got up from a nearby table and stepped between them. Diminov frowned, but the man did not move, shielding the Home Secretary from him. He could see the bulge of the pistol under the cut of the man's suit, his jacket buttons undone and his hands hovering at waist level in front of him, ready to give him a shove or draw his standard issue Glock 17 9mm pistol.

"Sorry," Diminov said, stepping around him. He ushered the girl around the bodyguards, glancing back at the woman that the man had been dining with. She was dressed a little austere and somewhat manly in a trouser suit, and he could see the earpiece she was wearing in her left ear. That made her righthanded, the earpiece being further away from her gun hand. She was looking worried but starting to relax as Diminov continued to walk away, but he turned and watched them, feigning enlightenment, and recognition. The Home Secretary. It happened all the time. The bodyguard was returning to the table where his partner was taking a sip of water. Diminov could see they had been dining on nothing but a complimentary basket of bread, their cutlery untouched, and an empty water jug with ice and lemon separated the two of them. "My fault," he mouthed with a smile. The bodyguard made a gesture like it was nothing.

Diminov took out his phone and typed a short text. Outside, he could see the black Jaguar the Home Secretary and her husband had arrived in, parked on the road opposite.

Parked three cars behind was the black Range Rover support vehicle. Inside both cars was a driver, and in the Jaguar's passenger seat the primary bodyguard waited, a mobile phone to his ear. Diminov could imagine the Home Secretary and her husband exiting, the two close protection officers a discreet two metres behind. Escorting them to the car, where the primary bodyguard would have already swept around the car and have the door open ready for them. The close protection officers veering off to the support vehicle and the convoy of two vehicles pulling seamlessly out and sweeping past the restaurant. But it would not happen like that.

Commander Robinson and his wife did not have the same degree of protection, but he did have an unmarked Jaguar saloon at his disposal, and a plain-clothed protection officer-come-driver. Diminov did not see the police commander's vehicle, but he imagined a short phone call would see it pull to the curb less than a minute later.

Timing would be everything. He checked his phone again, ignoring the escort's question regarding the rest of the evening. He hadn't been out to impress her, simply wanted the inconspicuousness of being viewed as a couple.

He had been told by the agency that sex would be by mutual arrangement, and on her terms. He still hadn't decided whether he wanted her yet. Diminov hailed a taxi as he crossed the road. The taxi pulled in fifty metres further up the street at the next available space. He checked his phone again, looked at the entrance to the restaurant, then pressed send to the text his thumb had been hovering over the whole time.

It was a go.

The Home Secretary and her husband paused on the steps long enough to exchange air kisses with Commander Robinson and his wife, the two men shaking hands. The lights on both protection vehicles came on as their engines started. A dark coloured van drove down West Street, past The Ivy, and put on its hazards and stopped in the road as another van stopped on the junction on Lichfield Street, the façade of the triangular-fronted restaurant occupying real estate on both streets. Robinson's Jaguar swept to the curb outside the restaurant on West Street and the driver got out and opened the rear door. A third van pulled up behind.

Diminov smiled. Textbook. The entire entourage was boxed in, a van at each point of the triangle. He opened the taxi door, told the driver the name of the hotel and slapped the escort's buttocks as she bent down and clambered inside. She let out a giggle, that sounded altogether fake. He was feeling powerful, the surge of testosterone thumping through him, his heart pounding at the exhilaration, and he would unleash it upon the escort as soon as he closed the hotel door.

***

Commander Robinson watched, the scene playing in slow motion. He was on his knees, crouching for cover beside his vehicle. He saw his driver glance behind him, the van stopping in the middle of the road. He had his weapon in his hand, and Robinson noticed it was shaking. The Home Secretary and her husband were climbing into their vehicle – the most vulnerable and dangerous time in any escorted journey was widely considered to be the embus/debus. The bodyguards knew it, and the Home Secretary knew it. And the seven, armed Russian agents that alighted from the three vans knew it, too. Robinson saw the muzzle flashes, heard the roar of automatic gunfire and was aware of his wife's screams. But the slow motion suddenly sped up to full speed, and it all happened so quickly. Bodyguards returning fire, their 9mm Glocks sounding like popguns compared to the roar of the Kalashnikovs. He could see the desperation in the bodyguards' faces, their movements as they frantically attempted to halt the tide, but to no avail. He could see the body armour worn by the attackers, the bandoliers carrying spare magazines. They were professional, too. Soldiers. Taking a knee and finding cover to change magazines, make their weapons ready again, before moving on. Amid the chaos, two bodyguards had broken cover to attempt to save their charges but were mown down by round upon round of 7.62mm short that left the barrel at thirteen rounds per second. The attackers gained ground, casually aiming head shots at the dying protection officers on the ground, not pausing or slowing momentum as they delivered an emotionless *coup de grâce*. He could see that one of the attackers had opened the door of the Home Secretary's Jaguar. His heart was pounding, he was aware of his wife's screams beside him, but he could not take his eyes off the scene of murder and mayhem. He looked at his bodyguard for guidance, but the man was down. A lone attacker crossed the road, briefly hesitated behind the body of his driver, and fired a shot into the man's head, splitting it like a watermelon. The muzzle of the assault rifle raised and then hovered in front of his wife's face.

"Please, no…" Robinson managed. His throat and mouth as dry as he'd ever known, and the words barely made it out. He swallowed hard and said, "Not my wife," he said quietly. "She is a mother of two…"

The gunman moved the weapon and aimed it directly at Robinson's face. The gunfire had ceased. The night eerily silent. The ominous sound of a battle won, a battle lost. Behind him, the rest of the attackers were heading for the vehicle further down West Street. The smoking wreckage of the two protection vehicles were blocking the road, and cars that had pulled up in the short time of the attack had been left abandoned as the other drivers had fled. He looked at Robinson, his eyes cold and hard and steady. The rest of his face was obscured by the balaclava. He checked his aim, and Robinson closed his eyes. The gunman then moved his weapon and fired three shots into the woman's face. Commander Robinson opened his eyes. Blood and brain matter and fragments of skull had smattered his face and his wife had fallen backwards, propped up against the wall of the restaurant, the top half of her head missing. Robinson stared at the man, his lips quivering and his hands trembling.

"Znay svoyego vraga…" said the Gunman. "Znay svoyego vraga."

20

Albania

King had rented the only car with off-road pretensions on the hire company's books. It was a Suzuki Vitara which had seen better days, but at least the taller wheelbase and larger tyres made the potholed road more bearable as he drove through the tight bends of the mountain road.

"Romanovitch is in St. Petersburg, I still don't see why we should have come to Albania."

King glanced at Alaina, battling with the jarring steering wheel as the front wheels found another pothole deep enough to grate the underside of the vehicle on the road surface. "I told you, I need to start the ball rolling here first. And for what I have in mind, I need considerable finances. Feel free to go after Romanovitch yourself, by all means."

Alaina folded her arms across her chest. "And feel free to go into the lion's den without what I know."

King shrugged. "I was all set to do just that," he said irritably. He worked best alone. Or at the very least with Caroline or Rashid. Big

Dave had gone back to London, an assignment he had walked away from still waiting for him, but he had made it quite clear that he thought Alaina should have remained at the property in the Urals. But King had not only felt for the woman, he had formulated a new plan after talking to her at great depth about Romanovitch's most trusted men. She had something he needed, only she did not know it yet.

"I miss her," she said quietly. "My sister did not deserve to die like that."

King nodded. "You truly believe her to be dead?"

"The cook had no reason to lie."

"She may have been mistaken."

Alaina shrugged. "And if she is not dead, then the life she would have in one of Romanovitch's brothels would be worse than death."

"Nothing is worse than death," said King. "No matter how bad it is, it's still living, and there is still hope that your situation can improve."

"You believe that?"

"Of course."

"Then you can't have known pain and anguish, or illness or despair." She paused. "What do you know of such things?"

"All there is."

"Because you are a tough guy? A killer? You think you know what it is to ache inside, in the way I do?"

King said nothing. He had nursed a dying wife, come back to her body and a curt note telling him that she would now be free from pain and that he should forget her and move on with his life. It had taken him five years before he had succumbed to another woman. And she had been a double agent, and he had held her hand as she had died, comforting her in her last moments. Told her to remember the love of her deceased husband. And not one day since had he not regretted her giving him no choice but to pull the trigger. He had killed many times, and he had been close to death himself. Nobody would ever convince him that there was a case for giving up, a reason not to go on. He believed it was a primal instinct, that survival was all there was, and he did not understand those who would succumb to a quick release.

He bumped over the last of the ruts and pulled the small four-by-four into the farmyard.

Flymo's vehicle was parked beside the large barn that had served as a hangar to the helicopter. He hoped the man had managed to procure what King had asked him to get. King parked next to the house and switched off the engine.

"What is this place?" she asked nervously.

"Somewhere for you to stay," he said. "While I do what has to be done."

"And what is that?"

"I work better alone."

"No way! I am not staying here!"

King got out, putting the keys in his pocket. He headed towards the large barn without looking back. Alaina followed begrudgingly, choosing to remain with King, rather than to risk losing sight of him. King wondered whether she was experiencing a form of Stockholm Syndrome, although he was not holding her against her will, since leaving with her she had only wanted to remain with him.

Flymo stepped out from the barn, cleaning his hands on a rag. He frowned when he noticed Alaina. "Who is this?"

"Long story," said King.

"Alaina Kopolova," she replied, walking

past King and holding out her hand.

"Leroy," he replied. "But they call me Flymo."

"Flymo," she frowned. "That is a strange name."

"I'm a pilot," he said. "A helicopter driver. I get so low, not even a Flymo can hover lower."

"And what is this *Flymo*?"

"It's a type of lawnmower."

"I see…" she said, but clearly did not. "And you are a gardener also?"

"No, a pilot."

"And this Flymo is good, yes?"

"No, not really. But it hovers on air, just above the ground. That was its unique selling point." He paused. "It's just a joke, and jokes aren't all that funny when you have to explain them in detail."

"Have you got the things I asked for?" King asked, interrupting the struggling conversation.

"All in the barn," he said.

"Right. I think it will be best to move the chopper out."

"Okey dokey," he replied amiably. "But we have a problem there. The pick-up died where I parked it. It struggled all the way up the mountain pass. I tried moving it this morning but no joy." He paused. "And the bird is on skid pans, ready for me to tow it out."

"Can you fix the truck?"

"I doubt it. I mean, I can have a go, but the engine is ceased solid and I tinker with helicopter engines a little, not cars. I'm certainly not a mechanic, I just do enough to keep a well serviced helicopter in the air. Do you have a tow hitch on that thing?" he asked, looking at the tiny four by four.

"No," King shook his head.

"Right."

"You could unfasten the skids and fly it out."

Flymo looked back at the opening. "I guess. I mean, it will be tight."

"Not for someone who has earned the name Flymo. You hover mere inches above the ground, after all…" King said sarcastically. He wanted to test him and was sure the pilot would take the bait.

"Fine," Flymo replied curtly and headed for the barn.

"A pilot? I was confused by the gardener

thing…" Alaina said, watching him leave. "You have your own helicopter?"

"The missing team did, yes," King replied.

"And you will use this to take down Romanovitch? How?"

"Not Romanovitch," King answered tersely. "His Albanian counterpart. The Russians and the Albanians are doing business together. The team were meant to disrupt their business, cause them a loss in profits and a break in the supply chain."

"But they went missing…"

"Yes."

"The Albanians visited the lodge in the Urals. Two men," said Alaina, her face sullen, like the memory pained her. "Something terrible happened. I did not see what happened and was told by Draco to remain inside. Then just one of the Albanians left. The next day I cleaned up the dishes and remains of a meal from the table on the pool terrace. There was dried blood on the grass. A huge amount. It had soaked in, but I could tell what it was. The other Albanian had died there, been butchered there. Later, there were many vodka bottles loose in the cellar. They should have been in the wooden crates, but they had been emptied out and the boxes removed. I think he was put into these crates, but I said nothing and asked nothing." She paused. "These are ruthless people. If your friends have been captured, then I do not hold out much hope for them. And you shouldn't, either. If they are not dead already, then they are as good as."

King ignored her and walked into the barn. The helicopter had been cleaned and polished. Flymo had been busy in his absence, and King could see the man had piled the things he had wanted next to the tarp hiding the safe from view.

"It's all there," said Flymo, standing at King's shoulder.

"What's the clearance?" King asked, looking at the doorway.

"A foot. A foot and a half at best."

"Great. Let's see if you can live up to your nickname, then." King walked to the double doors and opened the second one, pinning it back with a rock that had been purposed for the task. "Park it over there." He pointed to the middle of the yard, then looked at Alaina. "Best stand out of the way," he said, walking down the edge of the barn and perching on the bonnet of the Suzuki.

Alaina followed him and said, "Can he really fly that thing out of there?"

"No idea."

"There's barely any room."

"Call it his interview. Or audition. I haven't flown with this guy, don't know how he operates." The sound of the engines whining and the rotors slowly starting to turn was clearly audible, and gained gradually until the noise was familiar, unmistakable. "If he messes up, at least he won't have far to fall…"

King walked out into the yard, catching sight of the nose of the helicopter and the blur of the rotors. Dust and debris swirled out of the open doors like a dust devil in the desert, then dispersed in a blizzard once it was out of the rotor wash. The nose of the craft lifted by mere inches, then flipped up a few feet, but was corrected in time. The height of the barn was just sufficient to allow for the anomaly, but the doorway would not be so forgiving. The craft dipped lower, the skids catching the ground, then lifting slightly and in one smooth and swift motion, the helicopter glided out through the doors, inches separating the skids from the hard, sun-baked ground, and the spinning rotors afforded the same distance from the steel girder across the doorway.

King was impressed. He was about to say something to Alaina, but watched as the helicopter spun one-hundred and eighty degrees and took off backwards, banked hard towards the ground then spun around and climbed hard, the rotors close enough to the two of them for them to both duck their heads as the craft pivoted and climbed towards the sky, now righted and flying conventionally, but vertically with the turbine whining under both boost and strain. It climbed to around a thousand feet, then pivoted, looked as though the rotors were still and the craft was turning instead. King knew this was an illusion – although it was doing a bit of both – and then the helicopter was into a vertical dive towards them. Alaina screamed and fled towards the fringe of the woods, and King tensed, every fibre of his being wanting to run, but locked into a duel of nerve with Flymo as he rode the wave of inertia and powered flight downwards. King took a breath, stood resolute and hoped for the best. The helicopter corrected and levelled out, the skids just a foot above King as Flymo banked the craft hard and entered a controlled hover just a few feet above the ground and facing the barn entrance.

King was thrown to the floor by the rotor wash and was getting back up, dusting himself off as Flymo touched down the skids and shut the engine down. But he had not ducked, and he knew that Flymo had seen that, too. The rotors slowed, but King knew that Flymo would still be controlling the helicopter's overriding desire to flip over, until the rotors had powered down further.

Alaina made her way back out of the woods, looking sheepish and flushed with adrenalin and exertion. King noted her fight or flight instincts were strong. But he also wondered what in hell's name a psychologist would make of his own. Standing firm in a duel against man and machine and physics was not the sanest thing for a man to do. Especially a man with a woman at home and ideas about starting a family.

"Impressive," she said.

"Reckless," King replied.

"You don't like?"

King shook his head. "No, I like a great deal," he replied. "I've been left on mountainsides with ISIS hunting me because an extraction would mean an RAF pilot going over his limit for hours in the air, or that there is a bank of fog too near to take the risk. I've also been flown over because the landing zone is too hot with insurgents." He paused. "I can tell that none of these things will bother Flymo."

"Rather you than me…"

King made his way to the barn as Flymo got out of the cockpit. He lifted one of the skidpans out of the way and half wheeled, half dropped it into the corner. Flymo did the same with the other one.

"Sorry about that."

"You had an audience."

"I have been known to show off a bit."

"Well, you've earned your handle," King said, looking at the pile of items Flymo had procured in his absence. "I may have something else for you to do, but I'll work on that later. In the meantime, we need to get that safe open. What I have planned will depend on what pocket money we have left."

King kicked off the rocks holding the tarp in place and pulled it out of the way. somehow, the safe looked bigger and thicker and more daunting now that he had to try and break in. Early in his career with MI6 he had been trained to get into a variety of safes, and had put the practice into effect many times, but by his own admission, it had been a while now to say the least. He thought back to his first mission, stealing already stolen IRA funds, and planting the money in a criminal's property in France. Turning the rats against each other. Somehow, it seemed a world away, a lifetime ago, and yet simpler days. Then he realised those days had been no simpler, but he *had* been younger.

"You are breaking in?"

King looked at Alaina and replied, "Yes."

"Can I help?"

"Can you crack safes?"

"No, but I can learn."

"Okay, you can mix."

The inside of the barn was hot and airless. King took off his T-shirt and tossed it onto a clear area of floorspace. Alaina looked at him, then glanced away when he caught her. By his own admission, he was in good shape. Lean at the waist with a broad chest and shoulders. Working shirtless on the property in Cornwall had given him a tan and had shown up the road map of scars. Each one telling a story, and a reminder that he had won the battles, even if they had left their mark. He tipped the scales at fourteen stone and had the build of a light-heavyweight boxer. Indeed, he had boxed and fought in prize fights as a young man, and still trained on a bag most days to keep supple and hard and fast. He did not work too hard with weights, preferring to do press-ups, pull-ups, sit-ups, and squats. He had found that overly built or sculptured muscles tired quickly, and the strength he built through his routines allowed him to fight and get out of trouble through stamina.

Alaina took off her blouse, revealing just a bra. She tossed the blouse to where King's T-shirt lay.

"Christ, I'll leave you both to it if you want." Flymo quipped.

"It is hot, is all," Alaina snapped. "Now, show me what to do."

Flymo could barely take his eyes off the young woman. King tapped him on the back of the head and jolted him out of his lecherousness. "Give Alaina a bucket, and open that bag of chemical fertiliser."

King opened the packets of sugar and bicarbonate of soda and started measuring the quantities into a clean bucket. Next, he opened the bags of iron filings.

"We are making a bomb?" Alaina asked tentatively.

"Sort of," King replied. He looked through the boxes and found the saltpetre. "Okay, Alaina, tip half the fertiliser into the bucket," he said, handing her his bucket. "Then mix mine into it using the wooden batten." He pointed at two lengths of two-by-one pine batten. "Mix it well."

King picked up the bag of barbecue charcoal and tossed it at Flymo. He spread out the tarp and found a half concrete block beside the pile of rocks. He placed it on the tarp, brushed aside any debris and hunted for another piece of block. He found what he wanted and squatted down beside the tarp. "Empty a small amount of charcoal onto the block, and gently pound it into a powder with this…" He handed him the other piece of block. "Just like the women do in Africa with grain."

"Is that because I'm black?"

"No, it was an example."

"Couldn't find a better example?"

King shrugged. "No. Still can't."

Flymo pulled a face and started pounding at the charcoal. King noted his anger was getting the job done. He still couldn't think of another example, so he opened a bottle of concentrated bleach – sodium hypochlorite – checked the viscosity and poured it into another clean bucket. He stood up quickly and put some distance between himself and the bucket. "Shit, this needs a mask," he said pointedly. "It's strong stuff."

"The masks are over there." Flymo pointed to a bag with a home depot store logo on it. "Christ, I'll open the back door!" He crossed the barn and unbolted a single door and the barn filled with a blessed breeze. "I should have done that earlier. You two can get dressed now."

King was bathed in sweat. He wiped what he could from his eyes with the back of his wrist, then put on the mask and a pair of goggles and tossed one of each to Alaina and Flymo. He then returned to his bucket, where he spooned in quantities of petroleum jelly and started to mix in the iron filings. The mixture turned into a reddish soup, the bleach attacking the iron immediately. King turned to Alaina. "Here, bring your mix over. And pour it carefully into mine. And make sure your mask is on tightly."

Alaina struggled with the weight of the bucket, but she got her left-hand underneath and steadied it as she poured. King mixed it together with one of the battens until it became thick like porridge.

"How's the charcoal coming along?"

"Nearly there. Just like my mother used to do with my breakfast millet outside my mud hut as a child."

"Dickhead," King replied tersely. "At least she made you breakfast. I wouldn't see mine for days and sometimes ate out of the kitchen dustbin."

Flymo raised an eyebrow as he scraped the powdered charcoal into a bucket and brought it over. "Here." He placed it down beside them.

"Great. Now, unless you have any objections working for the *white man*, I need you to mix the two together while I work on the fuses." He stood up and left Flymo mixing and Alaina watching with great interest. King took the lengths of hessian string and a handful each of saltpetre and petroleum jelly and rubbed them between his hands. He then twisted the lengths of string into one strand and coiled it into a loose length around three feet in length. King returned to where Flymo was mixing and patted him on the back. "That's enough. Good job." He dropped the length of rope next to the safe and said, "Right, let's get this thing opened."

Flymo stopped mixing and tapped the loose mix off the batten. The mix looked like a brown sludge, and it emitted a vapour which could be seen and felt on the skin.

King put on a pair of blue plastic gloves – hospital PPE issue – and plunged his hands into the mix. He moulded it into shapes the girth and length of salami and pressed it into a line around the safe door. "The rear of the safe is the weakest part," he said, his voice muffled by the mask. "Rashid would have known this, which was why he set it in the concrete." He manipulated another handful, and after several applications, joining the lengths together, he had almost gone all the way around. He doubled the amount of mix at where he estimated the hinges and multiple locks to be, then scraped the rest of the mix out and finished the rectangle, pressing the joins together and making sure that there were no weak links.

"If this doesn't work, is there enough mix to try again?" Alaina asked.

"Not really," replied King. "Perhaps half as much again."

"Let's hope it works, then," Flymo commented quietly.

King worked the improvised fuse deeply into the moulded concoction on the thickest corner, to allow for an even burn in two directions. He fed the fuse out, then used his Swiss Army knife with its locking blade to trim a foot off the length. "Anyone got any matches?" Alaina did not smoke. Flymo looked impressively fit, so King doubted he did, either.

Flymo shrugged and said, "I'll get some from the kitchen."

King picked up his T-shirt and while he was bending down, he picked up Alaina's blouse and tossed it to her, trying not to look at the shape of her breasts straining against the sheer bra for a moment longer than he needed to. He supposed it wasn't necessary to look at all, but he was a red-blooded man and there had to be some sort of default setting. The over-ride switch to that setting was the last image he carried of Caroline sullenly watching him leave from the front doorway of their cottage. She had not smiled nor waved goodbye.

King used his T-shirt to wipe himself dry, then shook it out and put it back on. Alaina slipped her blouse over her and buttoned just three buttons in the middle of the garment. The top of her bra was visible, as was her pierced navel. She looked up as Flymo approached carrying a disposable lighter and three frosted cans of beer. She smiled and let out a gasp. King rarely drank alcohol in the daytime, but right now the ice-cold beer was looking good. He accepted the can with a smile and ran it over his neck and face in a bid to cool down.

Flymo handed King the lighter and he bent down and lit the end of the fuse length he had cut earlier, standing back up to set the bezel of his watch at the minute hand. He pulled the tab and drank through the froth of the icy beer. He did not recognise the brand, but it was weak and smooth and went down well on such a hot late summer's day. King stood back and watched the fuse burning on the ground. He had learned the hard way once and failed to outrun a fuse in time. He had been lucky, but now he always tested burning fuses. He checked his watch. The foot-long length had burned its length in just over twenty seconds. So, the four feet or so sticking out from the incendiary compound would give him plenty of time to get clear.

King drained his beer and dropped the can on the ground beside the barn. "Stay here while I go and light it," he said and walked into the barn. The smell of the compound reacting was enough to make him feel nauseous, and he adjusted the face mask and put on the goggles before his eyes started to water. In his back pocket he carried the 9mm Makarov he had left in the glovebox of the BMW. King had stopped by and collected it. The car had been intended as an emergency escape plan, and King saw no point in not keeping it for himself, parking it in a residential street near the airport. He took out the pistol and checked it before slipping it into his right jeans pocket. Neither Flymo nor Alaina had gained his trust yet and there was no telling what either of them would do if they liked the look of the contents of the safe more than their current options.

King studied the compound, giving it a final once over before lighting the fuse. The mix was volatile, but packed as loosely as it was, it would initiate rather than detonate. He had used the same mix packed tightly in plastic bags and sealed in a vacuum packer to create a highly destructive explosive for demolition purposes. He stepped back, making sure the flame was burning fiercely, the petroleum jelly fuelling the string, which burned like a wick. He picked up both fire extinguishers and carried them outside, handing one to Flymo when he reached him.

"When I say, we'll head in, but only use your extinguisher if I tell you to. Too soon and you'll cool the cuts in the metal, and it will fuse tightly together, welding itself back up."

"Okay…"

"The extinguishers are for the contents of the safe. Whatever is in there may well catch fire." He paused, then said, "Bugger!"

"What is it?" Flymo asked.

"I forgot to get something ready to prise the door off." He paused. "It's going to be heavy, and bloody hot as well." He glanced at his watch. "Thirty seconds, I reckon."

Flymo darted towards the house. He shouted something, but King could neither hear what he said, nor wanted to delay him further. He turned to Alaina and shrugged.

"Will it be loud?" she asked tentatively.

"I hope not. If it is, then I've done it wrong. It should sound like a massive fizz," he said. "And there'll be a flash of light, which is why we're waiting out here. It would be enough to blind you, otherwise."

Alaina nodded, but did not reply. She glanced over at Flymo, who was racing back with a bulky pair of oven gloves. It was the campest thing King had seen in a while.

"Better than tea towels, I suppose," said King. He checked his watch again, but it wasn't a science and he knew there was no real reason to check, other than he felt he had wasted enough time in Albania, when there was much to do in Russia. But he needed the funds for what he had planned next.

The fizz was an understatement. It was more like the roar of a forest fire after a dry summer. The flash was intense, brightening the yard which was already bathed in the late afternoon sun.

"That should be it," King said. "Follow me with the extinguisher." He snatched the oven gloves from Flymo and led the way into the barn, pulling the mask over his face and adjusting the goggles.

The smoke emitted from the flare of flame was white and acrid but was clearing quickly with the doors open front and rear. The flames were dying, the superheated iron filings had cut through the steel of the safe like a thermal lance. As King approached, he could see that the safe door had fallen inwards and he bent down, tucked his gloved fingers into the gap and pulled the door out. He struggled with the weight and heat, but after several tugs, he got a corner out and pulled it clear. He dropped it beside the safe, and the edges caught debris on fire, sparking like embers from a barbecue. Inside the safe, there were flames and Flymo stepped in and got his extinguisher ready. King nodded and stood back as the man doused the flames. King pulled off the oven gloves, the residual heat now burning his fingers. He looked at the gloves and could see they were scorched. At almost fifteen-hundred degrees centigrade, the compound had cut through cleanly, but had ignited the contents. Flymo was bringing it under control, and the inside of the safe was now steaming.

"Jesus," Flymo said. "We've incinerated hundreds of thousands of euros!"

King could see that the currencies had

been bundled in piles of euros, pound sterling, US dollars and Albanian lek. The outer notes of each pile had been scorched. He looked up at Flymo and said, "But it looks like there's several million left." King stood up and looked at Alaina, who was staring at the money in the ground. He was aware of the comforting feeling of the Makarov in his pocket, all the while trying to read their eyes. Money tended to do things to people. "Here, you and Flymo start getting it out. Make a pile for the ruined notes and another for the ones that are okay. I'm going to make a call."

King stepped out into the light, ditched the goggles and mask, and took out his phone, entered the man's number from memory and typed out a short text highlighting what he would require. He received the reply within a few seconds. Incredulity and surprise. King then asked for two. He would require shipping and the man would have to use his contacts and the full stretch of his bonded warehouse and storage remit. This would require the man's backdoor work with MI6 and the Ministry of Defence and several of the twenty-eight agencies it represented. Then came the question about payment. Normally cash on collection, sometimes King had used the allocated bank account details, or a credit card dedicated for a mission. But this would be different. This would require a courier to accompany the purchase, and to take the money back.

The text came back. Two million euros. King thought about what he had just seen inside the ruined safe. He could cover that. He typed his reply but added something else and told the man he would pay a further hundred thousand, then added his timeframe and waited for his response.

Deal. Shipping details to follow.

21

**Thames House,
London**

"It's too soon," said Simon Mereweather.

"Undoubtedly," Director Amherst agreed. "But there's no playbook for this sort of thing."

"He should be grieving."

"He will be."

"But at home. With his children."

Amherst nodded. "Let's see what he has to say."

"He can't possibly be heading the investigation."

"No, that had fallen to a dedicated murder investigation team and because of the crossover, there's a CTIU and CTU presence. As well as the team you've put on it as liaison."

Mereweather nodded. "And the Home Secretary?"

"Grieving. The Prime Minister is making a speech in the commons today, expect cross party platitudes. We all know she wasn't a popular choice, and has made many enemies within the opposition parties, but they all have families and this will be a reminder of the fragility of their own safety, the vulnerability and reality that comes with their chosen profession."

"It was so blatant," Mereweather said quietly. "To target their spouses like that. When they could have assassinated two leading public and political figures. I've seen the CCTV and the footage from the police updates, but the van the terrorists escaped in and the subsequent vehicles they were dropped at all had fake number plates and took devious routes. This was well planned. The police have most of those vehicles now, but the assailants have completely disappeared and are unidentifiable."

"Except for one man."

"Correct."

"Any news of his whereabouts?"

"He checked out of his hotel and took a direct flight to Moscow early this morning. He's already arrived and will no doubt be off the grid." Mereweather paused. "The Russian Embassy have been elusive. They have no records of an official visit by Major Diminov. But they have pointed out that the man is a registered diplomat, with the diplomatic immunity all that entails."

"So, no further action and no further assistance with our enquiries." Amherst got up from his desk and paced to the window. The Thames was its usual muddy self, made dark and moody by the grey skies and heavy rainclouds which hovered stationary above, ready to burst. Ominous and inevitable. "And we're meant to buy that he just happened to be at the same restaurant, and just happened to leave a few minutes before both parties, and just happened to take a flight back to Russia early the next day?"

"It's a message. Nothing more, nothing less. Like Tweedledum and Tweedledee in Salisbury. Two agents, a spot of sight-seeing and some selfies at the cathedral and then some Novichok nerve agent left on a defector's door handle. The Russians don't do subtle, and they don't do sorry. They just do what they bloody-well please."

The intercom on Amherst's desk sounded and his secretary said, *"Commander Robinson is here, Sir."*

Amherst turned his back on the window and walked back to his desk. He sat back down at his chair, straightened his tie with its immaculate Windsor knot, then pressed the button. "Show him in, please." The door opened, but Amherst decided he was appearing too formal and unwelcoming, so stood, and stepped around the desk.

Mereweather followed his boss' lead and stood up, adjusting his cufflink. A nervous gesture he often did but was unaware of. He nodded to the police chief but allowed the director to make the first contact.

"I'm so sorry for your loss," he said, gesturing him to take a seat. "Can I get you a coffee or tea?"

"No."

Amherst nodded, skirted back around to his desk, and sat down. "You really should be at home…"

Commander Robinson shook his head. His eye sockets were puffy and dark, and his eyes were red and sore-looking. The man had cried himself out. He now looked a hollow shell compared to the man who had been seated in the same chair at the beginning of the summer. "There *is* no home." He paused. "Thanks to you and your games."

"What do you mean?" Mereweather asked testily. "We came up with a solution to your inability to get on top of Russian and Balkan organised crime," he said defensively.

"Simon…" Amherst held up a hand. "Please, allow the Commander to speak."

Simon Mereweather picked up his coffee and sipped, more for a distraction than because he felt need of it. It was tepid and foul. He cradled the cup, nonetheless.

"It was a message," said Robinson. "A message to get our snouts out of Russian affairs. A Russian SVR officer organised the murder of my wife and the Home Secretary's husband. He calmly ate at the neighbouring table and left just ahead of us."

"But it just can't be," replied Amherst. "It's just too obvious for the man to have been there."

Robinson grimaced. He closed his eyes for a moment, reliving the events of the previous night. When he reopened his eyes, they were moist, and the soreness seemed amplified. "Before the man killed my wife," he said. "Before he killed the mother to my two children, he said something to me…"

"What?" asked Mereweather.

"Znay svoyego vraga."

"Good god!" Mereweather said quietly.

"What does that mean?" Amherst asked irritably.

"It means, *know your enemy*," Mereweather replied.

"Oh, dear god…" said Amherst.

"Exactly," Robinson replied. "The damned Russians are all at it. Government or organised crime, they're all in it together. You put your team of mercenaries on Romanovitch and his Balkan running dogs, and he's used his influence to have a Russian SVR hit team murder my wife." He shivered at the thought, his eyes welling with tears. "And as blatant as you like."

"But there's no paperwork, no connection to you," Amherst protested vehemently. "This is a black bag operation with no comebacks."

"But there bloody well *was* a comeback!" Robinson got to his feet and slammed his fists down on the large mahogany desk, forcing Amherst to flinch. Mereweather stood, but seemed unsure what to do next. "I must have been under surveillance, or the SVR had this place under surveillance. That seems the most likely scenario. But either way, word got back to Moscow that the terrorism police chief was meeting with MI5 mandarins and news filtered down to that weasel Romanovitch. He guessed the sudden and escalating attacks on his business interests was something we had cobbled together and hedged his bets!"

"But the Home Secretary isn't involved in our agenda." Amherst paused, regaining some composure. "She knows nothing about what we have set out to achieve."

Robinson frowned, shaking his head. "No, but she's coming down hard on undeclared Russian funds and property. Two birds, one stone." He paused. "She got the same message, apparently. Harold was collateral damage, because of us!"

"There's a COBRA meeting at mid-day. We may need to re-evaluate our agenda." Amherst said.

"Re-evaluate?"

"This can't come out," said Mereweather.

"No," agreed Amherst.

Robinson stared at the two men, cocked his head and said, "Really? That is all you two are worried about? I've got to look my children in the eyes and tell them that I have no idea why their mother is dead. I've got to keep this quiet from the cabinet, or I'll go to prison, and my children will be put in a foster home!" He shook his head. "Jesus Christ! I can't believe I went along with this, I can't believe that I involved the likes of you slippery bastards in police work." He paced to the door and stared at the two men in turn. "Well, that's it. I'm handing in my resignation. I have my children to think about and those Russian words will be swimming around my head for the rest of my days." He opened the door and sneered. "But I suggest you think on this... Those Russian bastards will know that whoever I spoke to here will be senior in rank, and they won't hesitate to do the same to you and your families if it means they get what they want."

22

Greece-Albanian Border

The food and water came in quantities barely enough to keep them alive. A piece of stale bread and a small plastic bottle of water once a day. The men had resorted to drinking their own urine the previous day, and with their unrivalled experience in survival training, they knew the desperation in this act. It would give them a few more days of survival, but little more. There were now dangerous amounts of waste in the form of nitrogen, potassium, and calcium in their urine and it was the colour of Guinness, and without fresh water the practice would soon have a detrimental effect.

Each man was handcuffed by their right wrist to a purpose made link set in the stone wall. Rashid could not vouch for the other men, but he had attempted to get the link loosened from the concrete from the moment he had been shackled. All he had achieved was to bloody his wrist until he could see the whiteness of the bone underneath the torn skin. It hurt so much, but a little less each day, and he realised that he was nearing the point of not caring whether he lived or died. He tried to snap out of his narcosis-like state, even prayed for the first time in years. He was a Muslim by birth and nurture and had worshipped at his local mosque throughout his childhood, but by the time he had reached his teens and discovered girls, his practice had dwindled. By the time he had established his military career and later passed selection into the SAS, he no longer practised Islam or any other faith. He couldn't explain why to his parents, and he didn't apologise either. His career had taken him to many places, and he had seen many terrible things. Some situations borne through oil and government agenda, but many by religion and colour and creed. His faith had been eroded. But in the cold confines of the cellar, with hope all but lost he found himself muttering a quiet prayer.

"Say one for me while you're at it…" said Mac. "I don't think my God believes in me anymore…"

Rashid smiled and said, "I'm not sure mine ever did…"

"Well, hedge your bets lad."

Rashid looked at him, figured he looked the same. Bruised black and blue, cut to pieces, and scuffed and grazed. He'd had a tooth chipped and another loosened. He thought it was firming up, but it didn't seem to matter anymore. He knew they had been on a deniable operation, but all he could hope for was to hold on.

Philosopher was unconscious, but thankfully he had been left face down. They had shouted at him for what seemed like an hour to move onto his side, but the man was out cold. He hoped he was still with them, but it wasn't looking good. The worst of it was Rashid had not been asked any questions on the last occasion he had been dragged away. Simply been given twenty-minutes of solid beating. The senior echelons of the Albanian brotherhood had not even been present, and it would appear the men were now the guards' playthings. Beatings for amusement. Rashid was trying to work out the scope for a counterattack. He was weak and running on empty, but he only needed the element of surprise. However, the guards seemed aware that they were dealing with tough, resourceful men and were wary of their apparent military service. When they took each of them from the cell, they were mindful to handcuff their free hand, shackle the chained hand before releasing the wall-mounted cuff. At no time during the process of taking them to or from the room where they were interrogated had the men ever had their hands free, or uncuffed from behind their backs.

The door unbolted and all three men tensed. They knew what would be coming next, a one in three chance that they would endure another beating. Another humiliating defeat at the hands of lesser men. But those lesser men had got the drop on them. They had been ready for them and the numbers had been overwhelming. Rashid supposed it was obvious, really. They had struck at so much within the brotherhood, that the key buildings and operations would be left waiting. He recognised his over-confidence, his feeling of invincibility. The property had been a stalking horse. Apparently empty. Apparently unsecured. But hiding an army within, that the men carrying out surveillance and not heavily armed, had been unable to overcome. And now they were paying the price for their over confidence, their blatant opportunism and guile.

Rashid looked up at the man holding the gun. He was a toothless ogre and the four men had given him the name *Shrek*. To be fair, that wasn't entirely fair on the cartoon character, the

Albanian version was simply hideous. The next man into the room was *The Runt*. Five foot three, single digits in stones and grey hair. He had a cruel mouth and even crueller eyes. He enjoyed his work, and the only redeeming factor was that he couldn't punch and hit as hard as he would have hoped. Rashid couldn't vouch for the other men, but he had grunted more than he needed to, begged more than he would have liked and feigned unconsciousness to buy him a few minutes respite from the beatings. Not that it was an easy task, there were still another two men who beat them regularly, as well as Shrek himself, but at least it was the saving grace when he saw the cruel face of The Runt. For a moment, he wondered whether to say something to them, perhaps curse them, and at least he would get a beating by The Runt. But he also remembered the first lesson a career corporal had told him during his training – don't volunteer for anything and make sure you are always the grey man. There will always be enough opportunities for trouble to find you, so you were best off avoiding it at all costs. Besides, he was leader of this team and the sense of duty within him told him he shouldn't opt for a lesser beating than the others.

"You…" The Runt pointed at Mac.

"There's no point doing this unless you ask us some questions," Rashid said measuredly. "Where's your boss?" Shrek stepped forwards and aimed the pistol at Rashid's face. He smiled, his wretched face both red and covered in perspiration. He looked the type of man to break into a sweat tying his own shoes. The pistol shook unsteadily in his hands, his sausage fingers making the Beretta model 92 look smaller than Rashid knew it to be. He cocked the hammer and stepped a little closer, before pulling the trigger. Rashid's legs shot out and he flinched as the hammer clicked. Both Albanians roared with laughter, and Shrek worked the slide-action, chambering a 9mm bullet. He aimed again, and Rashid settled, relaxed, and staring back defiantly. "Go fuck your mother, you fat piece of shit," he said. He could have cursed his reaction to the man's torment, but he was damned if he was going to go out begging and snivelling. The gun was loaded now, so if he was at the end of the road, then so be it.

"Rashid!" Mac exclaimed. "Don't give the fucker the satisfaction, mate!"

Shrek turned the pistol on the Scotsman, the same sadistic grin on his face.

"This guy must save a fortune on greetings cards," Goldie quipped. "What with his sister being his own mother and his dad being his own uncle." He looked at Shrek and grinned. "Family gatherings must be a bit confusing, but a small affair…"

Shrek stepped away from Mac and turned the pistol on the Londoner, his pasty white fingers gripping the pistol - and the trigger - more firmly than he should have. All three men knew the risks of a ND, or negligent discharge, and the risks of it happening right now was high. Rashid needed to defuse the situation.

"Let's talk to your boss again," he said calmly. "Come on, we're all men here. You know we had to hold out for a while. Maybe it's time for us to start talking?"

"The plan has changed," said The Runt in stilted English. "We have another use for you, now."

"Then whatever it is, we'll be more use to you if we're still alive. We need more water," he said calmly. "And food."

"We'll see," said The Runt. He nodded for Shrek to cover him, then produced a pair of handcuffs from his pocket. "But until then, we will still have our fun, no?"

23

St. Petersburg, Russia

King watched as the man approached. He was unhurried, a little unstable on his feet. He stopped, uninterested in people in the street around him and he leaned against a lamppost twenty feet from him, took out a pouch of tobacco and rolled a cigarette. He seemed drunk, but King knew it was merely part of his act. The man was a pro, and MI5 had invested thousands in him. Ramsay had told King that when he was no longer useful, or if he lived long enough without his cover being blown, there was a quaint stone cottage in the Lake District with his name on it.

King turned his attention to the woman outside the club across the street. She wore a leather miniskirt and stockings, with the tiniest amount of suspender belt visible when she moved, which was generally every few seconds to balance on the four-inch heels of the knee-length leather boots. Her legs were both long and shapely, and her hips swelled before pinching in at her waist. The warm late summer evening meant she could wear a silk top that showed most of her midriff, which was flat and firm and showed her pierced navel, which was adorned with a simple diamond stud.

King watched her as she waited outside the bar, phone in hand and looking to be seriously annoyed by something. She had turned down a couple of propositions from men as they passed, and he was sure there would be more. He certainly hoped so, at least.

Then he watched the man pause at the top steps of the club. King studied him, had a feeling this was his man. Something about the over-confidence, the arrogance of the man told him that he thought he was untouchable. The bar was one of Romanovitch's enterprises and was an exclusive caviar and vodka bar but served far more besides. A less than salubrious list of services. It had become popular with the so-called St. Petersburg elite, and offered a series of private rooms where high-stakes gambling took place, as well as transactions of the flesh which could be made with some of the hostesses. Nothing was truly off-limits and several of the barmen were casual 'acquaintances' of some of the regulars, both men and women alike. Romanovitch kept many of his more attractive, and somewhat more attentive women for this place and regular complimentary visits from the corrupt chief of police kept the facility and its much-coveted licence in place.

King looked back at the man leaning against the lamppost. He had barely started to smoke his cigarette, but he flicked it into the road. King watched the cigarette spark on the tarmac. The man walked away. Job done. He'd identified the target for King.

Vasyli lit a cigar at the top of the steps and exchanged a few words with the tough looking doorman. He nodded as if in agreement with something the man had said, then both men watched the woman talking animatedly on the phone, her suspenders showing as she paced around. Vasyli laughed at something the doorman said, and then tossed his match to the side and dropped down the three steps to the pavement.

King studied the man's body language. The big Russian hesitated for a moment, then approached her. King tensed. Vasyli asked the woman something, then nodded. The two of them talked for a few minutes, then he touched her on the shoulder. The woman laughed and he moved his hand towards her pert breast. She smiled, touched his waist and then the two of them turned around and Vasyli guided her towards his Bentley, which was parked twenty metres further up the street, under the watch of the doorman. King waited for them to get into the car, then started the engine of the Land Rover Defender 110. He watched the Bentley pull out, then drove steadily behind them, allowing a couple of vehicles to get between them, then he settled in at thirty-miles-per-hour and dropped far enough back to become invisible. Or at least insignificant. The Bentley's windows were heavily tinted, so he could not see inside, but he imagined what the Russian would be asking her. Or now that she was in the vehicle, ordering her to do.

The Bentley turned without an indicator and the street was lined with parked cars. No opportunity to stop. King flicked off dips and onto sidelights, which would give the impression he was a long way behind. He kept the turbo diesel V5 engine at medium revs in third gear, because timing would be everything and he wanted a good surge of acceleration if he was to do this right. The Bentley turned again, no indicators. King made the turn, too. He could see the luxury grand tourer slowing, the driver hesitant. Vasyli was clearly assessing where to do the deed, he wanted no streetlights, a quiet spot. King could see the best place for an illicit assignation up ahead on the right. He watched the Bentley pull across the crown of the road as the Russian saw it, too. King hit the accelerator and moved his thumbs to the edge of the wheel to avoid breaking them upon impact. The Land Rover's revs climbed as it surged forwards and he hoped that Alaina had remembered to wear her seatbelt. The Russians were without any reasonable doubt the worst drivers in the world, and he couldn't stress to her enough, that she should be buckled in from the moment she entered his vehicle.

The solid metal bumpers of the Defender tore into the Bentley's door and the two-and-a-half-ton beast was slammed into the kerb by the force of the impact. King reversed out a few feet, then got out and raised the pistol, firing three shots down through the Bentley's bonnet and into the engine bay. He aimed the weapon and shot out the front tyre, then the rear, and then fired through the glass beside the B pillar, missing Vasyli's head by a few inches and deflating the side airbag, as the dazed and confused Russian wondered what had just happened to his world. King jammed the pistol through the broken window and pressed the scalding muzzle against the man's temple.

"Get out," he said, coldly. "Slowly…" He looked at Alaina, who was looking just as dazed and confused as the driver. "Are you okay?"

"Y… Yes…" she managed, reaching for the door handle. She was covered in white residue from the resin in the deployed airbags, and the main airbag was deflating in her lap. King could see it had bloodied her nose when it had deployed.

King tried to get the door open, but it was jammed shut by the impact. He signalled for the Russian to climb over the centre console. He jabbed the man with the pistol again. Vasyli struggled to clamber out, scraping the leather and falling into the gutter the other side of the vehicle. King was already around the other side and he gave the man a kick in the ribs and side of the head to keep control of him, then dropped onto the man's back, his knees digging into him as he positioned his hands and attached two pairs of heavy duty cable ties to his wrists. He then reached inside the man's jacket pocket, retrieved a Makarov pistol, and tucked it into his own back pocket.

"Get up!" King shouted as he stood to the

side. He pulled him to his feet and jabbed the gun into the man's ribs as he frog-marched him around the ruined Bentley and into the back of the Land Rover. He used another two cable-ties to fasten him to the door handle, then waited for Alaina to get into the passenger seat.

"You are making a mistake…" Vasyli spluttered, his mouth bloody, his lips swollen. "You are signing your own death warrant…"

"Shut up!" King snapped at him, and punched him in the side of the head, rocking him on the spot and causing his head to loll as he battled unconsciousness.

Alaina got inside and closed the door. She was ashen and detached. She reached into the footwell and took out a bag, pulling items of clothing out as King started the Land Rover and pulled back out onto the street. "I need to get out of these stupid clothes!" she announced. "What kind of idiot goes for all this?" she smiled at King. "But it worked."

King dropped the .45 Heckler and Koch USP into the door pocket and looked across at her. "Well done," he said.

"I wasn't expecting it," she said. "I mean, I knew it was coming at some point, but holy shit!"

Alaina undid the skirt and pulled it down, then untangled the suspenders and stockings and ripped them off. "I feel ridiculous in these things."

King glanced and saw she was wearing only a pair of skimpy black knickers. He averted his eyes but caught the Russian sneering at him in the rear-view mirror. He turned his eyes back to the road and sensed she was pulling on her jeans, her pelvis pressed into the air to button them up. She pulled on her trainers and then set about tearing off the silk blouse and replacing it with a thin cashmere sweater. She bundled up the clothes and stuffed them into the bag, then pulled the seatbelt back over her.

"What do you want from me?" Vasyli asked defiantly. "You are foolish. My boss will cut you into tiny pieces and use you as bait when he goes fishing next. He holds records for pike in the Baltic."

"Pike are a freshwater fish," replied King nonchalantly.

Vasyli chuckled. "There is much you do not know. Like the Baltic Sea is the only sea in the world to contain pike, that also return to the rivers. And they grow to twice the normal size because of their life in the sea. Much like barracuda, who enjoy eating tiny pieces of human flesh." He paused. "And the fact that my boss will not only kill you for this, but your families, too."

"He's already killed my sister!" Alaina snapped. "That's why I'm here!"

Vasyli looked at her, then smiled as it dawned on him. Perhaps the plainer clothes helped. "You're the maid…" he said in Russian. "Oh, Romanovitch is going to like this very much!"

King was conversational in the spoken Russian language but would not indulge him. Instead he said in English, "Not as much as he when he realises you were instrumental in me ripping him off. Maybe he'll take you fishing, too."

Vasyli cursed him in Russian, and Alaina sneered at him over her shoulder. He looked at her and smirked. "You suited the clothes you wore back there. Maybe before this is over you will be working in one of Romanovitch's whore houses."

"Ignore him," said King, sensing her tense beside him.

"So, he killed your sister and you want

revenge? That would make sense. Even a worthless peasant means something to someone. But not Romanovitch. If he couldn't get an income out of her, then what was she worth? Just another filthy bitch from the Ukraine." He sighed. "What a place? All farm labourers with rough hands and tired bones. Your sister could pick flowers or cabbages all day long, but she couldn't make her sex convincing. Shame…" He paused. "I recognise her in you, now. The stuck-up bitch who wanted to succeed in business. The one who thought she was important enough, valued enough to turn down Romanovitch's advances and remain his personal assistant. Like it was a regular business. Silly bitch! That's why she fed the bears. But not before she did what she had never wanted to do all along. And when the boss had finished, we all had a go. Now, something like that will happen to you. Bears in the Urals, pike in the Baltic. You will simply disappear without trace," he smiled.

Alaina spun in her seat and tried to hit out, but her seatbelt tugged her back in place. She struggled against it, then undid her belt and rained her fists upon him. Vasyli ducked his head and laughed. "That's it, silly bitch! Put some spirit into it, like your sister could not!"

King slowed to a stop, pulled the handbrake, and put the gearstick into neutral. He picked up the USP, pushed Alaina aside, then calmly jabbed the pistol into the man's mouth. Vasyli recoiled and spluttered and spat out chips of teeth into his lap. King jabbed the pistol again, this time into the man's ribs and he wheezed. King heard the crack of breaking ribs. He turned around in his seat and placed the pistol back into the door pocket. He looked at Alaina, who was breathing hard and staring at the Russian, her eyes full of hate and malice. King recognised the look in her eyes. She wanted to kill the man in the seat behind her, wanted to kill anybody who stood in her way. She was dangerous to be around, like a caged animal wanting to escape. But he could see the spark of intelligence in her eyes, the resolve behind them. She had risked a great deal on her quest for a vendetta. She had infiltrated the Russian mafia, walked in the same footsteps as her sister, but she was still here. Even with the knowledge of what had happened to her, Alaina still hadn't been scared off.

King ignored Vasyli's groaning behind him and carried on driving until they reached the train terminal, then skirted the access road until he arrived at a dimly lit industrial complex. There were multiple compounds, each with the name of the company in Cyrillic lettering, many having no English translation. King could speak Russian, but he couldn't read it very well and Alaina was squinting through the gloom at the signs.

"You'll never get it open." Vasyli said thickly, his lips swollen, and teeth chipped and sore. "I will never help you get what you want."

King shrugged. "I think you will."

"I am not scared of you, Englishman. I have known tougher men than you." He paused. "Nothing you threaten me with or do to me will make me do anything for you. I am loyal to my boss."

"Then, you have a distinct lack of imagination," replied King. "As we shall soon see."

Alaina directed King through the maze of access roads, and they drove slowly past a security hut, but the guard on duty was busy watching a small portable television and drinking something from a mug. King glanced at Vasyli and could already see the doubt in the man's eyes. They would turn to fear soon enough. Nobody reacted well to the threat of pain and the unknown. Not when they were as vulnerable as the tethered Russian in the back seat. King had seen it before, and he had felt it, too.

King pulled the Land Rover to a halt under a row of trees, across the carpark belonging to a large warehouse. He switched off the engine and killed the lights. He opened the window a crack, not enjoying the feeling of being isolated from the outside sounds. The heavy semi-automatic pistol was threaded for a suppressor, which King now screwed into the muzzle. He dropped the magazine, took a handful of .45 bullets out of his pocket and replaced the six rounds he had fired back at the ambush. Back there, time had been of the essence and he had not wanted to wield the weapon with the heavy suppressor, nor take the chance of the weapon failing to cycle and suffer a stoppage because of the decrease in gas blowback. However, silence was of the essence now, and he already had the Russian mafia enforcer under his control. He glanced at Vasyli, noticing the man's apparent interest in the weapon. People tended to take a silenced weapon more seriously somehow. As if the threat of noise – and the .45 certainly made a great deal of that – would somehow offer an element of protection, whereas a silenced weapon lessened the threat of the user being caught and made the weapon altogether more useable. King wasn't sure what the theory was exactly, but he had found that screwing a suppressor into a weapon offered a sense of drama and threat that was inescapable. People stared at it, and they generally started talking.

"How do you know about this place?" Vasyli asked, his eyes still on the weapon in King's hands.

"We have our ways."

"Who?"

"We."

"Who's we?" Vasyli asked, then shrugged as he looked at Alaina. "Apart from a vengeful maid seeking retribution for a tragic whore."

King watched Alaina clench her fist and shook his head at her. "Plenty of time for that," he said, opening the door. He walked around the Land Rover and opened the rear passenger door, pressing the muzzle of the suppressor right up against the Russian's eyeball. The man gritted his teeth together tightly and flinched. "If you make a sound, try to alert anybody, then I will break your thoracic vertebrae. You'll spend the rest of your days in a chair and pissing into a bag at the very least." He let up on the man's eye, taking the pistol away and watching him blink profusely. Even in the gloom King could see the tears and redness. The man would be seeing white stars for a while, which would make him think twice about running. If he couldn't see, then he couldn't escape. King took out his knife, thumbed it open and sliced through the cable ties securing him to the door handle. If the Russian was going to try anything then it would surely be now, so King stepped back and held the pistol close to his ribs. Close enough to get off a couple of shots, but far enough away that he would not be able to kick the weapon from him or make a lunge with his tethered hands.

"There is nothing here," Vasyli said quietly. "You are wasting your time."

"That's not what I heard."

The Russian shook his head. "You will not get away with this."

"We'll see." King shoved him forwards. The man's legs were unsteady, and he rolled along the side of the vehicle. King remained at a distance, the weapon aimed from his waist. "Make a sound and I'll put a bullet in you."

Alaina followed them as they made for the door of the building. It was a brick-built factory, or at least had been once. King guessed it had been repurposed decades ago, and now modern purpose-built buildings had sprung up around it, like industrial estates the world over. King kept his distance and said to Vasyli when he reached the door, "Open it."

"No."

King reached out and grabbed a handful of the man's hair. He pushed him forwards and snatched his hand backwards, tearing out a sizeable patch. Vasyli howled, then turned and spat in King's face.

"You pull my hair like a bitch?"

King shrugged, wiped the spit away, then dried his fingers on his trousers. He glanced around him, the gloom emitted from the streetlamps not giving him the darkness he would have preferred. "I said, open it."

"And I said, no."

King studied the keypad and screen of the entry unit. "Fingerprint recognition?" He paused, taking his knife out from his pocket. He had the Russian's attention, and as he beckoned Alaina forwards, Vasyli frowned. King held out the pistol for her. "Cover him while I cut his thumb off," he said.

"Okay," she replied and took the pistol off him.

"No, wait!" Vasyli said quickly. King ignored him, kicked out the man's feet and pushed him against the door as he fell. He stepped into the back of the man's knee, grinding the kneecap into the tread of the step, and pinning him in place. King opened the blade and caught hold of the man's wrist. "No!"

King ran the back of the blade across the man's thumb joint, the cold steel making the man flinch. "Going to open it?"

"Yes! Yes!"

King pulled the man up to his feet and pushed him against the door. "Get it done, then."

Vasyli checked his thumb, scowling as he looked for blood that was not there. He was angry that he had been duped, but he knew the merry-go-round was already in motion. If he refused, then King may well cut him for real, and if he gave way so quickly before, then it was safe to assume he would do so again. King had bluffed, and Vasyli had been called. The Russian looked defeated, and he dejectedly pressed his thumb against the screen on the keypad and the door clicked open. King stepped back and taking the pistol off Alaina, he ushered the man inside with the muzzle of the weapon.

King could hear the hum of voices somewhere, the sound muffled by the sheer volume of the building. They were in a storage bay crowded with luxury cars and boxes, and the light emitted from a door at the end of the bay told King that was where they should head next. King counted a dozen BMW saloons and SUVs with as many Mercedes parked in rows behind. Stolen from Europe and ready for resale in Russia. As his eyes grew accustomed to the darkness, he could see the shapes of performance cars as well. Millions of euros worth of vehicles about to be lost forever. He suspected many would end up in China and Southeast Asia as well.

"How many men?" he asked.

Vasyli shrugged. "Two. It is the nightshift."

King thought his surmise was vague at best, but he did not trust a word the Russian said, so he figured there may well be more. He did not have a spare magazine for the weapon, so twelve rounds were all he had, with four loose bullets in his pocket. Not great. But on the plus side, it was a .45 and the bullets were soft-nosed hollow-points, so one shot per threat should be all he needed. He certainly did not want the situation to escalate to that, but after twenty years in this line of work, he knew plan B was always the way it worked out. If he was lucky.

The door to the office opened and the loading area was swathed in light. King jabbed the pistol into Vasyli's neck. He pushed the Russian forwards, then paused beside a Range Rover which had been parked facing the office. The vehicle broke their shape in the darkness. King glared at the Russian, daring him to make a sound. Vasyli looked back at him, but he did not say anything, did not move. They watched the man walk out of the office and across the loading bay to a stack of cases. He opened the lid to a crate, then sauntered back to the office carrying two bottles of vodka. King could hear voices and laughter, see movement within. As the door closed, he stared at Vasyli and said, "Two my arse. There's way more than that in there."

The Russian smiled. "Maybe you should go home?" He paused. "You're playing games you can't afford to play."

King looked inside the Range Rover, saw the key-fob resting in the centre console near the vehicle's retracted gear control. He was familiar with the vehicle, when the ignition start button was pressed, the giant chrome button rose proud of the console and it was a simple twist which would select drive or reverse. King looked at Alaina and said, "Keep him covered." He handed her the Makarov. "Just point it at his gut and pull the trigger if he moves."

She nodded. "My father had a pistol just like it, from his military service. He showed me how to shoot tin cans and bottles. I will not miss."

King stared at Vasyli. "Well, your gut is a damned sight bigger than a tin can," he said. "You want to bear that in mind."

Vasyli sneered, but said nothing.

King opened the door of the Range Rover and belted up. He pressed the ignition button, and the headlights came on as a default. He would have to be quick. He waited impatiently for the gear control to rise out of the centre console, then started the engine and twisted the selector into drive. The handbrake came off automatically as he crept forwards, and as the door to the office started to open – the sound of the vehicle's engine breaking up whatever party was in progress – King floored the accelerator pedal and the behemoth surged forward driven by a mighty V8 engine which vented through two throaty exhausts.

The door opened, but the inquisitive soul had no room to move as two tonnes of metal smashed through the office wall and deep inside the room. The airbags deployed, and King felt the force impact against his face, the seatbelt snapping him back into his seat. There was a cloud of resin in the air, the smell of explosives from the detonation of the airbags. King unfastened the seatbelt, his eyes blurred from the impact and resin in the air. He got out of the door, the room brightly lit from the light inside, the headlights of the vehicle and annoyingly, the hazard lights flashing amber either by accident, or by design.

King saw two men. One getting up from a pile of debris, the other reaching for a Kalashnikov in the corner of the room. He aimed and fired at the man reaching for the weapon. The bullet hit the man between his shoulder blades, and he was propelled forwards and rested still on the floor. The second man had reached inside his jacket pocket his hand now frozen to the spot, but King couldn't give the man any quarter at that stage. That was when bad things happened. He fired once, centre mass, and the man went down.

Gunshots erupted on the other side of the vehicle and King ducked down as glass blew out of the Range Rover's offside rear windows and bullets tracked towards him through the bodywork. King only saw muzzle flashes, and he aimed and fired two shots at them. He wasn't sure if he'd managed to hit the gunman, but he had stopped him in his tracks. King darted to the front of the vehicle, took a knee, and surveyed the scene through the sights of his weapon. He saw movement near some filing cabinets, then ducked as the muzzle flashes started up again and bullets rained all around him. He dropped onto his stomach and returned fire. Two shots. Six bullets remaining. And a few loose in his pocket, for all the good they would do him there.

King rolled across the room, the splintered door and smashed partition wall uneven beneath him. He found himself rolling over the man in the doorway. He was a mess, but quite dead. His Makarov pistol was still in his hand, so King relieved him of it and tucked it into his back pocket. He fumbled for the loose rounds and hurriedly dropped the magazine, reloaded, and slammed the magazine back in place. Twelve rounds and a new feeling of empowerment in place. He edged forwards, this time seeing a figure move cautiously between two desks. He aimed and fired, but clearly missed. The man ducked down, and King got to his feet and sprinted across the debris, the pistol outstretched in front of him. When the man chanced a look, King fired twice, then skidded to a halt, dropped to one knee, and fired two more shots through the back of the desk. He heard a thump behind the desk, figured he'd hit his target, so he stood up and edged around it in a wide arc. The man was dead, his eyes wide open with an Uzi 9mm machine pistol across his chest, the barrel still smoking. King continued past, checking the corners of the room and the other desks. Four men down. Four men guarding the warehouse, drinking vodka, playing cards. It was enough for a nightshift and he doubted there would be anybody else, but he would keep on checking the entire building after he returned to Vasyli and Alaina. He wondered how well the old building would have absorbed the gunshots, and whether he still had time to do what he came here to do, or whether he should cut and run. He glanced at his watch. It would take at least ten minutes for police to arrive on the scene, even if a patrol car was outside the complex, which he doubted. He still had time.

"Put the gun down…"

King froze, Vasyli's voice had taken on an air of confidence. He turned around slowly to see Alaina standing directly in front of him. She was a good few inches shorter than Vasyli, and King could see from the man's top lip upwards. The muzzle of the Makarov was touching her right temple. Vasyli was flanked by two men. Both aiming shiny stainless-steel Beretta automatics at him. The men were both tough looking with matching broken noses. King would attest to them being brothers. The blinking hazard lights lit up a network of tattoos that crept from their collars and teased at their faces.

"I'm sorry," said Alaina sheepishly.

"Don't worry about it," King replied. He had the .45 USP pointing to the floor, but near enough to them to cause at least one of them some discomfort if they fired upon him first. He figured that if they were going to shoot him then they would have done it by now. No, Vasyli wanted a little retribution. A beating, some cutting. King had a broad imagination, and it didn't take the darker recesses of his mind to come up with a playlist of these guys greatest hits. He looked at what he could see of Vasyli and said, "So, this is the part where you tell me to put down the gun…"

"I've already said that."

"Ah, yes. I heard it, but I didn't *feel* it."

"You soon will."

King smiled. "Right."

One of the men said something in Russian. Vasyli shook his head. King knew that he was asking if he should shoot him in the head. He didn't recognise the derogatory term the man had used about him. King had come to realise that most Russian insults involved having sex with farm animals. He wasn't sure what animal he'd been accused of doing, but he got the gist.

"You want what is in Romanovitch's safe," Vasyli stated.

"If you don't mind."

Vasyli glanced to the far side of the room and laughed. King followed his gaze, then looked back at him. "You are what the Americans call a wise ass." Vasyli paused. King could not see the whole of the man's mouth moving in sync with his voice with Alaina's head in the way and it sounded a little disconcerting, as if someone were narrating. "Now, hopefully you aren't just a wise ass, but you are wise enough to know that you are outnumbered, and that I hold all the cards. A gun to her head, and two guns on you. You must be low on ammunition, too. It's not looking good for you." He paused. "And less so, for your friends." King frowned and the Russian smiled. "You are part of the failed operation to get between us and the Albanian Brotherhood for Kontroll. What a ridiculous name?" He laughed. "Fucking peasants, fishermen and goat herders with an eye on easy money and who have watched too many Francis Ford Coppola and Martin Scorsese movies!"

King said nothing. He was judging the distance between himself and the three men. He was ten feet from them, and the men were evenly spaced. King noticed they were graded in height from left to right. Shortest to tallest. Not much, maybe an inch each. Three inches from end to end. Less than the amount of muzzle rise he'd expect from the .45, but about right for the recoil of a 9mm Makarov. King straightened, eased himself a little to his left.

"Drop the gun," Vasyli said coldly.

"What do you know about the men running this operation against you?"

Vasyli shrugged. "The Albanians have them," he said conceitedly.

"So, they're still alive?" King asked.

"Yes," he smiled menacingly. "But not for long. Not in any real sense, because Romanovitch is travelling there to see them. The Albanians have offered them to him in return for a bigger slice of the pie." He moved the pistol away from Alaina's neck and beckoned King with it. "Now, I won't ask you again," he said, placing the muzzle back against Alaina's head. "Drop the gun on the floor!"

King shrugged. He steadily moved a few inches to his left and felt the heft of the pistol in his hand as if weighing it as much as his options, before tossing it at the nearest man's feet. King was handy enough throwing knives and axes. It was a good discipline for accuracy, technique, and control, and he always reckoned it could come in handy one day. He was accustomed to estimating weight and volume and being familiar with the amount of spin and how many revolutions it would take to reach a target. In this case, the cocked hammer on the hard, concrete floor.

The pistol fired, the .45 resonating loudly inside the building. Alaina screamed and flinched to her left. The nearest man hopped somewhat ridiculously out of the way and Vasyli was reaching for Alaina. King already had the Makarov out from his back pocket and took a step forwards as he fired at the nearest man's forehead. He was aware that he had hit his target, but was already tracking the pistol across to Vasyli, just eight feet away. He fired, aiming right between the man's eyes, just over Alaina's head, then sighted on the third man as Vasyli crumpled to the floor. The man raised his pistol but could not get it around Alaina and on target. King fired and the man went down. No more than two seconds had passed since the USP had gone off, and Alaina was still moving out of the way. The .45 pistol was still sliding across the floor. All three men were either dead or dying and Vasyli's feet were twitching wildly, but he wasn't going anywhere. The men's height differences had helped, with each rise of the muzzle at the weapon's recoil, he found himself aiming exactly where he wanted to, simply easing the pistol two feet or so to the right with every shot.

King picked up Vasyli's Makarov and ejected the magazine. He switched it over with the one in his own weapon and pocketed the other, before tossing the man's weapon aside.

Alaina was stunned. She was shaking, staring at the three bodies on the floor. She hovered over Vasyli's body, staring down at his wide-open eyes and the gaping hole between them. "We need to get out of here…" she said quietly, not taking her eyes off the macabre sight of the bullet hole. There was brain matter visible and blood was draining from the unseen exit wound, the bullet hole looking like a bath drain, unplugged. She remained transfixed, and King broke her stare by touching her on the shoulder.

"We need to go," he concurred. "But I want what is in that safe, first." He stepped over the debris, bypassed another body, and headed for the filing cabinet Vasyli had glanced at. "Here, help me with this," he said over his shoulder. It was important to get Alaina moving. He could see she was bordering on shock, and then she'd be good for nothing.

She picked her way through the debris of broken tables and chairs, and where part of the ceiling had fallen in when the doorframe had been bulldozed out by the Range Rover. She tried to avoid looking at the bodies, but failed as she looked into the cold, dead eyes of the man with the Uzi. "Oh, god!"

"Romanovitch's men," said King. "Indirectly responsible for your sister's death. They are the lifeblood, or were, of his organisation, and that organisation cannot function without foot soldiers like these guys. From these lackeys to Vasyli and then all the way up to Romanovitch himself."

King bent down and looked at the cabinet. The other cabinet had moved when the man with the Uzi had taken cover. However, this cabinet had not shifted a bit. He gave it a shove with his foot, but there was no give. On reflection, the man with the Uzi should have tucked himself up against this, but there was never any sense in how people acted in a firefight. King had seen seasoned soldiers take cover behind bushes rather than sturdier options nearby. Sometimes the thought processes just didn't link up to the body's instincts.

"What is so important here?" Alaina asked. "Money? There were millions in the safe in Albania."

King pulled out the false drawer concealing the safe inside the cabinet. "Not money," he said, shaking his head. "Something far more valuable."

"What, then?"

King took the key he had made from Alaina's soap mould. He looked at her and said, "Power…"

24

Albania-Greece Border

Rashid slumped on the floor, the cold, hard stone jarring him to the core. The beating had lasted more than twenty-minutes. The equivalent of six rounds of boxing, but without corner breaks, gloves, a referee or being able to hit back. With four men taking turns. It was a wonder he was still alive. His nose had been broken, and he was sure his cheek bone and orbit had cracked. All his ribs had been bruised, and a few had been broken for certain. He had lost a molar as well, and the metal tang of blood filled his taste buds and stung his lips as he had spat, but his survival instincts had soon kicked in and he had swallowed every last drop of blood thereafter. The liquid was packed with precious nutrients he could ill afford to lose, and his stomach and organs would be grateful for the hit, even if it only served to balance the loss of blood.

"Well done, mate…" Goldie said. He watched Rashid roll carefully onto his side, then shouted at Shrek as he yanked him across the stone floor to tether his wrist to the wall. "You bastard!"

The Runt aimed his pistol at him and smiled as Goldie flinched. "Big man..." he leered. "Your time will come again soon."

"Aye, and so will yours, yer wee cock!" Mac growled. He grinned manically as the pistol was turned on him. "Ah, away with you, yer little shit..."

The Runt stared at him, and Shrek stood behind him menacingly. Rashid tried to sit up but rasped as his ribs moved and sent a stab of pain through him. The two men turned to him and smiled gleefully.

Philosopher had barely moved since he had been brought back into the cell. He was lying on his stomach with his left hand outstretched to the shackle. He was breathing shallow rasps. Before either of the men could protest, The Runt aimed his pistol at the back of the man's head and fired. The gunshot sounded like cannon-fire in the confines of the room, and the stonework bounced the sound around, echoing both in noise and ominous finality. The bullet ricocheted off the stone walls, no telling how many times, and landed at Rashid's feet in a twisted, deformed mess of copper and lead.

Philosopher's body twitched before resting still, but the spread of blood washed across the floor like a tsunami, a single wave followed by a swell of mass, crimson in colour with a viscosity that meant it appeared to constantly push forwards, contaminating all before it. The blood reached Mac, who at first pulled his feet out of its path, but was soon left sitting in it, resigned to the fact there was no escaping the torrent.

Rashid watched his friend bleed out. The brain did not shut down immediately after such trauma. He had seen it before. But that did not mean he would ever get used to it. There were pints of it, almost a bucketful, and as the men stared transfixed at the macabre scene, powerless in their restraints, the flow slowed suddenly, then ceased altogether.

Nobody said a word. Nobody taunted their captors. The stark reality of what may yet be their fate, a constant reminder in front of them.

The Runt and Shrek closed the door behind them as they left. Still nobody said a word. But Rashid slowly opened his hand and looked at the twisted bullet he had picked up as both of his captors had watched Philosopher dying on the floor. His palm was bloody and dirty, but the bullet glinted in the light, the gleaming copper as bright as the opportunity that had just been presented.

25

Albania

Flymo had collected the freight from the port of Vlore using the details King had forwarded to him. The freight was being held in a bonded warehouse and the usual customs checks had been bypassed under the Diplomatic Act. The manifest had simply said: Farm Machinery. The crates were yet to be unpacked, but he had installed two external fuel tanks underneath the fuselage of the helicopter, and a complex bladder system was now under the rear seats that served as an emergency fuel supply. If his calculations were correct, then the craft would now have a range of seven hundred miles. However, the calculations changed when he factored in the use of fuel and the weight difference the burned fuel would make. He was coming up with a figure closer to eight hundred, but he preferred to err on the side of caution. The extra fuel would greatly affect the helicopter's speed and handling, a factor he would have to consider along with the altitude at which they would be flying. He was now contemplating the crates, and how in god's name he would fly anywhere without sparking a war footing with Albania's military forces.

King had made a brief report and uploaded it into the shared cloud. Ramsay would already be sifting through it. Along with the report, King's movements were being data logged via his mobile phone. He had risen early and taken a run, showered with the house's limited hot water supply, and eaten a breakfast of fried eggs and toast, washing it down with several cups of tea. Alaina was showering, but only drank black coffee in the mornings.

Flymo walked into the kitchen and nodded at the kettle. "Tea?"

"No, I'm fine," replied King.

"Successful trip?"

King thought about the USBs he had collected from Romanovitch's safe and nodded. He had couriered them to a safehouse address in Kensington, where they would then be forwarded to Thames House. It never paid to write MI5's address on anything sensitive. The offshore account information, the details of his empire waiting to be picked apart by MI5's forensic accountants, the task force that would soon be put in place, possibly with Interpol but perhaps not, as the Russians would then become involved and the waters would become muddied somewhat. Either way, Romanovitch would be lucky to come out of it unscathed, his organisation in tatters. Alaina had taken great solace in this, retribution for her sister, but she wasn't done just yet. She wanted blood.

"So, you've tackled the fuel problem," said King. "What about the *farm machinery*?" he asked.

"I'm going to start after this," he said, holding up the mug. He tossed in a teabag and poured on boiling water. "I could do with a hand," he added.

"You'll get it." King paused. "Alaina can help, too."

"Help do what?" She breezed in, her hair damp from the shower, her half-empty cup of coffee in her hand.

"Some lifting and holding, while I do the welding," Flymo replied.

"Oh, alright," she replied. "I will make another coffee," she said, looking at King. "Do you want one?"

King shook his head. He was thinking about St. Petersburg and the deception he had left in place, and he was wondering just how long it would last. After he had stripped the safe of every scrap of information that could be used against Romanovitch, he had tossed the bundles of currency into boxes and stacked them in the Land Rover, along with Vasyli's body, which he had wrapped in packing sheets and secured with parcel tape.

Outside, the night had been still, and the drizzle had seemed to envelop the glow of the sporadic streetlamps, encapsulating the industrial estate in an orange hue. Sirens had been audible in the distance. No surprise really, somebody would have heard the gunfire inside the warehouse, but the token security presence must have called a report in and remained in his booth watching his portable TV and sipping on coffee or vodka – or perhaps both – and earning his basic wage without risk.

King had driven to an area near the docks where he had earlier scoped out a stony beach with a steep drop off. Unbeknown to him, the same beach Rashid and his *Penguins* had used to launch from to take down Romanovitch's shipping warehouse months before. King had ditched the Land Rover along with Vasyli's body inside, watching it sink slowly and pirouette to the bottom, lost to the black waters of the Baltic, a sliver of moonlight glinting on the surface. His Bentley would soon be found, and it would quickly be assumed by the police that there had been a gang takeover attempt, or a carjacking gone wrong. However, King hoped Romanovitch would see Vasyli's disappearance and the missing contents of his safe as treachery at the hands of his number one enforcer.

"Are you alright?" Alaina asked, snapping King back. "You looked a little zoned-out there."

King nodded. Since she had recovered from seeing the eyes of the dead man with the Uzi, lifeless, accepting and final, Alaina had not baulked at preparing Vasyli's corpse for transportation, nor at sending it to the bottom of the Baltic Sea. In fact, King could swear she had looked gleeful, but had later denied it when he had mentioned it on the plane. They had flown out before dawn, slept little and she had not once seemed troubled by the events. "Just wondering whether what we did in St. Petersburg will work for us," he replied. "Or whether I've wasted time that could have been better spent looking for my friend."

"But you've continued with the brief," Flymo commented. "It's a game of chess, not snap. If Romanovitch is unsettled, then he may make a mistake. And now you've taken measures to see him put out of business." He shrugged. "And we don't know if the team are being held at that mountain fortress, whether they've been moved or even if they're still alive. Either way, you've greatly weakened Romanovitch's organisation."

King nodded. "I suppose," he said, then drained his cup of tea and stood up. "Better get to it, then."

26

They had come for Philosopher's body the next morning. The blood had congealed, smelling both sweet and pungent. Rashid had watched his friend's body move throughout the night. The gasses building within him. Rigor mortis had set in and both The Runt and Shrek had given the body a kick, decided it would be too awkward to move and returned later that afternoon after the chemical process had worn off and the body had turned flaccid once more. The men watched, subdued. Shrek had returned with a hose and sluiced the blood away, then tossed three bottles of water and a whole loaf on the wet floor.

"See you next Tuesday…" said Mac, just before the door closed. Shrek turned and looked at him, then slammed the door and bolted it behind him. Mac blew out a deep sigh.

"What?" asked Goldie, reaching for the bread. He tore it into three pieces and tossed them towards the other two.

"You spell it out, using the first letter," Mac replied, kicking one of the bottles towards Rashid. "So, C U Next Tuesday…"

Goldie laughed. "Daft bugger." He

glanced at the space Philosopher had once taken up, then looked at Rashid. "What the hell are we going to do, boss? We're fucked…"

Rashid put the damaged bullet down on the ground beside him. He had worked his nails into it, had managed to peel some of the copper coating away from the lead core. His nails were broken, and his fingers were bleeding. They turned the bread pink as he picked it up and tore off a piece. He found it difficult to chew, his broken tooth sore and jagged. His gums and lips were raw. He swallowed as best he could, the bread going down like glass. "We hang in there," he said. He had not told them about the bullet. He did not want to give them false hope. He drank the whole bottle of water down, the cuts inside his mouth stinging as if he had chewed upon nettles. He picked up the bullet and slipped what was left of his thumbnail between the copper and lead and continued to worry it. "They won't turn their backs on us."

"MI5?" Mac scoffed. "We're as good as done for!"

Rashid shook his head. "Not everyone will sit back and do nothing," he said. "Just hang in there…"

27

King looked at the mountainside. It was rocky and wooded, but also with vast clear areas of scree and cactus, with tufts of grasses growing from the crevices. It was a harsh environment and although it was late summer, the temperature was still around thirty degrees centigrade.

"It's quite a hike," said Alaina.

King shut the boot down on the Suzuki Vitara and locked the vehicle with the fob. He held the key up for her to see, then knelt and placed it in the springs of the front suspension. "Just so we don't lose them," he said, but he really meant, *just in case something happens to me you can still get away...* "It is a hike, but I don't want to give ourselves away with the helicopter."

King and Alaina had set off hours before in the car. King had texted Flymo the coordinates of where they had parked and given an approximate time that he expected to reach the property. He now knew that the Albanian Brotherhood's safehouse was called *The Eagle's Nest* and was high on a peak five miles beyond where they had parked. It was accessible by road, however, the road in question was ten miles further north of their position. King was relying on both stealth and guile to get himself close enough for a reconnaissance. Or hard reconnaissance, he called it. Whether he made a strike or not depended upon the intel he gleaned from the recce. As a result, he carried all he would need, including some items shipped over by his weapons contractor contact who fulfilled contracts for MI6 via bonded delivery and warehouse through diplomatic channels. King's primary weapon was a Heckler and Koch G36 with a x4 scope. He also carried one of two Walther P99 pistols. He had given Alaina the other and had shown her how to use the hefty little 9mm pistol back at the farmhouse. She had been a quick learner and had pulled on the experience using her father's Makarov. King was confident she could hold her own. His worry now, was whether he should have brought her along at all.

Flymo would now have reached his LUP - or laying up point. He had scouted out a decent landing site using Google Earth. It was an area of rough ground at the base of a peak five miles to the west. The nearest road to it was a few miles to the northeast. There was no guarantee that the helicopter would not be seen, but the area was off the beaten track and as quiet as they could have hoped for.

King had been adamant that the helicopter had worked for the team but had also been its downfall. This time, the chopper would be used as a fast extraction method only. If the recon was negative, then they would return to the car and make their way back, while Flymo flew hell for leather to avoid being seen. If the recon was positive, and King could find a way, then the helicopter would swoop in and pick them up. It wasn't the greatest of plans, but considering they were so few in number and had no support, it was fluid and all they had. Alaina would use the powerful field glasses she carried around her neck, and together with a dedicated frequency two-way radio which was encoded with the radio in the helicopter and the one King carried, she would keep watch and call in what she saw. King needed to have an extra pair of eyes to alert him of threats, and if things went south, she could make the call for Flymo to come and do his thing.

They set off, the incline deceptively steep, the terrain hard and unforgiving. The heat reflected off the ground and the sun bore down on them from directly above. King had planned it so they would arrive early in the afternoon. The sun would be behind them and dusk would give King the opportunity to get close to the building. With Alaina holed up and watching through the field glasses, there would be no sun against her lenses to give her away. The dimming light would also hide her more effectively in the cover, although it looked as if a recent fire had thinned the undergrowth and the trees were sparser on the approach.

King's legs ached as he neared the summit, and he drained his first water bottle when he reached the top. The climb had taken forty minutes. Alaina still had a hundred metres to go. King used the time to survey the next peak. They had a welcome traverse and descent of around five hundred metres, although this could often put strain on the thighs.

"Drink the whole bottle," King said as Alaina joined him, breathing hard. "It will help stave off cramp."

She nodded, wiping her brow with the back of her hand, and taking out her bottle. She drank thirstily, drained the bottle after a minute.

"We take the empty bottles with us, don't leave a thing behind." She nodded, wincing as she adjusted the straps to her backpack. "Here," he said, taking the weight of the pack. "Tighten them, get the weight further up your back."

"Thanks."

"You still want to do this?"

"You don't need my help?" she asked, her expression not best hiding her annoyance.

King nodded, then turned and started over the ridge. "Sure," he said behind him. In truth, he was pleased she could act as a second pair of eyes, pleased she could act as a relay to Flymo and his heavily converted helicopter. But he had felt since he started the climb, that just because she could help, it didn't necessarily mean she should. He longed to have that feeling of trust, of complete and utter reliance that he could place in Caroline, and Big Dave, for that matter. Rashid always had his back, and he had failed him. Failed to see the bigger picture, failed to keep one of their team safe. He had rolled the dice, and somebody had paid the price. And things had never been the same between himself and Rashid ever since. And yet, when he had needed it, on a mission of vengeance in the US, Rashid had been there providing support from afar with his sniper rifle.

"You don't seem all that convinced."

King stopped and turned around. She was beautiful, and she was determined. The burning within ignited a beauty that was almost animalistic, and it had burned more fiercely and with more striking allure the closer they had become to rocking Romanovitch's world. She was young, but King was quite sure had he not been with Caroline, then he could easily have made a fool of himself with her. There were not many women to have caught his eye since the death of his wife, and Alaina would have sat firmly in the running. The thought filled him with guilt, but to his dismay, not as much as it should have.

"This is dangerous," he said. "I shouldn't have allowed you to convince me to bring you along."

"You didn't take much convincing."

King shrugged. "Meaning?"

She brushed past him and to his annoyance, took the lead. "Some tears, some cleavage and vulnerability and you were only too happy for me to tag along."

King shook his head, although she did not see, striding ahead of him. "I don't buy that," he said. "I saw the fear and hurt in your eyes."

She stopped in her tracks and turned around. "Of course, you did! Because it was there, and it is all true!" She paused. "But why did you agree to get me out? Because you wanted me. Like all men, you saw a chance and thought you'd exploit it."

"Bullshit!" King snapped. "I haven't made an advance on you. Not a single move…"

"You didn't exactly pull away from me on that quadbike!"

"It was made for one!" King shook his head. "The bloody seat was only two feet long and we had five hours together on the damned thing!"

"Then why?" King walked past her, setting a fearsome pace diagonally down the slope. He didn't answer her. She broke into a run to keep up. "Wait!" she called after him.

King turned and held a finger to his lips. "We need to be quiet."

"It's miles until we get there!"

"They may have roaming patrols," he said tetchily. "They may even have audio receivers and trembler devices. We don't yet know what we are up against." He trudged on and dipped into the fringe of trees as he started the next incline.

"Sorry," she said as she caught up with him. "You are a good man, Alex King. I can see that. And I know you are committed to Caroline. She is a lucky woman. To have a man so faithful these days."

"What's so different about these days?"

"Well, people are so narcissistic now. It is no longer a personality disorder, it's simply a common trait. People want instant gratification. They are egocentric and want instant credit, notoriety, satisfaction, and recognition. People don't wait for things or turn down opportunities, even though that opportunity brings on nothing but self-destruction. We do not guard against false prophets. We accept all too willingly. That is why half of all marriages end in divorce. People can't remain faithful to somebody if there is the hint of the possibility of a sexual conquest. You are rare being."

King shrugged. "I suspect there are a few of us left."

"I blame social media. It has created the idea that everybody is a celebrity, everybody is more important than everybody else, just so long as their audience continues to enable them." She paused, stepping over a rain gully worn into the rock. "So, somebody posts a picture of their expensive lunch and gets a load of likes or positive comments. What they really need is to be told that with starving children in the world, their picture is an obscene image of narcissism, and that they should be ashamed of wanting their ego massaged. That would go a long way to curbing this trait that is eating away at the heart of society."

"Why would somebody post a picture of their lunch?"

"You're kidding, right?"

King shrugged. Social media was lost on him. He checked the summit through the sight of the G36. They would have a better idea of their position once they cleared the next ridge. "I guess I generally have more to worry about," he said.

She nodded. "Like what?"

King thought how his life had changed since he had left MI5 behind. Maybe he didn't have much to worry about these days. And the thought made him wish that he had. In truth, he had enjoyed being back in the field and the thrill of the close quarter battle at the warehouse in St. Petersburg had cemented that. Not at the time. He never enjoyed the killing. But afterwards, as the adrenalin subsided – there was no feeling like it.

Unperturbed by King's silence, she continued, "That is what I want," she said. "Something more to worry about than the day to day monotony of a home in a small town. I wanted to find out about my sister. Hoped I could save her, but I was too late. Now, I just want to kill Romanovitch."

"It's a hell of a thing to kill a man," said King. "You take away all he has, all he ever had and all he ever will have."

"Good."

"He has a wife and children," said King. "You make your mark on them, too."

"I can live with that."

"Because of your sister? It won't bring her back. Killing someone for vengeance doesn't heal the wound. In fact, the wound only festers."

She hesitated before answering, then said, "I suspect it will not make me feel better. But the apple does not fall far from the tree. Any child of Romanovitch will end up causing misery to someone, sometime. My actions won't change that fact. So perhaps I pay it forward."

King knew she was right. It was a family

business, and Romanovitch's wife would have known what her husband had done to butter the bread. Perhaps she was a prisoner to it all, but King doubted that. The woman had enough freedom to shop in London, Paris and Milan without too much trouble, and the endless properties, furnishings, cars, boats and parties came at a price where you either questioned it, or turned a blind eye.

They reached the summit and King could see the property atop the next but one peak. They would have to be careful now. Whether or not they had security measures in place surrounding the grounds, they were at visual range now. A guard with a pair of binoculars could spot movement from a window. It was as simple as that. King looked for the best route and found it after thirty seconds. It looked to be a tough and undulating route, requiring some free climbing. He was confident he could do it. He just hoped Alaina would be able to follow.

28

"I can't climb that."

"It's just a case of putting one hand in front of the other and having a good, strong foothold before you release your grip. Short steps and reaches."

"But I've never climbed before!"

King shrugged. "Well, you'd best wait here, then." He checked the G36 was secure to his pack and stepped up onto the first boulder. He reached for the first handhold and straightened. "Take cover and wait for me. If I'm not back in three hours, set back the way we came, but remember not to step out from the forest until you're over the first peak." King took another step and was soon eight feet above the ground and on a path through the gully.

"But what if Romanovitch is there?"

"I'm hoping he will be."

"No! I want to kill him!"

"Too bad…"

Alaina watched King climb. The face of fallen rocks wasn't quite vertical, but it was only marginally off the plumb. He was making good progress, when she cursed and scrambled up the first boulder and followed the path he had taken.

The climb was around two-hundred feet, but it brought them up within the pine forest, and closer to the property than they could have hoped to get without detouring more than a mile, and still they would have had to cover open ground to get to an advantageous position.

King paused two thirds of the way, his hands sore and sweating. He dried them on his chest, both feet pressed into a gap between two rocks. He waited for Alaina to near him, then held out a hand for her to hold, before hoisting her up to his tiny ledge.

"Not so bad, is it?"

"I've had more fun."

King took out his water bottle and drank down half. He offered it to her, and she accepted, drinking the remainder thirstily. She handed him back the bottle and he tucked it back into his rucksack. "Not much further," he said.

"Good."

King started to climb again but had to traverse around a large gap created by two giant boulders. The gap was too high to reach over, so he needed to get around it. His powerful legs and arms meant he soon left Alaina behind and was close to the top. He turned around to guide Alaina to him but ducked when chips of rock scattered into his face and a gunshot resonated around him. He flattened himself to the rock and struggled to get the G36 off his shoulder. It was tied on tightly to the rucksack and he could not get his arm back far enough to unhitch it without raising his head above the rock. He gave up and drew the P99 from his belt holster. Another gunshot rang out and more fragments of rock peppered him.

"Get into that cave!" he snapped at Alaina behind him. He watched as she took out the pistol and shuffled into the gap between the two boulders. Her face was ashen, and her eyes were wide.

King lifted his head a touch to try and spot the gunman. Another shot frighteningly close this time, and he felt more than rock debris, the bullet clipping his shoulder, tearing his shirt, and grazing his skin. He winced, cursed under his breath. He checked the movement in his hand and wrist. It was unaffected. He touched the wound with his fingers. Bloody, but not overly so. Probably the luckiest gunshot wound he'd either experienced or witnessed. A true graze, less than half a millimetre.

"What do we do?" Alaina shouted in a hushed tone.

"Sit tight. I'm going to try and draw him out."

King sprang up and climbed the remaining five feet, then rolled onto the ledge which was thick with fallen pine needles. A plume of needles and earth leapt into the air, and then another – closer to his feet this time. King fired three shots as he ran to a fallen tree. He ducked low and fired another three shots in the direction of the gunman. He holstered the pistol and finally got the G36 off his shoulder and checked the area through the scope. The gunman returned fire before he could spot him, but King was sure he'd seen a muzzle flash as he ducked down again. This time, when he raised the rifle, he fired a short burst, then got up and charged forwards to the thicket of trees, dropping onto his stomach, and using the largest tree for cover.

"We have you surrounded!" came a shout.

"Bullshit…" King said quietly, but with that, he ducked his head as a bullet clipped the tree near his right ear. "Shit!" he raged and spun around, rolling to his left.

The bullet had come from the other direction and he knew he was up against more than one opponent. He kept rolling until he reached the next tree, but as soon as he did, he scurried around it to place himself at the tip of the triangle between the other gunmen. He raised the rifle and scanned the ground between the two points. He had barely taken in the ground when a bullet slammed into the rifle and he was thrown to the forest floor. King's jaw had taken the full force of the bullet, cushioned only by the metal action of the rifle. He felt as if a brick had been thrown into his face. He picked up the rifle, but it was twisted, and the action had been forced open by the impact. He dropped it and drew the Walther, but he had nowhere to retreat to for cover. Instead of being at the tip of a triangle, he was now in the centre of it with a gunman on each point. He had never been in such a position before, and the realisation that he was beaten was not only something new, but thoroughly abhorrent. What goes around, comes around. After all these years, he'd finally been outdone. He rolled over again, hearing the gunshots, and feeling the debris on his back and then his face as the bullets drew nearer their mark. King got out his mobile and opened it. The text was already in the folder and assigned to various numbers. He pressed send. It was done. He did not wait to see if it had been sent, but dropped it onto the ground, then aimed and fired a bullet through the screen before tossing the pistol onto the forest floor and standing up slowly and walking out into the open.

29

Neil Ramsay tended to ignore his texts. He would catch up with them in batches. Otherwise he would get nothing else done. However, he had assigned a dedicated alert to King's messages for the duration of the operation. He looked up from his computer monitor and searched for the phone amid the opened files on his desk. When he found it, he read the text, his heart thumping against his chest. He leaned back in his chair and swivelled towards the window, where he had a much-coveted view of the Thames. The water was green, and overhead, the sky was grey and heavy with rainclouds which were growing darker by the second. Only Ramsay's mood was even heavier and more foreboding.

30

She had worked hard that morning. Deadheading the hanging flower baskets and even getting to grips with the strimmer on the edges of the lawn before wiping down the window sills and giving them a coat of gloss so that the afternoon sun would have enough time to dry them.

Caroline looked out across the fields at the glistening ocean. The colour reminded her of King's eyes. Blue-grey, cold looking. But they could sparkle, and she swore they had sparkled more since he had left the world of intelligence behind. She'd never told him. Partly because she would have felt silly casting such a revelation, and partly because King would never have believed her, anyway. She cursed him again. She'd lost count how many times she had, several times yesterday and this morning alone. The man had made a clean break. Turned his back on that world while still in one piece. Physically, at least. The mental toll was yet to truly be seen.

Caroline sighed. He'd bloody well jinxed it now. Off on a fool's errand through some misguided sense of duty and friendship. And she knew, deep down, that it was because he had not had friends as a child, and had never been able to cultivate friendships while he had worked in the shadows for MI6 and handing out permanent sentences for people who had avoided Her Majesty's justice or posed a threat to the nation and its interests. So, after a lifetime barely able to count his friends and loved ones on the digits of one hand, he had developed friendships within his new work with MI5, in particular Rashid, who Caroline knew King not only felt a close sense of kinship, but had seen something of himself in him. Something before the tarnish of his dirtier assignments had seeped through his skin and worked its way into the marrow.

Caroline walked over to the outside furniture on the patio and sat down heavily in one of the wooden chairs. She leaned back in the chair and sipped her tea. She wasn't a fan. Not least because it had turned cold, but because she had forsaken her beloved espressos for the sake of her blood pressure. King didn't know, but she had started on a fertility fitness drive. No alcohol, no caffeine, only whole foods, and plenty of exercise. Five months of letting nature take its course and she had grabbed the reins and taken control.

She welcomed the warmth of the sun on her face. It was late summer and so far, the bite of an early autumn was holding off. In the distance, clouds scudded over the sea and the calm surface switched from grey to blue and back to grey, glistening in the sunlight. She found herself wondering what the winter would be like here. The wood burning stove glowing and the rain lashing against the windows. She thought of snuggling up to King on the sofa, not a care in the world. And then she was angry again. At the pig-headedness of the man and his misplaced sense of loyalty. He should have realised what he would be leaving behind. What they both risked losing if things went wrong.

The car was visible way off. A speck of black heading her way. The road only went out to two neighbouring farms and the old coastguard cottages, and she could see that it had bypassed the first farm turning, and then the second. She felt a flutter in her stomach. The car slowed and took the first lane on its right. Caroline took another sip of tea, briefly wishing it was something stronger, then replaced the cup, stood up calmly and headed inside. King's snub-nosed revolver was in the bureau. She checked it over. Simplicity redesigned. King had sawn off and filed down the thumb piece of the hammer making it double action only and reducing the chances of it snagging as it cleared his pocket, and he had removed the ramp foresight and notch rear sights and welded a simple guttersnipe sight along the top of the frame. This was just a channel to line up on the target, but in essence it was a point-shoot weapon for distances of twenty metres and under, although with the 125gr .38 Special soft-nosed hollow-points, packed an almighty punch at close range. She felt the heft of it, then held it down by her side as she returned to the porch using the edge of the cottage as cover and studying the approaching vehicle through the foliage.

The car was a Jaguar saloon with tinted windows, and it swept over the gravelled driveway with authority and abandon, throwing loose chippings in the air. It lurched to a halt, rocking on the front springs and the passenger door opened immediately. Ramsay stepped out, buttoning his suit jacket as he walked up the pathway. The driver's door opened, and Dave Lomu got out, filling the opening of the cabin completely as he manipulated his limbs out of the vehicle and followed.

Caroline's knees buckled and she had to save herself from falling, scrabbling her hands and the revolver against the granite wall. Ramsay stopped when he saw her, then lunged forwards to her aid.

"Tell me he's okay…" she managed to say, before taking his arm. She tucked the revolver into her pocket, the feeling gradually coming back to her legs. She pulled away from him, walking unsteadily to the garden table.

Ramsay picked up her half-full cup and handed it to her. She took a sip, this time not seeming to notice how cold and foul it tasted. "We just don't know," Ramsay eventually replied. "He's gone off the radar. An asset he was working with reported over her two-way radio to the one remaining member of Rashid's team that he had been captured."

"Who was the asset?"

"Alaina Kopolova. She was working with Interpol against people trafficking in the sex trade."

"The sex trade?" Caroline exclaimed. She had taken two sabbaticals from MI5 with Interpol. She had been on a crusade after being kidnapped by someone running a trafficking ring. She had escaped from a holding centre, but the girls she had been held with had not been so lucky. "What the hell has that got to do with Rashid and his team going missing?"

"It's gang interests, not a specific factor, but part of the bigger picture. The mission started off with a clear remit. Putting a halt to an ever expanding Albanian and Russian drugs trade, and the copious quantities getting onto British streets. Along with that, weapons, counterfeit goods, and people trafficking closely follow. The gangs want a quick profit on their trade in human flesh, so slavery and in particular, sex revenue is the most lucrative method, " replied Ramsay. "I knew of an Interpol operation looking into Romanovitch's involvement in the sex trade and did a deal. We would get intel and the woman would get a new identity and a start over here." He paused. "It's classic mission creep. Alex was working with her to get to Romanovitch."

"Who the hell is she?"

"An asset…"

"Who?"

Ramsay hesitated, then said, "A maid. She was searching for her missing sister. She turned informant."

"So, no training."

"No."

"But with a personal interest in this," she commented flatly.

"Yes."

"Which clouds judgement." Caroline shook her head. "You've placed him in danger. Searching for Rashid is one thing, but working with a civilian is quite another…"

"We're all civilians…"

"An amateur then!" she snapped. "Christ, Neil, stop being so bloody pedantic! Where is this Kopolova woman now?"

"She went missing as well. Our man hasn't seen her since."

"Jesus…"

Big Dave ambled past them casually and said, "I'll get us some tea."

"Coffee," she replied adamantly. "This is a job for coffee." She turned to Ramsay and asked, "What do we know?"

"It was his call," said Ramsay. "He met with Big Dave, who had been reconnoitring the region for him. Unofficially, that is. A favour to King and for Rashid. Big Dave said that King came back out with the woman, and a man was shot while getting her out. A low-ranking bodyguard of Romanovitch's named Draco. King told Big Dave that the woman had had enough, feared her time was up. Romanovitch was making his feelings for her obvious, and she feared that if she rejected his advances, then she would end up swept away by the sex trafficking trade and spend the next ten years in one of his many brothels."

"Oh," she said quietly, shuddering at the thought, those same fears resurfacing and conjuring up memories she hoped she'd one day forget. "Well, of course he would help…"

"As for where he was last seen, that was near the Albanian border with Greece. The Albanian brotherhood has a rear echelon headquarters there. It's called *Shqiponja Stofull*, meaning Eagle's Nest. That's the national bird, and features on the Albanian flag. Or a double-headed one, at least."

"Thanks for the primary school geography lesson." She paused. "Anyway, Eagle Nest was the Third Reich's building paid for by the Nazi Party, and where Hitler did vital planning during his campaign. Do the Albanians share their views?"

"Kehlsteinhaus, on the summit of the Kehlstein," Ramsay nodded and said, "There are plenty of neo Nazi beliefs and ideals shared with the Albanian brotherhood, but I'm not sure that they took the name for their headquarters because of that link. They are proud of their eagle and it epitomises their flag and national heritage."

"And Big Dave ended his aid after Alex came out with the girl?"

"Yes. He felt it was unwise."

"He maybe had a point."

"Lomu did what King asked, but he was doing it between assignments and returned to London. I believe they did not part amicably on account of the girl."

"Right," she sighed. "What was Alex doing next? Or at least when you lost contact with him," she asked quietly.

Ramsay looked up as Dave Lomu stepped out into the sunlight carrying three cups of coffee. He placed the two in his right hand on the table and reached the one in his left across the table to Caroline.

"That'll put hairs on your chest," he said. "Good and strong, and there's a couple of sugars in there, too. Help you get over the shock."

Caroline smiled and sipped some of the coffee, her first caffeine hit in weeks taking the edge off. "I'm not, though," she said. "Shocked, that is." She shook her head. "This was always going to happen. He was out. We both were. And then he goes on a damned fool's mission to get Rashid back. Well, here's the heads up; Rashid was playing games against two mafia factions. He's most likely already dead. Which means Alex probably is, too." She turned away, tearful and flushed red with anger. "Why did you and Mereweather ever have to come down here and ask him to do another job? He's now gone after Rashid because he feels guilty that he turned the assignment down. Then, you offered him just the training element and Rashid went in his place. He could have probably stepped away from it, had it just been Rashid's mission. Shit happens. Lord knows we've lost enough friends along the way." She paused. "But you asked him to train those guys up for the task. Alex would have felt he had let Rashid down."

"I'm sorry," said Ramsay.

She turned to Lomu. "I understand you and Alex fell out about this girl?"

The big man shrugged. "It wasn't a falling out, as such. And she ain't no girl. Not from what I saw of her. I'd say she knows a thing or two about the world."

"Oh…"

"I just thought we'd gone in for one reason, to find Rashid and his team, and came out with baggage that could only expand the parameters of the operation." He paused. "I saw it enough in the Afghan. We'd go in after a target and the next thing, some Rupert has us shepherding women and children to a better life and good men get killed along the way. And guess what? The women and children didn't want to go, the officer knew less than he thought he did about hearts and minds, and the innocent women and children were more than likely executed by the Taliban to save face and send a message back to the allied forces. Mission creep. I couldn't see that taking the women would do anything for Rashid," he said. "When I got back, I told Neil, but he seemed to think that her insight into Romanovitch's organisation wouldn't be a bad thing for King to have at his disposal. My bad, I suppose. So, I'm here to help."

"Well, not so much to help," Ramsay shrugged. "But I thought we'd come and tell you in person."

"Tell me what?"

"That he's missing, of course," he frowned. "I'm sorry."

"So, MI5 are writing him off?"

Ramsay shrugged. "He knew it was a deniable operation when he agreed."

Caroline nodded. "I see."

"I really am sorry."

"So, you say."

"If there's anything I can do?"

Caroline sipped a mouthful of coffee, then put the cup down measuredly. "Yes, well, there is just one thing."

"Name it."

"You take all your heartfelt apologies and you shove them right up your own arse." She paused, glaring at him. "I'll need tickets and some operating capital."

"But..."

"Shut up, I'm talking!" she snapped. "When these lips are moving, pin your ears back and do some listening, Neil! How dare you come down here and give me such terrible news and offer me insincere platitudes! Now, as I was saying, tickets and expenses. You can drive me back with you. And then you can call in sick. Call it stress. That seems to be all the rage. I don't care what you say but make it believable because you're taking a leave of absence and you will not be coming back until this is resolved." She paused, swallowing hard and drying her eyes with the back of her hands. "Or at least, *confirmed*." She turned to Big Dave and said, "And that goes for you, too. I'll need a safe pair of hands and some back up, and Alex trusted… *trusts* you."

Big Dave shrugged. "Works for me. Like I said, I'm here to help. I thought he was operating well off his remit, but I can now see why he did it. He's a sucker for helping people, sure, but that young woman would also have a year's worth of knowledge surrounding Romanovitch and his organisation. So, I'm in."

"Now, look here…" Ramsay started.

"Neil, don't. Just listen to me. You are coming along with us. You are going to help me find out what has happened."

"But there are only three of us!"

Caroline shrugged. "Well, if you hadn't offered him such a ridiculous mission, then it wouldn't have come to this." She paused, glaring at him. "And coming all the way down to Cornwall to tell him that Rashid was off the radar was a calculated move on your part. MI5 were washing their hands of the entire situation. What was the man we all know, and that I love going to do with that? This is the guy who got himself arrested as a terrorist just to find out the location of a secret prison! A man who doesn't know when his limits have been reached, just because he's still alive! There is always fight in him, always the desire to win. You knew that when you delivered the news. You knew he would be Rashid's best chance without MI5 having to do a bloody thing!"

"She's got a point," Big Dave commented.

"Oh, for Christ's sake!" Ramsay stood up, shaking his head. He trudged towards the car, then turned and stared at them, his gaze switching between Caroline and Dave Lomu. "This is bloody madness!"

"Go pack your bag, sugar lips, the car ain't leaving without you," said Big Dave, leaning back in the wooden garden chair, cradling his cup of coffee.

"Lomu?" Ramsay stared at him.

"That's mister Lomu, to you." He paused. "Broad's got a point. You've made a mess, so you'd better get cleaning it up."

"We'll need his data logging. I presume he had activated his phone?" Caroline asked.

"Of course," Ramsay replied tersely. "His

movements and locations have been recorded, right up to the moment the signal was lost."

"Have you tried to override?"

"Yes, but there's nothing, which would indicate the phone has been destroyed."

"And did he make reports via text to his cloud facility?"

Ramsay nodded. "The salient facts. King was never the best at that. He didn't like a trail that he could be accountable for later."

"No. Makes you wonder why, doesn't it?" she said sardonically. "Okay, let's do this. We'll take up where Alex left off. If we move fast, we may at least stand a chance of getting him back alive."

"Bloody hell!" Ramsay kicked the gravel at his feet. "We can't do this! It bloody well can't be done!"

Caroline stood up and stepped closer to him. "Then, you should have thought about that when you came to see him. I blame you, Neil. You should have thought about our new life here before you laid on what it meant for Rashid if Alex did not step up. You used him, and you've thrown us both under the bus in the process."

31

Goldie had been taken away and brought back almost an hour later. He had been beaten, but this time he looked to have been broken. He had been thrown to the floor and shackled once more by his wrist. The Runt had taken out his pistol, aimed at the back of the man's head and smiled at Rashid and Mac as he pulled the trigger.

The hammer fell on an empty chamber and The Runt had laughed at both men before leaving the room, with Shrek patting him on the back, laughing enthusiastically.

Goldie was sobbing quietly. All men break eventually. Given the right amount of time and the severity of their conditions. Rashid turned his attention back to the mangled bullet. He had no idea how long it had been since Philosopher had been killed, no clue whether it was night or day, or when they had last been fed. But he had used the time well, and had removed almost all of the copper, and although his fingers were raw and his fingernails were broken down to nubs, he kept going, while Mac spoke softly to his comrade, telling him to hang in there and to think about slotting the two bastards when they got the opportunity. He looked over at Rashid, watching him work on the bullet. Rashid had caught him watching a few times before, but the Scotsman had not said anything. Rashid figured he had known how low Goldie had ebbed. There was no use getting the man's hopes up only to have them dashed, which could finish any resolve altogether.

Rashid cringed, his last effort removing his thumbnail completely. He gritted his teeth together, looked at the bloody mess, but forgot about the pain when he saw the copper had separated. He smiled, wasting no time in trying to fold it, using the edge of the hard metal handcuff to press it against the stone cobbled floor.

32

They had flown into Tirana, hired a car at the Hertz desk and had driven southeast, stopping only for some dry filled rolls and bottled water at a service station. Big Dave was driving while Ramsay was seated in the backseat using a dongle to get online on his laptop and study the cloud King had uploaded the last of his reports to. Ramsay had read out the GPS coordinates of the farmhouse and Caroline had punched them into the satnav.

"Put these into your phone," he said, then read out the GPS coordinates of The Eagle's Nest. "King was heading there with Alaina."

Caroline scowled. "What about this pilot, Leroy Wilkinson?"

"They call him Flymo," said Ramsay. "On account that he…"

"Hovers so low, yeah, I get it," she said humourlessly.

"He sent a message to his cloud, or the cloud the team were using. Only Rashid performed the updates, but Flymo added to it when the team disappeared. He uploaded the report that King and Alaina had disappeared. He hasn't added anything since. I imagine he'll be thinking about bailing."

"Better get there before he does, then," Big Dave commented, putting some extra weight on the accelerator. The Audi surged forward. They were hovering around the ton. Big Dave filled the seat, his hands making the steering wheel look small. "Another three miles and we take a mountain road. Looks small and twisty."

"They usually are," said Caroline distractedly.

"What's the plan when we get there?" Big Dave asked.

Caroline shrugged. "Hope for the best?"

Big Dave laughed. "Seems to be the mantra of this unit…"

33

Flymo had bugged out. He had been torn between buzzing over the mountainside fortress and searching for King, but he knew the operation was finished. King's text had unnerved him, and he knew that the man had been sent as a last resort. He had flown low to the ground, living up to his namesake. He decided to set things in motion for his withdrawal, and that meant his withdrawal from life as he knew it. There was a great deal of money left in the safe. King had burned his way through it, given him a substantial amount for the delivery to the bonded warehouse. What was left would set him up for the rest of his days. There was a lot of money that had been damaged in the heat, but there was still a fortune. He'd set some aside for the men's families, and he would retire someplace hot. But first, he had to torch the farmhouse and the helicopter and anything else with his fingerprints and DNA on it.

The helicopter would be easy, but dramatic. He would have to rig a fuse to make sure he was far enough away, and he would need to be in the car and driving away, because the fire and smoke would be vast. He worried that he would not get down the mountain road and to the main road in time before the fire services and police got wind of it and he would meet them on the mountain road. And yet, he would have to be sure the fuse would work, as he wasn't going to risk returning to relight it.

Flymo had started to fill two sports bags with the money. A mix of euros, leks, US dollars and kunas. He discarded any damaged ones as they would be more trouble than they were worth, and he still had more than enough. As he zipped one of the bags up, he looked over at the helicopter and the work he had done to it. King must have been insane to think they could use something like this and get away with it. The alterations were simply too great, and he had flown as close to the ground as a tired snake to avoid being seen. He started on the other bag. He was glad to be done with this folly and was looking forward to slipping into a quiet life.

He froze when he heard the vehicle on the gravel yard, cursed leaving his pistol in the farmhouse with his things. He was a pilot, not an agent. And now he was the last man standing. He zipped the bag, then dropped them both behind the fuel drums and crept across the barn to peer through the gaps in the boards. He watched the white Audi turn a lazy circle and stop outside the farmhouse. He looked around for a weapon and picked up a large wrench. Back with his eye at the gap in the boards, he watched the woman get out of the driver's seat. She was of medium height, slim and athletic looking. She casually put her mousey blonde hair up under a black baseball cap and studied the windows of the farmhouse. He shuffled along and paused at a couple of planks that were more warped, to take in a better view. This time a man of about five-ten and slim build getting out of the passenger seat. He wore casual clothes, but they didn't seem to suit him. Like he'd be more at home in a suit, shirt, and tie.

Flymo looked at the wrench in his hand. He had come too far for his clean getaway to be thwarted. He had no idea that the two people he spied upon were with MI5, and he wasn't going to wait to be discovered, his run money put at risk. He gripped the wrench tightly and made his way out of the gap that King had made in the side of the barn. He pushed out through, the wrench leading the way. As he ducked his head, he was aware of a shadow. An eclipse.

"All right, sunshine?"

Flymo looked up into the face of a man with skin as black as coal, shoulders as wide as a doorway and towering six-foot-four. He grabbed the wrench from him as if it were a pencil in a child's hand and caught hold of him by the shoulders. He tore him through the gap, pulling two more planks out with him, and kept hold of him as he dragged, pushed, and pulled him down the side of the barn and into the bright sunlight of the yard.

"Look what I found," Big Dave bellowed. He propelled Flymo in front of him, no real lightweight himself, he took off and landed a few feet further forward, stumbling to remain on his feet.

"What the hell?" Flymo protested.

"Leroy Wilkinson?" Ramsay asked, already knowing the answer.

"Where's King?" Caroline asked urgently, not waiting for the man to answer.

"Who are you?"

"I'm Caroline Darby. I'm with MI5."

"Well, technically…"

"Shut up Neil!" Caroline snapped.

"Christ, he only went missing yesterday…" Flymo looked at them, bemused.

"But it was a broken arrow scenario. He sent an emergency text and we think he destroyed his phone, which meant imminent capture. Alex is my partner. Fiancé, even. So, I have a vested interest, hence the fast reaction." She pointed to Ramsay. "He's with MI5, officially at least."

"I got a text," Flymo said lamely. "I suppose it was generic when I think about it now. I was waiting for his call. To see if he needed me. He took Alaina with him, by car. He didn't want to give himself away. The Albanian's wised up to us hitting them using the chopper. They shot at us last time, hit the fuselage trying to hit the rotor base. King felt that they would have taken measures by now, got some hardware to take us out of the sky. I was there as back-up and exfil, if needed."

"I got the same text," said Ramsay. "That's why we're here. As Caroline said, it was a broken arrow scenario. A last communiqué."

"Jesus, it's good to have friends like you." He shrugged. "But I don't know what we can do," he said, thinking about at least two million pounds in various currencies sitting on the barn floor.

"You fly the bird, we'll do the rest," said Big Dave. "What weapons have you got here?"

Flymo shrugged. "There's an assault rifle, a few pistols, some ammo for each."

"That'll do." Big Dave looked at his watch. He had recently bought himself an oversized Casio G-Shock to better suit his thick wrist and dinnerplate hands, and it looked like a small wall clock. "Get the pre-flight checks done, we're going in." He paused. "Where are the weapons?"

"In the house," Flymo said. He had been caught off guard, had made plans for his future. But the team had become his friends, and he thought about the man who had come out here to go in alone and get them out. He decided his plans could keep. "I'll get things sorted." He turned and walked back to the barn.

"Dave…" Caroline said quietly. "Go with him, while I get the weapons."

"Everything all right, Caroline?" asked Ramsay.

"That guy was the only one left from Rashid's team, and twenty-four hours ago, he makes it out when Alex gets compromised? You earn trust, and he's a long way off that yet."

34

His hands and fingers were ruined. A bloody mess of cuts and tears and broken nails. Through sheer dogged determination, Rashid had managed to fold the copper into something resembling a lock pick. He had hidden it when The Runt had entered and thrown three bottles of water and three flat breads onto the floor between them. Thankfully, he had not taken one of them with him and all three men were almost shaking with relief.

Goldie was sitting against the wall with his legs outstretched. He had said nothing since he had broken down, and he had a faraway stare in his eyes. Mac was doing his best to keep chatting, but the tough little Scotsman was on his last reserves. Another beating or two and they would beg for a bullet. Rashid would not allow that to happen. He had worked on his handcuff for almost an hour, the copper too soft for its purpose, but a ratchet had finally given, and the cuff had expanded a notch. A relief not only in terms of hope but giving a little respite to his wrist which had rubbed raw. He had to reshape the pick, but if he could get some more movement and hold the pick steady, then the ratchet would lift, and the lock would open. However, if he had to do it one turn of the cog at a time, then so be it.

"How's it coming along?" Mac said quietly. He hadn't spoken about it until now, but he had seen the look in Rashid's eyes and there was a flicker of hope in his own. Goldie simply stared into space, oblivious.

"It's hard going," he replied quietly. "Just hang in there, mate…"

35

Yosef and The Shepherd were flanked by nine men as they watched the black S-Class Mercedes pull steadily across the gravelled driveway and ease to a halt in front of the house. Built in the late nineteenth century as a vineyard, it had fallen foul of Italian occupation at the start of the Second World War as part of the puppet state, and then a succession of German occupation, partisan liberation and communist repurposing and then eventually, private liberation by the Albanian mafia after the collapse of the Soviet Union and its satellite states. The building had been modelled on a French chateau, but the vineyards had long gone, taken over by scrub and cactus and pine forest. Vines needed irrigation, labour and investment. They needed husbandry at the hands of experienced horticulturalists, not years of abandonment as the property's occupiers drank the cellar reserves and allowed nature to encroach on a hundred years or more of design.

Yosef's brotherhood each cradled AK-74 assault rifles, some with folding stocks and others with folding bayonets. They looked an imposing sight.

A black Mercedes ML SUV followed the luxury saloon and pulled a wide arc, facing back out of the driveway. Three of Romanovitch's men got out of the SUV and took up positions. They made a show of adjusting their holsters, checking their pistols, but in this company, they were clearly outgunned.

Before Romanovitch could show himself, a member of the Albanian brotherhood jogged over and sidled up to Yosef.

"I have found the patrol," he said.

"And?"

"Their buggy went over the cliff at the south end," he said breathlessly. "They are all dead."

"An accident?"

"It looks that way." He paused. "Their weapons are with them, the buggy is burned out. I saw smoke and followed it. They must have got too close to the edge."

"Gregor being a fool again and driving like a racing driver, no doubt." Yosef shrugged. "When we are done here, get it cleaned up. But now, go and tell them to get the prisoners ready for the exchange."

"Yes, Sir."

"I don't believe that," said The Shepherd, watching the man walk towards the chateau. "What are the chances?"

"You are suspicious of everything," Yosef replied, adjusting the sling under his jacket. The bullet which had killed his boss on its way into his shoulder had been removed, but it had taken surgery and twenty stitches, and it was yet unclear whether he had suffered nerve damage.

"And I have the privilege of being an old man because of it."

Yosef nodded, smiling sagely. "Have a look around the grounds," he said, still watching the S-Class with the blacked-out windows. "Take a gun and a couple of men with you."

The Shepherd shook his head. "I have my knife," he said. "And I move silently alone."

36

"There's movement in the trees," Ramsay said into his phone. "I have a good view from here. Three black Mercedes SUVs have parked in a logging track further down the road and men have spread out across the forest."

"How many?" Caroline asked.

"Not sure. But I see a flash of solid colour every now and then, and there were three men walking in single file. I'll say nine or ten at least."

"Has anyone remained with the vehicles?"

"I'll have to go and check. I'll do a drive past."

"Well, be subtle about it."

"Subtle is my middle name."

"I thought it was Patrick…"

"Funny."

Ramsay started the Audi and pulled out onto the tarmacked mountain road, which was narrow and only bore white lines in the widest sections. The Road led to North Macedonia and to Greece. They had chosen it not only for its proximity to the chateau, but for its tactical importance, too. Three countries, three different directions.

He slowed as he passed the logging track. The vehicles all had tinted windows, but the windscreens were clear. He used his mirrors to try and spot if someone was inside but could not see anyone. He drove on past and when he was around the next bend, he slowed and performed a three-point-turn and slowly made his way back. The three vehicles were parked in a row. Ramsay pulled in and switched off the engine. When he stepped out of the car, he listened for a moment. The forest was quiet, and he could hear his own thudding heartbeat over the silence.

Cautiously, he crept forward and crouched at the first car. He unscrewed the dust cap, then retrieving a silver ballpoint pen from his pocket, he worked it into the valve and let the air out. The hiss of air was surprisingly loud, and he was aware that it could probably be heard from a long way away. He wondered whether the trees absorbed the sound or echoed it more acutely. Ramsay worked his way around the cars, letting out the air in just the front tyres. Those were the wheels that did the steering, and being four-wheel-drive, he figured they would do a good bit of work as well. By the time he worked on the third vehicle, he had almost zoned out to the noise of the hissing air but was suddenly aware of a shadow. He glanced up and looked right into the man's foot as it came scything towards him, catching him in the face.

Ramsay yelped as he fell backwards into the dirt, still clutching the pen. The man was hitching up his shirt to reach his pistol and Ramsay struggled forwards and jabbed the pen into the man's thigh. It punctured the heavy cargo pants and plunged two inches into the muscle until it hit bone. The man screamed, but Ramsay pulled the pen back out and got to his feet. He didn't square off, didn't work out a strategy. King had once told him that rage and speed was what would work for him in a fight, and Ramsay had not had one of those since his first day at secondary school. He lunged at the man, flinging himself inside the man's guard, and as he took several rabbit punches to his back, he drove the pen deep into the man's throat.

Ramsay fell back onto the ground, the bloody pen still in his balled fist. The man clutched his neck, but the blood was spreading far more quickly than the man had any hope of staunching its flow, and he wobbled on his feet, staring angrily at Ramsay the entire time. When he fell backwards and crashed heavily to the ground, it was a huge relief to Ramsay, who scrambled to his feet, tossed the pen into the depths of the forest, and ran back to the car.

He started the engine and tore out of the gravel track and onto the road, catching sight of himself in the rear-view mirror. He had tears in his eyes and had turned pale. He slammed the steering wheel with his fist. He was an analyst, a planner. He should never have been here, or on any of their missions. He felt ashamed having taken the man's life, but relieved that he had lived through the incident, and as he thought about what had happened, he felt overwhelmingly guilty and further ashamed of his relief. He slammed the mirror with his fist, smashing it from its fixings and putting a six-inch crack in the windscreen. He would not mention this to anybody on the team. He had no desire to join their club.

37

Rashid had moved the ratchet four more times. He still couldn't get his hand out, and in trying, he had closed the ratchet one click. Frustrated, but high on the knowledge it *could* be done, he had set back to work, his fingers raw from the work of getting the copper away from the lead, as well as aching from the awkward dexterity required. He could now hear footsteps approaching. What if they took him for another beating? They would snap on the handcuffs and release his own, putting him back at square one. What if they discovered the pick or wondered why his hand and fingers were so bloody? They would know what he had been doing for sure. In desperation, Rashid continued to work on the lock, feeling the ratchet give another notch. The footsteps grew closer, and Rashid grit his teeth to bolster himself and positioned his thumb and little finger together, took a breath and squeezed the two digits together with his right hand. The thumb cracked and he gritted his teeth through the agony, panting through the pain as he squeezed the broken thumb enough to get the handcuff over his hand and set himself free. He tried to straighten the thumb, but nothing happened. It merely flopped loosely, the source of such unbelievable pain.

The door unbolted and opened, and Shrek and The Runt walked in. They had not come to drop off food or water, nor empty the communal bucket each man had been forced to slide to one another with their feet. Which meant they had come to take one of them away.

"Time to go," The Runt said, grinning through broken, yellow teeth. "All of you."

Rashid and Mac shared a look. Could this be it? A bullet in the head and a shallow grave outside?

Shrek held up the shackle in one hand and the keys in the other. He stepped towards Rashid but was caught off guard when he lunged towards him, rugby tackling his legs. The big Albanian recovered enough to whip Rashid across the back with the shackles, but he was already going down and Rashid was too invested, too focused to acknowledge the pain anywhere else but in his hand, and he was doing a good job of ignoring that. Shrek went down hard, and Rashid reached up and caught hold of The Runt by his scrotum and yanked him down into the melee. The Runt screamed, fell to his knees, and reached for his pistol, but Rashid was already upon him. He pounded him in the face but recoiled as he felt every bit of it through his broken hand. Instead, he grabbed the man by his ear and pulled him over him and kicked him towards Mac, as he concentrated on the ogre beneath him.

Mac wasted no time and seated on his backside, he clawed at The Runt with the heels of his feet, pulling him across the stone floor towards him, using his legs like mechanical backhoes. Once the slightly built Albanian was close enough, he straddled him and clutched the man's throat with his one free hand, gripped like he had never gripped before, and straightened his arm until it was rigid. He then leaned down on him and watched the life leave his eyes second by second. He was gritting his teeth, saliva drooling from his mouth, like a rabid dog as he used all his strength and willed the man to die quickly.

Shrek had recovered and was overpowering Rashid, slowly bringing him closer to him in order to put a wrestle hold on him. Rashid kicked and fought wildly, resisting, but short on both energy and strength. The beast of a man got his forearm around his throat and Rashid knew he was running out of time. He flung his head backwards and there was a sickening, but comforting crunch as the ogre's nose flattened against his face. Rashid did it again, and a third time, but Shrek had wised up and turned his head to the side. He fiddled with the shackles, then got the chain around Rashid's neck and started to strangle him. With every ounce of strength Rashid lost, he could feel the strength gain in the man who was trying to kill him. He grabbed for something, anything – a flap of skin, the man's groin – anything that would cause his opponent momentary pain or discomfort to buy him some time, but he was at a loss. The Albanian was twenty-stone or more, and he was as strong as an ox. Smelled twice as bad, too.

Rashid knew all about the term, *circling the drain*. He wasn't sure how it had come about, possibly the blood in the shower scene in the film *Psycho*, but he knew it was meant to describe someone about to enter the death throes, the point of no return. His vision was blurred, he couldn't breathe, and he felt lightheaded. His hearing was starting to become impaired, every sound echoed and rang, distorted and unworldly. But, as he felt close to passing out, he heard a muffled sound and the beast on top of him fell forwards and rolled off him. Gradually his hearing, sight and breathing returned to him and he was aware of Mac's booming voice calling him. He rolled over, the side of his face wet with blood, but he soon registered that it did not belong to him. He looked at Mac, who was looking at him earnestly and holding the smoking gun in his left hand. At his feet, The Runt was dead, his throat and neck misshapen, his head flopped to one side at an impossible angle.

"Get the keys and get us the hell out of here, boss," said Mac.

Rashid looked at him and smiled. "On it." He turned his attention to Goldie, who still stared at the wall, oblivious of what had taken place. "Goldie! Get to it!" he shouted. He got to his feet, tossed the bunch of keys to Mac and gave the Londoner's foot a kick. "Get up, soldier!" Rank or seniority did not dictate who carried a liberated weapon, so he allowed Mac the privilege of carrying the pistol. He had enough problems with his broken thumb, anyway, so he snatched the keys off him as the man's shackle hit the floor and set about unlocking Goldie's handcuff. "Come on soldier, on your feet!"

Goldie looked up at him, his eyes seemingly hard to focus. He nodded, got unsteadily to his feet and Rashid put his arm around his waist, moving him towards the open door.

38

The door of the black Mercedes S-Class opened and Romanovitch stepped out, his foot crunching on the thick gravel. He fiddled with his mobile phone, a cigarette pursed between his lips. He ignored the Albanian mafia boss, something that did not go unnoticed by the men of the brotherhood. Tension was taken up on the grips of the weapons and they looked to their leader, who remained impassive. Better to ignore a snub and pretend that it went unnoticed, than to take offence and do nothing.

Romanovitch's guards fanned out, but their weapons remained holstered. The Russian said something to one of them, then walked over and stood before Yosef, looking up from his phone.

"I believe you have something for me…"

Yosef smiled. "This was a winery, for many years. There are a great many wine crates in the cellar, but fear not, you will not be going home in them. I shall extend to you the courtesy you did not afford to my brother…"

"Very wise," Romanovitch commented, seemingly unintimidated.

The Albanian smiled, although it was

mirthless and thin. "I have the advantage. My men are well-armed."

The Russian nodded. "We do not want more bloodshed. Let us start a new accord. You give me the men you have captured, and I will increase supply and logistics by one hundred percent."

"Not forgetting the ten million euros bounty I put on them." Yosef paused. "One of the men was killed. But in light of what you did to my brother, the price remains the same for three."

Romanovitch frowned. "I thought there were four."

"As I said, one of them was killed."

"And that leaves four."

"No, that leaves three."

"I see…" Romanovitch frowned and glanced at his phone once more, then typed out a short text. "Forgive me, but I have to finish ordering a hit on someone. A competitor who has outlived his usefulness."

Yosef smiled. "Business. It never stops," he said. "Anyone I know?"

Romanovitch sent the text and put the phone back in his pocket. "Yes, my friend. I believe you do…"

Yosef's head blew apart as the high velocity round hit him between the eyes. Romanovitch dropped to one knee and pulled out a tiny 9mm Ruger LC9S pistol and fired two shots at the nearest brotherhood member in the line, dropping him and aiming for another. The men had barely any time to react before they were cut down by automatic gunfire from the forest. It was over in just a few seconds and Romanovitch's bodyguards stepped forward and aimed shots at the heads of the men lying either dead or wounded on the ground. The gunfire died down and when it became silent, Romanovitch stood up and walked back to the car. He opened the rear door and helped the passenger out onto the gravel.

39

Twenty-seven hours earlier

The smell of the pine was almost nauseating. King could both taste and smell the heat of the forest, the warmth in his mouth and nostrils. He was reminded of hot summers on the southwest coast of France. The pine smelling so hot that he could imagine it about to combust. The ground was almost completely made up of rock, but for the thin blanket of pine needles and pine mulch beneath that. King watched as the first of the gunmen stepped out from a thicket of trees and crunched across the ground towards him. He carried an AK-74 assault rifle with a scope attached. That made sense, considering the accuracy in which he had forced King to keep his head down.

King stepped on the small Motorola two-way radio and ground it into the pine needles underfoot. If he was to convince them he was alone, the last thing he wanted them to find was a two-way radio. He had his hands raised slightly, walking tentatively out from the trees. He never went full surrender with his hands on his head, once you made that pose, the people holding the guns didn't like you breaking it. Better to let them come up with the terms, and whatever they stipulated gave you an idea of how professional they were. Another man stepped out, and then another. Both carried assault rifles. Sure enough, all three had formed a triangle, decreasing in size with every step they took towards him.

"Who else is with you?" one of the men said in half-decent English with a thick Balkan accent.

"I'm alone."

"Bullshit!" said another. "We heard voices!"

"It was my phone. I answered it on speaker by mistake."

The third man closed the gap and said nothing. Instead, he swung the rifle and the butt smashed into King's jaw. He spun and fell to the ground, and the man jabbed the butt into his right kidney. King gasped for air, contorted in pain. He rolled onto his side, tucking his knees to his chest, and shielding his head with his elbows, but the rain of blows he was expecting did not come. Instead, two pairs of hands grabbed him by the shoulders and heaved him to his feet.

"We have your friends," said the first man. "You will join them, and then you will be sold tomorrow when the Russian comes."

King said nothing. Vasyli had said as much. A new deal between Romanovitch and the Albanians. A new partnership, sealed on Romanovitch getting the people responsible for interrupting his business, making him lose face. He could only guess at what the Albanians gained, but he suspected a stronger foothold. For now. Organised crime alliances were uneasy and short lived.

They marched King to a curious looking all-terrain vehicle. The ATV was like a giant quadbike, but with seats and a roll bar. A steering wheel was on the left, and the screen had been folded down like an American Willie's Jeep from the Second World War. King stiffened, pressed his weight down into his pelvis, hips, and thighs. He gradually became a deadweight for the men to push and as they reached the vehicle, they had to exert some strength to position him near the rear. The silent one stepped in towards him, but instead of butt beating him, he put the muzzle of his rifle near King's face and practically growled at him.

King snatched his left arm back, rotated his wrist and broke free from the man's grip, caught hold of the muzzle of the rifle and simply locked out his arm. A round from the weapon was never going to hit him, and he snatched his right arm free and clawed at the gunman's left eye, striking with both his index and middle fingers pressed firmly together. But not quite straight. Just enough bend in them to get behind the man's eyeball and hook it clean from the socket. The man was out of action, falling into shock as his optic nerve was severed and sent all kinds of signals to his overworked brain. There was no coming back for him, it was done, and the shock could well kill him.

King barrelled his right shoulder into one of the men, then headbutted the other on the bridge of the nose. The man was going down and fell onto his knees. King caught hold of the other man's head with both hands and ripped downwards, smashing the top of the man's head with the other man's face. The ATV stopped the felled man from collapsing backwards, and King bludgeoned the man's face into his companion's head two more times. Both men were out cold, and the man who had suffered the eye gouge who had clearly been in shock and had remained silent until now, was screaming and clawing at his face. His legs were shaking, and he looked like a drunk about to lose the use of his legs at any moment. King picked up the man's rifle and applied the safety catch, before turning it over in his hands and holding it by the barrel. He raised it high above his head, then brought it down with all his might onto the top of the man's head with a sickening crunch. The man fell, poleaxed. His right foot twitched a few times and went still, just like the rest of him.

King retrieved his pistol and spare magazine. He saw that one of the men carried a 9mm Browning and he took it out of his holster and tucked it into the back of his waistband. He checked the pulses of the other two men. Nothing doing. So, he loaded them into the ATV and picked up their weapons. He checked his watch. Forty minutes had passed since the first gunshot, so he trudged back to the clifftop and called down for Alaina. There was no reply. He called again, dropped down onto the ledge, and made his way down to where she had taken cover between the two enormous boulders. He called again, but he knew it was in vain. He saw her two-way radio on the ledge below. King peered down the near-vertical drop, then studied the ground all the way to the far ridge. No movement. She had simply disappeared. King assumed she had used the time to run. He would have to adapt his plan. The text he had sent had been set up to multiple recipients. Flymo and Neil Ramsay. It had simply said he had been compromised and they had to assume he had been captured. He was a realist, and he knew his chances of rescue were around nil. But he hadn't wanted to disappear without trace, and he had wanted them to know his last location.

King returned to the ATV, clambered inside, and pressed the start switch. The engine fired into life, and he checked the controls, realising it was an automatic, single gear set-up, like a snowmobile or a jet ski. He turned the vehicle around and drove back down to the cliff, stopping right on the edge. He got out and moved one of the bodies into the driver's seat and called once more down the cliff for Alaina. Nothing.

King dabbed his foot on the accelerator and the ATV shot forwards. He moved his leg out as the front wheels went over the edge and the vehicle plummeted down the rocky face, crashing down onto the ground some two hundred feet or more below. It hit the ground with terrific force and two of the men were thrown out, and the vehicle eventually rested on its roll cage, the wheels spinning and smoke billowing from the engine.

King regretted not taking one of the assault rifles, but anybody discovering the scene would know how the men had been armed. He briefly gave thought to tossing the Browning over the edge, but it wasn't out of the question for a single pistol to have become loose from a holster and get lost in the gaps between the boulders. He turned his back on the scene and made his way into the trees. Behind him a whoosh of petrol igniting filled the air and smoke billowed high into the sky.

40

From her vantage point high on the slope, on the edge of the forest clearing, Caroline had seen the grisly scene in front of the chateau. She had separated from Big Dave, both circling the property, to do a full reconnaissance and they had planned to meet on the east side. She eased back into the fringe of trees, her foot catching a rock and sending it bouncing down the slope. Almost at once, gunfire erupted behind her and she took off into the trees.

She did not know how many men were chasing her, but there was an array of gunfire and as she pounded through the trees, she could make out both pistol and rifle rounds pinging past her. The muted tones of pistols and the sharp crack of a rifle on semi-automatic filled the air. She had fifty or sixty metres on them, but it wasn't enough. She veered right, where the gradient increased. If she could run at full pelt down the slope, then she would hit the belt of trees way ahead of them and be able to use them as cover as they headed down the slope. Tactically, it was a sound move. But she slipped and fell, and by the time she got back to her feet, she could tell they had gained on her.

And then the ground shook and the air around her seemed to vibrate and her insides slushed erratically, and she was lifted off the ground and thrown down into the dust and pine needles and forest debris. She rolled onto her back, her ears ringing and her chest aching. She struggled to breathe and wiped her eyes with the back of her hand as she rolled onto her knees and finally took a deep breath.

There was no more than three metres between her and the man directly in front of her, and ten more between her and the man directly beyond the first. The third man was twenty-five metres away, but he had an AK2000 assault rifle in his hands and that more than changed the game. She had fallen onto her side, the grenade knocking her clean off her feet. Again, she thought how crazy it was for her to be here. No back-up and an ill-conceived plan at best, but she was fully committed and so tantalisingly close to her objective, to get to the man she loved, that she couldn't afford to weaken at the thought of being injured or outnumbered.

Because outnumbered she may well be, but outclassed, she was not. The concussive shock of the explosion had reverberated inside her, feeling as if her insides had been shaken loose. She had lost her baseball cap, her mousey-blonde hair spilling out and cascading around her shoulders. Slowly, she got back to her feet, turning to see the man now standing in front of her. His 9mm Sig Sauer pistol aimed at her, his eyes blinking disbelievingly and the expression upon his face telling it all. A woman. Unexpected and at odds with the Albanians and the grisly scene he had just witnessed.

    She held up both her hands, but as she straightened, she feinted a stumble. The man momentarily forgot himself, leaned forwards to assist her. Maybe he'd been brought up right. A long time ago. Before his chosen career path. Before the Russian mafia had eaten at his soul. Showing respect to women, instilled into him by his sisters, his mother, his grandmother. It was all Caroline needed and she faked another stumble, looking up and making sure that he now stood directly in front of the man with the AK2000. He was, so she drew the small but heavy Makarov pistol from her back pocket and shot him in the throat. He hadn't even begun his slump to the ground when she took another step forward and steadied her aim. When the man fell, she already had the vee and pin sight aimed at the man with the assault rifle twenty metres distant. She fired a single well-aimed shot at the man's forehead, then double tapped centre mass as he went down. Dropping to one knee she twisted to her right and fired three rounds in quick succession at the man in between, and adjacent to, the two bodies. He had been pulled in by the sight of her being a woman and putting up such resistance to their pursuit, and hadn't known it was she who had fired until he had seen the second man drop to the forest floor, and by the time he managed to fire back at her, he had already been hit by two of the punchy 9.2mm bullets, but his own bullet went desperately wide of his target and the next three went high and wide as he fell to the ground and the pistol flailed wildly in the air.

Caroline stood back a few paces and shuffled to her left. She did not want to be where the men had last seen her when his comrades had fallen. She had not yet confirmed that he was dead, and she did not want to be there if he managed to steel his resolve and fire wildly. She dropped the magazine, slotted another in place, but did not work the weapon's slide. She could count, after all. Now she was nine up. She aimed between the three bodies, rubbing her stomach gently, comfortingly with her left hand. She had grazed herself on the ground and could feel splinters and pine needles and wood bark on her skin. She was shaking, the adrenalin subsiding after such a peak of endorphins and the exertion of running up the slope and sprinting down the other side.

One of the men was still moving. Her compassion told her to walk over to him, kick his weapon aside and walk away. Let him die in peace or give him time to be recovered by the rest of his team. But she'd seen what he had done. He was a ruthless killer and would offer her no quarter if their situations had been reversed. Besides, she had been with King too long now, and her instincts had been honed through training, if not osmosis from working - and living - with such a man. There were too many variables involved in such an act. Too many things to consider and counter. She was outnumbered, after all. She aimed and fired, and the man's head rocked, then he rested still. The brutal action could well have saved her life and the lives of her friends and acknowledging the fact made her feel nothing for what she had just done. They would have done worse to her, once they had gotten over the fact that she was a woman. Undoubtedly, they would have soon taken advantage of that fact, considering who these men were and who they worked for. They deserved no mercy, and least of all from her. And, as she picked her way through the forest floor, she just prayed she was still in time. Prayed that the man she loved was still alive.

She picked up the AK2000 and checked the action. She looked around her to get her bearings and headed downhill.

Big Dave came crashing out of the trees and lowered his rifle when he saw her. "The fucking place is crawling with hostiles!" he said breathlessly. "It's no good going that way!" He charged past her and said, "Follow me!"

"I'm okay, thanks," she said sarcastically as she struggled to jog behind him.

"I can see that." He paused. "I've just seen King…"

"Really!?"

"Fucking Romanovitch just went apocalyptic on the Albanians!"

"I know, I saw," she said breathlessly. "Now, where's Alex?"

"He's chasing two people into the woods!" He paused. "South and west. Get

Flymo on the phone and sort out a shoot 'n scoot!"

"A what?"

"He'll know what you mean. Just tell him the north side only."

"But we're on the north side!"

"Then pick up the pace, sweet cheeks! You don't want to be here when he flies over!"

41

King was tired and hungry. He had used all his water and the biscuits and packets of pre-cooked rice he had put in his rucksack had been eaten, but he was a world away from a steak dinner and a good night's sleep. He had completed his thorough reconnaissance of the property and had holed up in a thicket in front of the house, waiting for an opportunity to get closer, but the area had become a hive of activity with numerous guards checking the grounds. He had seen that the ATV and bodies had finally been discovered and had skirted the chateau on his way back. The man he had followed had reported to his leader, and then he had watched the Mercedes S-Class arrive, followed by the SUV. In his heart of hearts, he knew he was too late. Too late for a plan at least and would have to see what happened and play it by ear.

King had a feeling when he watched Romanovitch's body language. He had been involved in enough ambushes to know, and he had seen the muzzle flashes in the fringe of the forest as soon as Romanovitch had taken a knee. By then, the Albanian leader was already dead, and the Albanian brotherhood only had mere seconds before they joined him.

The Russian gunmen had emerged from the trees, ten in all, and then a sudden movement further up the slope, where there was a fire break, had sent three of the gunmen in pursuit. King had watched Romanovitch return to his vehicle, then open the rear door and help a woman out onto the gravelled driveway. His heart pounded, and he rubbed his eyes, struggling to make out the woman's features at this distance. But he knew enough to recognise the height and shape, and the gait as she walked across the gravel and stood staring at the chateau.

Gunfire erupted further up the slope, and then the sound of a grenade. Below him, small arms fire sounded, and he watched two of the remaining Russians fall at the side entrance. A small, fit-looking man with a crew cut of red hair edged out of the doorway, a pistol in his hand. He ducked as he experienced incoming fire, then eased the pistol out and returned fire. King could see two men crouched beside a low wall with their backs to him. He watched them aim and fire, saw the man in the doorway return a volley, but he knew he would be low on ammunition, and he could see he looked weak.

King broke cover and ran down the slope. When he was thirty metres from the two gunmen, he slowed and fired a double tap into each of their backs. Closer to the building, he could see that the man in the doorway was Mac. King had familiarised himself with Rashid's team, and he recognised the man's features from the photographs in the file. Behind him, two figures struggled to remain upright. King took a step towards them, but a trace of gunfire sent him into a dive towards the wall for cover. He pulled one of the bodies towards him and wrenched the Steyr Aug 5.56mm assault rifle out of his dead hands. He already knew from the track of the bullets where the gunman had been, but that did not necessarily mean they were still there. In the same situation, King knew he wouldn't have stayed put. The Steyr Aug's fixed optic was one of the best in the business, but King did not look through it to acquire his target. Anyone who did would risk seeing too much magnified detail and most likely be looking in the wrong place. Instead, he looked above the sight and saw the gunman aiming at him from one-hundred metres away. King lowered his eye to the scope, placed the tip of the post on the man's upper body and fired three rounds. The man went down on the third shot. King looked back towards the doorway where Mac was firing at someone closer but blocked from King's line of sight by the Mercedes SUV. He took out the Walther P99, on account that it would probably stand up better to what he was going to do next, then lobbed it high and far. It tumbled in the air, then bounced on the gravel and skidded to Mac's feet. King stood up, stepped closer to the SUV and opened up with a sustained burst through the windows at an unseen target beyond. When he looked back at where Mac had been, he was no longer there.

  King got to his feet and set off to where he had seen Romanovitch running south and west of the chateau. As he reached the rear of the chateau a helicopter roared overhead. He was thrown to the ground by the rotor wash, but as he rolled over and watched it climb to around eighty feet, he could see it was the Bell Jet Ranger with Flymo's 'optional extras' bolted in placed. There was no mistake. The M-134 Mini-gun – a gatling gun which could fire six-thousand 7.62mm bullets a minute – flared up and whirled away, the sound curious, but unmistakable. Five seconds after the first burst, and the helicopter now a hundred metres further up the wooded slope, the sound of brass shell casings raining upon the gravel sounded like a thousand windchimes. The chopper pulled a hard-starboard turn, and the mini-gun flared again, and King could see branches fall from the trees and men scattering through the forest. Now the craft rose high into the air, banked hard before straightening up, and the mini-gun fired in shorter bursts, before the first Hellfire missile fizzed away in a puff of smoke from its mounting under the fuselage. The forest erupted in flame and the helicopter banked away, flames licking at the belly of the craft.

King turned his back on the scene and sprinted across the garden and towards the scree slope on the other side of the property. He could see Romanovitch ahead of the woman, who was almost into the trees. King stopped, aimed the rifle, and fired. Romanovitch went down. The woman stopped in her tracks, hesitantly looked down at the Russian for a moment, then bolted into the trees. King started to run again, but Romanovitch got to his feet and limped after her. King stopped and aimed again but lost him to the treeline. He fired three shots, about a metre apart and the rifle dry clicked on empty.

King tossed the weapon onto the ground and took out the Browning 9mm pistol. It was the weapon he was probably most practised with and it felt comforting in his hand. He started out across the slope made up of scree and larger boulders but headed uphill. When he reached the treeline, he was sixty metres higher than where Romanovitch had entered the forest, which gave him the luxury of heading downhill through the trees. He knew that they could not have covered the ground before him, especially with Romanovitch limping, and he had time to assess the situation as he stalked them through the trees.

King heard the hiss of wind, ducked, and held up his hand. The knife sliced deep through the meat of his forearm and he found himself falling forwards, half by the impact of the blade and half by his own reaction to the surprise attack. He rolled and made it smoothly back onto his feet, but he had lost the pistol. He looked at the man in front of him. He was old and his hair was grey, but he looked wiry and fit and King would guess his life had not been easy. His eyes were cold and grey, and his brow was furrowed enough to hold a hand of playing cards in the creases. King realised he had seen the man with the Albanian leader. He'd put him down as a senior figure, but not the boss. An old hand. The way the man had used the knife, King now suspected he was a killer and enforcer for the brotherhood.

The man charged forwards and King darted to his left, snapping a roundhouse kick with his right leg. It caught the man in his stomach, but he was fast and experienced and stabbed King's calf muscle. King grimaced. His arm was wet with blood and he knew the wound was deep and suspected the knife had cut its whole, and not inconsiderable length. King took out his own knife. It was a modest folding lock knife with a three-inch blade. It looked puny in comparison, but as he whipped it open, he saw a glint in the old man's eyes.

"I am Galanis. They call me The Shepherd, but many from my village call me the Butcher." He spun the knife in his hand and the blade glinted in the shafts of sunlight between the trees. In the distance there was the sound of another significant explosion. King reflected both Hellfire missiles had done their job, now the helicopter would be down to its gun. "I kill my goats for village celebrations. I can butcher an entire beast for the fire grill in twenty minutes. What do you say to that?"

King gripped the knife firmly in his left hand. His right arm was aching, and his grip was weak. He took a step forward. "I say you talk too much, old man. And I'll tell you right now, I'm not a scared little goat."

Galanis lunged forwards, whipping the knife in the air and slashing great arcs back and forth ninety degrees or more. King came in hard, but at the last minute he lashed out a front kick to the man's abdomen, beating his reach, then swiped his blade across the man's wrist. He yelped, but King jabbed his knife twice into the man's bicep, then ran it across his side as he backed away. Galanis swapped hands with the knife. His confidence had gone, and he steeled his resolve, coming in for another attack. King swung his arm up and under the man's attack, and when he blocked the knife across his body, Galanis' left side was exposed. King stabbed but caught the rib bone and the blade deflected. The old man screamed, but he caught King across his left shoulder, the razor edge of the curved blade slicing a good two inches and half an inch deep. King darted one way, then another and as he faked a stab, he slashed the man across his forehead and stood back. The man backed away, too. The blood ran down his face, like a theatre curtain closing. He wiped the blood with the back of his hand, squinting to see through the blood in his eyes.

"I have used that cheap knife fighter's trick, myself. Gimmicks will not win against me. I have carved up dozens of men!" Galanis panted, but he managed a thin smile. "You know, as do I, that only one of us is leaving here alive…"

King nodded. He bent down and picked up the Browning that was now at his feet, both men parrying above it. The difference was, King had planned it that way while Galanis was busy having a knife fight. He shot him in the face and turned around to head after Romanovitch, but almost walked into Alaina.

She was holding the Walther P99 that King had trained her with, then given to her before they had set out.

"Put the gun down," she said confidently. Her weapon was aimed at King's head, while his own was pointing to the ground.

King looked at Romanovitch. He was breathing heavily, his hand covering the wound to his side. He was bleeding, but nothing vital appeared to have been clipped by the bullet on its way through. King could tell by the colour of the blood, and how much of it the man was losing. King dropped the pistol for the second time in as many minutes.

"Surprised?" Romanovitch asked. "You complete fools at Interpol and MI5! How easily you can be played! You follow your *emotions*, never your *instincts*."

King shrugged. "I do as I'm ordered."

"But you showed mercy and compassion to a woman putting on an act. How easily you were manipulated. How you only saw what we wanted you to see!"

"I take it our mole in St. Petersburg is a double agent?" King asked, his arm throbbing and the blood running over his hand, droplets patting on the forest floor.

"Double, treble, I forget," Romanovitch smiled. "But, yes, he works for me, not you."

"And Vasyli?"

"Stealing from me. A great deal over a long time. He had to go, so better to use him in a charade than to simply waste him." He paused. "Vasyli killed Alaina's brother in a card game. I offered her the chance of retribution if she worked for me, played a part in the deception." He touched her waist, and she smiled.

"Amongst other things…"

King had witnessed the passion in her hate for Vasyli, the way she had stared transfixed at his body, her eyes locked onto the bullet hole between his eyes. It must have brought her great solace, or perhaps guilt. King reflected it was usually the latter. But whatever she had felt, she must have taken on her role like a method actor, substituting her love for her brother and her hate for Vasyli for an anonymous young woman and the mafia boss. He looked at Alaina and said, "Was it worth it?"

"Yes," she nodded.

King shrugged. "And the real Alaina? Did she come in search for her sister? If indeed there really ever was one."

"Oh, there was," Romanovitch said before she could answer. "And Alaina joined her. Foolish girl."

"And Draco?"

Romanovitch shrugged. "Collateral. Wrong time, wrong place. I'll send his family some flowers."

King stared at Romanovitch and said, "Is this about your brother?"

The Russian frowned. "*My* brother?"

"In Georgia." King shrugged. "We

crossed paths. I killed him. Sorry, I should have sent flowers."

Romanovitch stared at him for a moment, then broke into a wry smile. "My brother was a bastard. I took over after he was killed. I should thank you. I now have all I could wish for."

"Don't mention it."

"We need to go," said Alaina, or whoever the hell she was, glancing at her watch. "Ten minutes until our lift to Bulgaria arrives. Let's do this and get going. Do you want the honours?"

Romanovitch nodded. "I guess so," he said. "For my worthless brother, because it's what my mother would want me to do." He took the P99 from her and aimed it at King's forehead. "So long…" He pulled the trigger and the internal hammer clicked. "For god's sake!" He snapped angrily at Alaina, took his hand away from the gunshot wound and quickly worked the slide backwards, his bloody fingers momentarily struggling for grip, but he got it done and fired again.

Another click.

King bent down and picked up the Browning. His hand was slippery with blood, but the bulky chequered walnut grips could stop anything from slipping. He nodded to Alaina and said, "You put on a good show. I was baffled by your hate towards Vasyli, it almost had me doubting myself, but now it makes perfect sense."

"You suspected?" she asked incredulously. "When?"

"Well, a long time before I removed the Walther's firing pin, that's for sure," King said. "In my room up in Novyalaski, you said that Interpol gave you Ramsay's details and you contacted him. I found that odd. But by then, of course, the real Alaina Kopolov was already dead."

Romanovitch chuckled, but his face was humourless. He was clearly in pain. "And then some," he said. "Just like her stupid sister. But it paved the way for our little charade. My snake in the woodpile…"

King nodded, looked back at the woman whose name he did not know. A woman who had set out on revenge herself and sealed the fate of another young woman in search of her own justice. God only knew how many lives Romanovitch had ruined, how many souls were left searching for answers to lies, and retribution. "It was Draco," King said decisively. "That was what started me doubting you. Right there at the beginning. He wasn't on to you or investigating a break in. He was at the pool house to meet you. You lured him there with the promise of sex, but really you had me kill him to add weight to your story." He shrugged. "And your reaction when you saw him was forced. There was no need to scream like that. And you got in my way when I stepped towards him. You didn't want him knocked out, you wanted him dead, so you gave me no choice. Afterwards you didn't act like someone in the role you were supposed to be playing. That response didn't belong to the frightened and desperate young woman in search of her sister, or the truth about what happened to her. Your comment about his death was callous, much like the person I suspect you really are."

"Fuck you!" she snapped.

King turned to Romanovitch. "No, when something's not right, it's just not right. I wasn't convinced from the start, but I wanted to see where it would go. I suppose, when it comes down to it, it's not like you said, that we follow our emotions, never our instincts, but the other way around entirely." He shot Romanovitch through the forehead, then turned the gun on Alaina.

"No, please…"

King fired and started to walk away before her body hit the ground. He looked up and saw Caroline and Big Dave standing twenty feet in front of him, each taking cover behind a mature pine. Big Dave lowered the rifle. King didn't know how much they had seen, but he guessed they had arrived after Romanovitch had fired the defective gun. Or at least, he hoped they had.

"Alex!" Caroline flung herself at him and he winced. "Are you okay?"

He hugged her close, smelt the familiar natural scent of her and her silky hair against his face. "Never better," he said quietly. "Never better."

42

Flymo had already landed the chopper and had taken up a defensive position with a rifle he picked up off the ground. He was kneeling beside the Mercedes S-Class and was firing single shots into the trees, with the helicopter's engine running and rotors engaged. Not the sort of thing learned in a civilian flight school, but something he had done many times flying in Afghanistan. Rashid and Mac were loading Goldie's body into the aircraft. An unlucky bullet. But Rashid would later tell King that the former SAS soldier had died in that cell, or in the interrogation room where the beatings had been handed out so freely. Rashid knew that he would never know the catalyst, what had broken the man entirely, but he had his own demons to live with and had to let it go.

Big Dave opened the door of the helicopter, keeping his head down beneath the rotors. At six-four, he had the most to lose. He retrieved the medi-pack and handed some gauze to King. "Pad the leak!" he shouted above the noise of the rotors and engine. "I'll take a look when we get back!"

King rolled up his sleeve and pressed the pad against the gash, as Caroline struggled with some tape to hold it in place.

Rashid was staring at Goldie's lifeless form on the deck of the aircraft. There was simply no time to look for Philosopher's body, sporadic gunfire erupting from the forest, almost at once being suppressed by Flymo and Mac from their positions. Rashid looked at King and nodded, but his eyes gave all the thanks King would ever need.

"Let's go, let's go!" Flymo shouted above the din. "Everybody in!" He clambered into the helicopter and put on his earphones. Immediately the pitch of the engine changed, and the rotors sped up.

Rashid got into his seat, facing backwards. King sat opposite on the row of three. Caroline followed and Mac closed the door, leaving Big Dave to ride in the left-hand seat to balance the craft. They each put on their earphones, taking relief at the dramatic reduction in noise.

The helicopter lifted as they were all putting their belt harnesses on, and Flymo was bringing the craft around in a lazy spin as they climbed in height. "It's heavy," he said. "We have far more fuel than standard and we're full to capacity."

King reflected that the two Hellfire missiles used on the men in the forest had lightened the load considerably and there was a hell of a lot less 7.62mm bullets than before. He glanced down at Goldie's body, but said nothing. He did not know the man, but three people on board had, and Flymo could be the one to make the decision if he decided one-hundred and sixty pounds needed to be jettisoned anytime soon.

King could see men in the trees. He could see muzzle flashes, too, but they were climbing and heading out of range with every second that passed. He rested his head against the bulkhead. He was tired, not just because of the lack of sleep and exertion, but because by his estimation, he had lost more than a pint of blood. For the first time since he had boarded the aircraft, his leg hurt, too. The old man with the knife had been a fearful and experienced opponent. He glanced down at his desert boot and saw that blood had discoloured the laces and suede. His sock seemed to be soaking much of it up.

Caroline rested her head upon his shoulder. She still had the Makarov in her right hand. They hadn't said much to one another, especially now the voice-activated comms linked all their earphones. It would have to wait until they got back on the ground, but already there was communication between the way their legs touched, and the weight of her head against his shoulder. An unspoken comfort and familiarity.

King turned and looked at her. She was attractive, but far from glamorous. Her mousey-blonde hair had cascaded around her shoulders and she was covered in dirt, but she was beautiful and stubborn and tenacious and all the things that kept a relationship exciting. He grinned and she smiled back at him. She pursed her lips and raised her head for a kiss. King was thrown back against the bulkhead and Caroline screamed as the helicopter banked and dropped so violently, that Goldie's body levitated several inches from the deck as gravity momentarily fell to zero, then dropped down heavily again as the craft levelled out and physics was restored once more. Only their belts held them in place, but everyone had shifted in their seats.

"Incoming! Incoming!" Flymo shouted. He banked hard and a missile shot past them, a great white trail of smoke streaming behind it as it fishtailed, recalculated, and turned in the air. A second later and it was coming back at them.

Rashid craned his neck to see, but soon got sight of the missile as the helicopter switched course and dropped several hundred feet in height. King turned, saw the missile gaining impossibly quickly and he braced for impact. The helicopter banked again, dropped lower, and turned violently back on its previous heading. The heat signature change from the Bell's jet engine confused the missile's heat-seeking system, and it raced on past, caught the new heat signature, and turned once more.

The helicopter climbed and Flymo rolled the helicopter in a loop before descending straight back down to earth. King swung his legs out and pinned Goldie's body to the floor. Rashid glanced at him, then did the same.

"Oh, mother fu…" Big Dave didn't finish his sentence as the ground loomed ahead of them. He had a clearer view than most of the ground coming towards them, but he had now closed his eyes.

Flymo flew them down a fire break in the forest, the helicopter's skids just feet off the rocky ground and the rotors clearing the trees by no more than a few metres on each side.

"It's on us!" Rashid shouted, staring at the missile gaining on them. Only the sudden change in direction had slowed it down.

King reached up and snatched a flare gun from its mounting above Rashid's head. Rashid looked at him, guessed what he was thinking and pulled the pin on the emergency door released, then pulled the lever down and the door spat out into the air and the cabin filled with wind, blasting all around them. King cocked the pistol and fired ahead of them and to the right. Flymo cut the engine altogether to lose the heat trail and banked hard left and pulled up on the stick. The missile raced past them and detonated on the bright phosphorus head of the flare. The concussive shockwave vibrated through the craft and they were blown sideways by the force of the explosion.

The helicopter started to fall, and warning sirens filled the cabin, and the wind noise clearly audible now that the jet engine had been switched off. Flymo turned into the natural spin of the craft and fired up the jet engine, using autorotation to cut the friction of the rotors and take the path of least resistance. He struggled on the controls, but the craft was mercifully back in control, just feet above the trees.

"Oh my god!" Caroline exclaimed.

"I know," said King. "That felt intense..."

Caroline shook her head vehemently. "Not that! Look!" She pointed and everyone turned, their eyes wide. Ahead of them an attack helicopter, laden with an array of missiles and cannons was hovering above the trees less than two hundred metres away.

"Holy shit..." Big Dave said quietly.

Flymo was already on it. He built the helicopter up to maximum revs and they banked hard and accelerated towards the craft. The attack helicopter answered with twin cannons, but Flymo dropped down, the skids of the Bell skimming the trees.

"He's going closer!" Caroline screamed, unsure to whom, but her outburst mirrored the feelings of everyone on board.

Except for King. He knew that some opponents only fought well when they had the advantage of reach. Get close, and they struggled. King snatched one of the AK-74 rifles off the deck and got it to his shoulder. As Flymo banked hard left, he opened up with fully automatic fire on the cockpit of the attack helicopter and the great leviathan, banked hard defensively, exposing its belly. King kept firing, but the weapon clicked empty before he could do any real damage.

Mac got the other weapon ready and jettisoned the door on his side. It had the effect of alleviating the air pressure inside as the wind blew straight through.

"Where the hell did that come from?" Caroline shouted above the noise.

"Romanovitch had a lift organised to take them to Bulgaria," King said. "I'm guessing that was it. He must have known all about our chopper and the weapons Flymo added to it from Alaina, or whoever the hell she was. He raised the stakes."

King looked behind them and saw the attack helicopter banking hard above the trees behind them. He heard the cannons over the wind noise and the Bell's rotors and engine. Tracer fire streaked past them to the sides and carried on for what looked like forever ahead of them. Every tenth 20mm bullet was packed with phosphorus and lit up in the sky like laser blasters in a sci-fi movie, and there were enough of those to be concerned about, let alone the other nine bullets following the same path. Flymo heaved back on the controls and the helicopter climbed and banked and the rotors sounded as if they were straining under full throttle. An alarm sounded and kept sounding until the turn levelled out.

"Oh god, no…" Flymo did not finish his sentence, but he sent the craft down vertically and everyone lifted in their seats.

King and Rashid kept Goldie's body pinned to the deck, but their steep dive at once turned into a steep climb and a victory roll which ended in a hard banked turn so violent that the body shot out of the open door and was gone in an instant.

"No!" Rashid shouted and banged his fist on the bulkhead.

The attack helicopter was now directly in front of them, the missiles fishtailing back on course with the heat signature. Flymo opened fire with the 7.62mm gatling gun and the attack helicopter veered to port. Flymo kept on course and sparks lit up all over the hull of the beast, but the Vulcan soon whirled soundlessly, its ammunition spent.

"Bugger!" Flymo shouted. "I used up too much on the forest."

They hadn't slowed and were gaining on the enemy and being nimbler they countered its turns and as the attack helicopter banked and then straightened, they were close enough to feel its rotor wash. Both missiles streaked past, climbed high into the sky and self-detonated. The attack helicopter carried a beacon which emitted an electronic code that was paired with its own missiles. It simply couldn't shoot itself down. It had been quick thinking on Flymo's part, and a gamble to say the least.

"Stay on his rear!" King shouted. "I have an idea!" He looked at Mac and said, "Switch to the rear-facing seat."

Mac frowned, but he undid the harness, caught hold of the opposite harness, and tentatively stepped past the doorless opening and fell into the seat, buckling himself up. He kept the AK-74 across his knees, looking at King incredulously.

King looked at Caroline and shouted, "Get into Mac's seat!"

Caroline undid her belt and scooted over, but the helicopter dipped and banked, and she stumbled forwards towards the doorway. King unclipped his belt and grabbed hold of her ankle as she fell, and Rashid bent forwards and gripped onto King's leg.

"Fucking hell, Flymo!" Mac yelled. "She's out the door, help get her back!"

The attack helicopter was firing flack behind it – an incendiary countermeasure against missiles. Like fireworks filled with white-hot shrapnel which would home missiles onto the intense heat and away from the aircraft. The onslaught was creating super-heated debris and they were flying straight into it.

King gritted his teeth, every fibre of strength gripping Caroline around the ankle and taking all her weight in one hand, as he battled to heave her back in, while holding on with his left hand gripping the seatbelt harness of the empty middle seat. Mac dropped the rifle and it clattered out of the open doorway. He cursed, but caught hold of Caroline's other ankle and heaved, and as they were gradually bringing her back inside, Flymo dipped the controls and banked, and the inertia threw her back inside. King heaved her into his arms, hugging her close, then helped her into Mac's vacated seat and helped her on with the harness. Rashid kept a vice-like grip on King's leg as he lifted the middle seat and pulled out a large canvas duffle bag, with a hose attached. It was considerably heavy, and he struggled to get it out and onto the deck, especially as Flymo was countering every move the attack helicopter made in front. He whipped out his knife and cut the hose, spilling fuel all over the deck.

"Here, take this and fold the end, then hold it tight," he said to Caroline, handing her the leaking hose from under the seat. He tied the other end in a knot and tucked it inside the duffle bag. Inside was twenty-five gallons of aviation fuel in a rubber camel pack. Flymo's hack for extra mileage. He just hoped the Bell wasn't running on it yet. "Get us above that bastard, Flymo!" he shouted, dropping heavily into his seat, and fixing the harness around his waist only.

Rashid had let go of him, and now undid his own harness, and followed King's lead, just clipping it over his lap. He looked at King as he helped drag the bag closer to the doorway. "I've missed this," he said.

"When the hell have we ever done this?" King hollered back at him.

Caroline, who looked like she was trying to stop herself from sobbing, broke into a laugh and said, "You're bloody crazy."

"Fuck me, you all are!" Mac grinned.

"What's going on? I haven't opened my eyes in ten minutes…" Big Dave chipped in.

Flymo was directly behind the attack helicopter, following its every move. The rotor wash buffeted them, and the flak was showering the canopy with hot metal, but as the attack helicopter entered a dive, Flymo climbed first, then accelerated and followed the dive towards the mountainside below. When the attack helicopter levelled out just fifty metres above the rocky terrain, the Bell was directly above it with no more than fifty feet between them.

"Get on top of him! Squeeze him downwards!" King shouted. "Let's see how close you can get! See if you can live up to that name of yours…"

The Bell dropped in altitude and Flymo put the skids just feet from the rotors below them.

"Tell me when its away and hang on!" Flymo shouted.

King could see the blur of the rotors below him. They were so close he could see the trees and rocks below them through the whirling rotors. He glanced up at Rashid and nodded. They dragged the bag right up to the doorway, then heaved and helped it out with their boots.

"Away!" shouted King and the helicopter banked hard to port and rose high in the air.

Behind them, the bag of fuel fell into the rotors and was instantly shredded, fuel covering the entire craft. The twin exhausts of the jet turbines, glowing red with heat ignited the fuel vapour and engulfed it in flames, the force of the ignition unbalancing the rotors with enough severity to deviate its course. Unable to correct in time, the pilot could not save it from skimming the ground and crashing heavily, bursting into flames where live ammunition and the rest of its missiles exploded moments after impact.

43

**Ten days later,
Cornwall**

King and Caroline had not been to Thames House for the debrief. Instead, they had returned to their cottage and reflected on a number of things. King had been stitched by Big Dave using a battlefield medi-pack to clean the wounds and suture them. Simon Mereweather had met them at Gatwick Airport and taken King to his Harley Street doctor, and the man had confirmed nothing more could be done by private medical practitioner or NHS hospital alike. King was now exercising gently, mainly walking the cliffs and thinking things through.

King had built the barbeque pit by cutting a forty-gallon oil drum with an angle grinder and using two wire baker's trays as cooking racks. He fixed them to bricks he had cemented to the patio. It was rustic, but functional and by lighting just a small amount of charcoal in one, and having a roaring flame in the other, he could work between the two and had quite a system in place. Caroline had laboured over half a dozen various salad dishes and dips, and they remained largely untouched as Rashid, Mac and Flymo, led by Big Dave, made light work of the steaks, chicken drumsticks, pork chops, burgers, ribs and sausages King had spread over the two grills.

"I've said it before, and I'll say it again, Rashid, but you really are a shit Muslim when it comes to food," King said, putting out the fire engulfing a particularly fatty piece of pork.

"The way you cook it, Allah isn't going to know what the hell it is anyway. Everything you cook looks like burned beef, anyway."

"And tastes like a burned shoe," Big Dave chuckled.

"Well, I don't see you queuing for Caroline's salads," King replied testily. "Besides, it's better crunchy." King loaded a burger onto his own bun and looked at Ramsay, who was picking somewhat absentmindedly at a sausage. He noticed a change in the man. He didn't know what he had seen in Albania, but if it was anything like the burning and strafed forest after Flymo's handiwork with the gatling gun and the Hellfire missiles, then he had a good idea. But it was more than that. King had seen it in men before, knew that Ramsay had seen, or done, something that had affected him. When Ramsay had finally returned to the farmhouse in Albania, he had thick lips and a swollen eye, and there was blood on his shirt. The man wouldn't talk about it and King had decided that he would continue to top up the man's glass throughout the afternoon and get him talking later.

King looked at Flymo, who was talking animatedly with Rashid. No doubt, about the money he had liberated. Flymo's *Costa Del Retirement* dream had ebbed away as it had been agreed a share should be set aside for both Philosopher's and Goldie's next of kin, and King had suggested a donation be made to the family of Alaina and Dina Kopolova, two young women he never knew, but whom had suffered at the hands of Romanovitch. Mereweather had agreed, and the remainder would be used for clandestine operations of national importance.

A champagne cork popped and everyone except Ramsay turned and tensed, then visibly relaxed. Simon Mereweather laughed and said, "Crikey, I should learn to pick my audience!" He started pouring the champagne into glasses on the table. "Here's to a successful mission!" He handed out the glasses, then held his own above his head in a toast. "All's well that ends well."

King had not been pleased when he had seen the half case of champagne. Mereweather had picked up the six bottles of Dom Perignon from Fortnum and Masons. King felt champagne was too much a celebratory drink, and while they were all glad to have got Rashid and Mac out, two men had not been so lucky. To King, champagne was for weddings, christenings, and New Year.

"No. To absent friends," said Rashid, holding his glass in the air.

Everyone concurred, Mereweather looking slightly foolish, especially given that when Rashid and his team had gone missing King was billed as their only hope. Likewise, falling to Caroline to railroad Ramsey to help her when King went off the radar, albeit with the willing help of Dave Lomu. But like any true mandarin, he got over it quickly enough and was likely to never look back.

Mereweather walked over to where King was busy cremating some sausages, he eyed Ramsay on the way, and he followed. He wasn't a fan of champagne and had swapped his untouched glass for a glass of *Pimms* that Caroline had made in a large glass jug with all the accompaniments that went with it.

"The USBs are useless," commented Mereweather.

"Figures."

"But Romanovitch is shut down, as are the Albanian brotherhood." Mereweather paused. "So, all in all…"

"Two good men are dead," said King. He looked at Ramsay and said, "What about you, Neil. Do *you* think it was worth it?"

"Why are you asking me?" Ramsay responded irritably.

"As liaison officer, you must have a view. Was what we, *you*, went through worth it?"

Ramsay raised his glass. "All good things," he said. "For queen and country…"

"Neil…" Mereweather glanced at him awkwardly.

King turned to the deputy director. "So, Simon. Clean up time."

"Meaning?"

"You've got a double agent in play," he said. "Are you going to send a message or wait for him to align himself with the person who picks up the reins?" King rolled the sausages onto the other grill, but it was too late. All hope was lost for the flaming pork links. "Clearly, if you leave him in play then you can take the bullshit that he feeds you and shovel it back on him at a later date."

"That was our take on it."

"Cowboys and Indians."

"What?"

"Games," replied King. "I think after a hundred years of playing games with the enemy, it might be time to simply shut them down altogether. We take one of theirs and turn them, bribe them, they go back and renege on their deal, feed us a load of crap, we discover what they're up to and change the feed. They realise and counter… Christ, it's bloody endless! It's just foolish games!"

"What do you suggest?" Mereweather asked, sipping his champagne.

"The Home Secretary's husband, the SO15 Commander's wife, for a start. They were slaughtered to send a message. A message from a mafia boss via a Russian intelligence officer." King paused. "The SVR killed the counter terrorism police chief's wife! And the husband of one of the top three ranking ministers!"

"Well, what are you suggesting we do?" Ramsay asked sharply. "Another mission, another fruitless operation where we lose more of our people?" He shook his head. "We know who these people are, and we can use that to our advantage."

"Or we stand up and show we won't take it."

"To the nation with the second largest military on earth?" Ramsay replied.

"It's not about military. Otherwise we wouldn't have been playing these games with the East for the past eighty years. We have alliances with the right people, the right numbers. And we're a nuclear power." King paused. "But we need to be tougher. Not reckless, just tougher."

"So, what do you suggest?" Mereweather asked quietly.

"I know where we should start."

"We?" Ramsay shook his head. "I thought you were out?" He glanced over at Caroline, who was trying to get Big Dave to eat some of her salads. "I thought you both were."

"We need a different approach," said King. "We operate so much in the shadows that we have lost our perspective of how the world looks in the light of day."

"I agree," said Ramsay. "We should continue with our embrace of technology and cyber intelligence."

"We have GCHQ for that."

"And that's the way the world is going."

"Neil, I think after this mission you of all people know that sometimes the work on the ground is horrible, but necessary."

Ramsay frowned, but looked vacantly into his glass. "I need a refill," he said and headed over to the table where Caroline had given up on Big Dave and was sipping her champagne. She smiled, picked up the jug and topped up his glass.

"Something I should know about?" asked Mereweather.

"I think it'll come out when he's ready."

"Where should we start, then?"

"Major Diminov of the SVR," said King. "He didn't pull the trigger, but he clearly organised it and that can't stand."

"My thoughts entirely."

44

Three months later
Russia

Autumn had closed in and winter had announced itself with freezing winds, flurries of snow and the promise of harsher days to come. Moscow was set to retreat into itself once more.

Major Diminov had taken a leave of absence. He was suffering from exhaustion and had found it difficult to carry out his tasks. The thought of a winter in Moscow, confined to his apartment and longing for the boredom to end filled him with dread.

He had been promised the rank of Colonel and a posting at the embassy in Stockholm, Sweden. A gentle posting as a reward for his services to the Motherland, and he had received the *Orden Svjatogo Georgija I Stepeni*, or Order of Saint George 1st Class, in a private ceremony with the Russian President. He had been allowed to hold his medal for a few moments before it had been taken away and put into safe storage, along with the report of achievement that would, along with the medal itself, forever remain a secret.

Diminov drank some water, but he had trouble keeping it down. He had checked his temperature. There had been so much illness in the world, that he had recently purchased his own thermometer. He made his way into the tiny bathroom, opened the cabinet, and took out a jar of paracetamol. He swallowed two of them and put his mouth under the tap to chase them down. Again, he felt sick and straightened himself, holding onto the sink. Catching sight of himself in the mirror, he looked at his eyes more closely. They appeared sunken, and his eye sockets looked dark. He ran a hand through his hair but frowned when several large strands came out effortlessly. He checked again, horrified that it pulled out so easily.

Diminov padded back to the living area and switched on his laptop. He waited for it to boot up, cursed when the battery indicated it was low and he pulled the charging cable out of the drawer and plugged the device in to charge. The battery seemed to have no capability to hold charge. He guessed they never really lasted long, style over substance, lightness, and ergonomics over practicality. It smelled hot, too. Like it was about to burn out. Perhaps the fan wasn't running properly? But it was a relatively new machine. The keypad felt hot to the touch. He needed it for work, despite being sick, he still had tasks to assign, reports to make and agents to contact. Diminov brought up *Yandex* and typed in his symptoms. The search engine brought up localised services offering some of the keywords he had typed in, so he went onto *Google* and searched again. The keys were hot to touch, and he knew he would have to either buy a new device online or get a subordinate to take his laptop off for repair. He did not hold out much hope of that. Even Russia was becoming a throwaway society these days.

He read the results, clicked and clicked back, scrolled and skipped until he found what he was looking for, but as he stared at the screen his heart beat faster and his stomach knotted as he matched his symptoms with the possibilities. One stood out more than the others.

Thallium poisoning.

Diminov rested his hands on the keys, then took them away, the heat of the laptop enough to make him uncomfortable. He rubbed his aching, tired face, then froze, staring at the device in front of him. He switched it off, unplugged it and stood up quickly enough to knock over the chair. Diminov raced to the chest of drawers and returned with a set of electrical screwdrivers. He started to unscrew the back of the laptop, his hands shaking and his heart racing. It seemed to take forever, but he unscrewed the panel with little regard in keeping the screws, allowing them to roll off the table and onto the threadbare carpet.

Diminov removed the panel and stared at the silvery-white metal, which switched to a dull grey against the light. He could see that the battery had been swapped for a smaller design and around it the silvery metal had been folded and pushed into place. More had been packed around the two tiny fans. He pushed the laptop away from him and picked up the landline phone. He dialled and placed the phone against his ear, then froze, took the phone away and looked at it in his hand. He took one of the screwdrivers and jemmied the case open. Again, more of the silvery-white metal in the earpiece. Diminov threw the phone against the wall and screamed as it shattered on the painted block wall. He got up, but felt his balance going, like he was six vodkas into the evening. He picked up his mobile phone, but suddenly he was aware of its weight. He returned to the table, used the screwdriver, but already knew what he would find. Alongside the battery, a sliver of the silver-white metal. He was about to throw the phone, but something caught his eye. The battery was smaller than it should have been – he knew because he had changed the SIM card many times for security protocols and the battery had to be removed first. Something lay underneath the battery. He tapped out the battery and a small fold of card fell into his hand. Diminov dropped the phone to the floor and unfolded the card. He recognised the logo and writing, the name of the establishment and the address.

The Ivy.

He flipped the card over in his hand and read the scribbled words out loud. "Know your enemy…"

Diminov dropped heavily into the worn fabric armchair and smiled. He knew enough to know the end was near. He had enjoyed his lifetime playing cowboys and Indians and he had always thought himself a worthy adversary. Only he knew that the longer you played the game, sooner or later you would be beaten. It was the way of things. Sooner or later the Reaper would come to call.

Author's Note

Hi – thanks for making it this far. The fact you did means you hopefully enjoyed the story, and if that is the case, then I hope you enjoyed it as much as I enjoyed writing it!

As always, I would be profoundly grateful of a review on Amazon and/or Goodreads – just a quick line when you have time would be great. It really helps with the Amazon algorithms and visibility.

It's a pleasure to write for a living and I can only do this because of people like you who have bought or borrowed my work. You can find out more about my books, sign-up for my mailing list or learn a bit more about me at www.apbateman.com

Thank you, and I hope to entertain you again soon!

A P Bateman